Winter in Chicago

For Jack,
with affection —
Chicago Rocks!

David Hamlin

David M. Hamlin

Published by Open Books

Copyright © 2016 by David M. Hamlin

"Wrigley_Building_Across_River" © Mike Warot

Learn more about the artist at flickr.com/photos/--mike--/

ISBN-13: 978-0997806243

ISBN-10: 0997806249

For my extraordinary, endlessly delightful family; and for Wallace, Violet, Kate & Caroline because JD the DJ is right: "You can't know where you're goin' if you don't know where you've been."

To Sydney, the muse who sings to me every day.

.

1.

Emily slid her arm from under the covers at 3:18 in the morning. She tapped the alarm clock button, squelching it two minutes before it sounded. She remained still for a moment, listening to Ben's steady breathing, and then slid gently off the bed.

She stood, gazing at Ben, and smiled. Her goal every morning was to let him sleep undisturbed and she succeeded more often than not. She snatched up the robe from the foot of the bed and wrapped herself snugly. It was cold in the apartment and she was fully awake quickly.

She padded quietly out of the bedroom and down the hall to the living room's bank of windows facing Lake Michigan. There was a dash of dampness in the air, illuminated by an occasional set of headlights on the Outer Drive and floating beneath the street lamps. A modest wind occasionally shivered the bare bone trees in the park. She laid the back of a hand against the window, confirming that it was very cold out there, then turned and went back down the hall to the second bathroom.

She showered, toweled her short hair dry and applied a

minimum of make-up, switched off the bathroom lights, opened the door and moved quietly and quickly across the hall to the guest bedroom. Her clothes were laid out on the bed.

In the kitchen, Emily read Ben's note about dinner plans, added "OK" and then "Love you" and went back to the windows to watch the street. When the cab turned into the driveway from Wellington, she took her heavy, ankle-length high collared pea coat from a dining chair and shrugged into it. A bit over five feet tall, she was nearly smothered by the thing, but that made it deliciously warm. She snatched up her large canvas satchel and left the apartment.

"Good Morning, Max."

"Howya doin', Emmy?"

As soon as she was old enough to do so, Emily had made it quite clear, first to her family and then to the world at large, that her name was *Emily!* No Em, no Emmy. She didn't like either, she said, because they were "cute." She backed up her manifesto by steadfastly refusing to acknowledge any who violated it; even her father gave up on Em, pleased in the end to encourage his daughter's spunky streak.

Ben's uncle Max had turned out to be every bit as insistent on Emmy as she had been to the contrary as a toddler. She eventually recognized Max as an equal—every bit as idiosyncratically stubborn as she—and stopped correcting him. He became her one and only exception.

"I'm good, thanks. Ready to go. Cold out there, Max. Cold."

"Here."

Max passed a cardboard cup of coffee and a paper sack to the back seat, took the wheel and eased the cab forward.

"Warm you up."

"Not fast enough. Thanks."

Emily picked up the first of three newspapers stacked on the seat beside her. By the time Max pulled onto Lake

Shore Drive from Belmont, she had scanned all three front pages and read several lead paragraphs in the metro and regional sections. As they motored along, Emily took the faintly warm bagel out of its bag and turned to Kup's Column. She scanned it, stopping several times to read specific entries, some for work, others for the fun of it. As Max exited the Drive at Michigan Avenue, Emily set aside the previous evening's late edition of the Daily News and watched as her aggressively handsome city rolled by.

She was looking west down a quiet street when she saw several police vehicles, an ambulance and a coroner's van.

"Max, take the next right."

"That ain't right, Emmy. We always go down the Avenue to Wacker. Same route every day."

"No. The next right, Max. There's something going on near Rush Street."

Max moved the cab into the rightmost lane and slowed to a crawl.

"So, you get out and start schmoozing, we run up against the clock. On time, every time, that's the deal, right? What'll I tell Ben, he asks?"

When the opportunity for the morning drive radio news position came to her, Emily and Ben knew she had to accept it. Ben's only concern was her safety on lonely pre-dawn city streets. They had no car and he wasn't comfortable, Emily walking streets alone or riding in busses with whomever might be found in them in the wee hours.

So Ben called his Uncle Max, a retired widower who had, to the family's amazement, filled the empty spaces in his life by becoming a cab driver. Max, childless, was Ben's permanent best friend. Max always got Ben the birthday presents his parents had nixed, Max called when he landed great seats at Wrigley, Max had corralled a superior caterer for their wedding at a discount so steep that Emily suspected skullduggery. When Ben asked, Max happily promised to be there every morning. Thereafter, at every family gathering Max bragged that he was the reason the news on "that rock station" was so great every morning.

Emily said, "Max, it could be a story. It's my job. What if it's something big, I might actually get on the air? We'll tell Ben you're the reason I broke through.

"Besides, I have a watch, you know. I can tell time real well, Max. Big hand, little hand and all. I won't make us late, I promise."

Max didn't say anything. He turned in his seat and gave her a look.

"I won't stay a second longer than I have to, okay? "

"Don't make me regret this, Emmy."

He took the next two right turns, then a left.

Emily wrestled a bulky, expensive broadcast-quality portable tape recorder from her satchel and slipped its shoulder strap in place. She extracted her microphone and plugged it in, hit the Record button, said "Test one two" twice and played it back. She put the bagel back in its bag and stuffed the bag in the satchel.

Max spotted the collection of vehicles before she could point them out. He turned the corner and pulled to the curb.

Climbing out, Emily reached back to the satchel for her ID tag, clipped it to her coat lapel and checked to be sure the ID faced out. It did, her name above WEL NEWS STAFF, her photograph below.

Across the street, Emily saw a handful of uniformed cops, a couple of men in Virginia Hotel blazers, two ambulance attendants leaning against their vehicle sipping coffee and the coroner's team standing around a slab of canvas on the street.

She swept the gathering again, this time to confirm that there were no other reporters on the scene. There were none and a little smile appeared for just a moment.

There were three men in suits and trench coats. Two wore knit Bears caps, the third a broad brimmed fedora. Emily headed directly toward them.

The fedora saw her and separated from the group, walking up the street to greet her.

"Hello, Nails. Long time, no see." He lightly touched the brim of his hat.

Emily grinned and gave him a wave.

"Detective Jack Potter. How the hell are you, cop?"

"Just fine, news hen. You wanna know what's goin' on?"

"That'd be good," she said. "You'll give me something for air?"

"We'll see," he said. "Let me fill you in first."

* * * *

Emily graduated from college determined to become a television news reporter. She started in the quad cities on the Iowa Illinois border. Only when she moved to Moline did it emerge that the station's definition of "female, on-air news" was confined to appearing on camera, in costume, as the pixie-like assistant to a kids' game show host. They told her the kiddy show led into the early evening newscast and was therefore an important part of the news operation.

When she quit, the station's General Manger told her that she'd only been hired in the first place because of her height.

"You're the perfect elf," he told her.

"We're even," said Emily, "you're the perfect jerk."

The experience did tell her where she belonged, or at least where she didn't, so Emily went home to Chicago. She bounced from copy girl to part-time production assistant to talk show gopher to music library secretary. She relentlessly contacted local TV news shops and built a network of friends in news, chatting and probing for openings constantly. One of her colleagues told her about an opening for a radio news position and she applied, thinking radio exposure might generate TV news notice.

In her interview, the radio station's News Director told her the position had been "suggested" by the station's network affiliate offices in New York, where there was growing concern that "some women" seemed far too eager to bring discrimination suits. He said he wasn't happy about the edict, but was powerless before the network's pressure.

Still, he'd been impressed when he saw the degree from the University of Missouri's Journalism School on her resume.

"Never went to college, myself, only couple of the guys in this newsroom did. Didn't graduate. Maybe you can teach us something."

"I'm hoping it will be the other way around," said Emily.

"Oh, you can count on that, honey," he said. "You start on Monday."

It took Emily less than two weeks to figure out their plan. If they had to hire a girl, they would make sure she didn't last.

Emily was told to straighten out the newsroom filing system, change the ribbons in the typewriters, load paper rolls and ribbons into the wire service machines, keep track of water cooler orders, make coffee and run to and from the deli or the News Director's dry cleaners.

The only time news copy came into in her hands was when a smirking guy at one end of the newsroom had her carry it to a smirking guy in the studio. She spent most of her time sitting between assignments. Her desk was a table in a corner of the break room; it had no phone.

She understood that if she quit another woman would follow and stay only until she couldn't stand it. And then another. At some point, the guys would confidently report that "It just doesn't work."

So, at the first available opportunity, Emily flagged down her News Director.

"Jerry," she said, "I have a question."

"Yeah? What?"

"Can you find more for me to do, please? I just love working here, I want to contribute more. It's just so exciting, being in a newsroom, I can't believe how lucky I am. What else can I do?"

She punctuated her deliberately perky request with a smile of considerable wattage.

The next day, she was told that she was to be transferred to the overnight shift at the Chicago Police Department headquarters press room.

She said, "Thank you. When do I start?"

The guys in the station's news room had been unpleasant. The reporters who worked over night in the cop shop press room were openly and aggressively hostile. She wasn't one of the boys and she had a degree. They were seasoned tradesmen, offended at the notion that their real-life, deadline-driven work could be taught in a school, never mind to a girl. They were determined to preserve their domain.

On her first night, somebody at one of the desks growled "Hold on to your balls, boys, there's a skirt here" when she walked into the room.

For days, that was the only interaction she had with any of them.

The door to the bathroom was locked, a hand-lettered sign announced Men Only—Key At Trib Desk. There was a packet of rubbers in the center drawer of her desk, atop three editions of Playboy. Two of the reporters nearest to her desk brandished penis-shaped ball point pens.

On her fourth night, the Department's press office issued notice of an armed confrontation between CPD and someone at the Cabrini Green housing project. Emily saw the reporters heading for the doors, each with the CPD notice in hand. She scurried over to the Tribune desk where Ralph Raines, the senior reporter in the room and the acknowledged leader of the pack, sat. In his trash can, she found a copy of the notice. By the time she gathered her equipment from her desk, the room was completely deserted.

She was last to arrive and for the first time they were only too happy to talk to her.

"Where ya been, skirt?"

"Geez, girly, get a move on. We're headed back already."

"Stop to fix the make-up, honey?"

She brushed past them, her face stern and tight, to the perimeter the police had established. She asked the first uniform she saw who was handling press.

"You want Detective Jack Potter, sweetie. Guy in the suit over there."

She walked up to him and showed him her credentials. She switched on her mike and pointed it at him.

"I gave the guys everything we have, ma'am. Drunk up there on the fourth floor, kicked out a window, started firing a .22 rifle at the asphalt plaza down here. Wasn't aiming, didn't much care what he hit. This late, plaza's empty, nobody got hurt. We sent a couple uniforms up, they talked him into handing over the gun. End of story."

"Okay," said Emily, "Thanks. Now give me something the guys didn't get."

"Like what? That's all there is."

"What did the uniforms say?"

"Huh?"

"The two cops you sent up to talk to him, how'd they get him to give up?"

Potter grinned. He spoke directly into the mike.

"The officers offered to trade the suspect a six pack of Colt 45 for his Remington .22. The suspect agreed and surrendered himself. Thanks to their resourcefulness, no one was hurt during the incident."

Back in the press room, the print reporters didn't bother to file anything. A couple of radio guys filed brief stories which aired only once or not at all. Emily wrote and sent a 30 second synopsis and patched the recorder to her phone, transmitting the taped quote from Potter. The station used her copy and Jack Potter's quote all morning, teased through the hour as "Cops Swap Booze For Barrel!"

The next night, Jack Potter strolled into the press room to give a quick follow-up.

The shooter had sobered up and expressed great remorse. He now faced reckless endangerment charges, the DA seeking only probation and proof of participation in a rehab program.

Nobody paid much attention until Potter moved from the doorway to Ralph Raines' desk, a sly smile on his face.

"Yeah?" said Raines.

"Just wondering. How's it feel to get scooped by the college chick? The rookie found a story, you guys all missed it."

Raines snorted. "Beginner's luck, is all."

"I don't think so, Ralph. I think the kid's got what it takes. In fact, I think you guys better watch your backs. That lady's as tough as nails."

The next night one of the reporters called out "Hey, Nails!" when she arrived. She smiled and waved at him. The Playboys and rubbers had vanished and the two guys put away their tacky pens. The lock on the door to the bathroom and the warning sign remained in place.

A few days later, Emily caught up with Jack Potter as they were leaving the building at the end of the shift.

"That was a pretty neat thing you did with Raines the other day."

Potter nodded.

"And I wish you hadn't done it."

He cocked his head, eyebrows up.

"This is complicated. First, I think I can take care of myself."

"I have no doubt."

"Thanks. But here's the thing, Jack. My work has to stand on its own and I know it can. That was the whole point of my question to you at Cabrini, show them I know what I'm doing. You gave them the who, what, where and when, but not the how. I got the how."

"Point taken," said Potter.

"There's more. Don't take this the wrong way, I really do appreciate what you did, but I can't have a man stepping in every time I hit a pothole. I'm not trying to fit in a man's world, I want it to be my world too. When the knight in shining armor rescues the maiden in distress, everybody knows it's because the maiden is a weak helpless idiot in high heel shoes. If they accept me only when a guy says it's OK, then I'm right back where I started. That make sense?"

"I get it. And it makes a lot of sense." said Potter. "Can I say something?"

"Of course."

"First, I'm sorry. Should have thought it through, I guess, but the chance to needle Ralph was right there, you know? Anyhow, the point is, damsel, I wasn't trying to be the knight. Chivalry had nothing to do with it. I was extending my hand to a fellow exile."

"Exile?"

"That's why you're here, right? Couldn't handle you so they moved you to the pits, hoping you'd break and quit? Yeah, well, me too."

"No kidding."

"Short version, okay? Tried college, didn't care for it, joined the force, top honors in my class, superior rookie evaluations, all's right with the world. Nam comes along, I enlist and serve a couple of tours. Come back to the force, looking forward to it, only it's not the same. Not the same at all. There's anger everywhere, most of 'em believe anyone who doesn't wear their uniform is the enemy and they're way too hungry for action. The war's in country. There are no Cong in Chicago.

"Anyhow, I kept shooting my mouth off when I shouldn't, next thing I know they got me sitting on the press desk, midnight to 8 AM, minimum six months. I'm doing my time in exile, waiting until they remember I'm a good cop. Which I am."

"Doing time and waiting" said Emily. "I can dig it."

* * * *

The ambulance crew began packing up to leave as the officers first on the scene drove away. The coroner's truck and staff were still there, some dancing in place against the cold.

"Almost certainly suicide," said Jack Potter. "She came out that window, eleven stories up."

He pointed to the room, its old-fashioned up-and-down sash window fully open. Emily could discern movement in the room and watched as someone leaned out to measure the window's width and height.

"You're sure about suicide?" said Emily.

"Pretty sure. We'll wait for the coroner, but there's nothing to suggest otherwise. The room is pretty much the way it was when she checked in. No furniture tossed around or tipped over, the bed's rumpled but the cover is still in place. Desk staff say they don't think she had any visitors. A fair number of the rooms in this place are on long term leases, a few are on that floor. We've interviewed a couple of full-timers, home all night, say they didn't hear anything out of the ordinary."

"Young? Old?"

"I'd say she's about your age, 30, 35, no older than that." Potter winced. "Lovely girl, really lovely. Hard to imagine why she'd take the dive. A shame."

"Can I see?"

"Really? It isn't pretty, you know."

"Jack, I covered the mob girlfriend, supposedly threw herself through an apartment window on the 91st floor of the Hancock? She was raw hamburger on the street. I can probably handle this."

"Okay, Nails."

They walked past his two colleagues and both gave her a look. Emily gave them a wave.

"Hey, guys. Sorry about da Bears. 4 and 10 isn't much to cheer about, is it? And that last game? 42 to nothin'? To the 'Skins? Lousy way to close out the season, you ask me. They'll turn it around next year, right?"

They both frowned. Jack Potter made sure he was past his colleagues before he shook his head and grinned at her sly style, embracing the very men who were convinced she didn't belong. Potter was confident they frowned because they weren't quite sure what had happened.

He led her to one corner of the canvas, nodded to the attendant and said "Show her."

The attendant pulled the canvas away. Emily looked at the contorted body and then at the face.

She staggered back on shaky legs, her breath gone, her heart racing, tears flooding her cheeks.

She spoke so softly that Potter had to lean in to hear her.

"That's Beni. My God, Jack. That's Beni Steinart. Benita. I know her, we went to Lakeview High together, we were two live wires, always in talent shows and productions. We did a duet my senior year, the sisters' song about leaving Ohio. We've stayed in touch. She always sparkled, even on the phone. She called me, right after Thanksgiving, she was fine. She was sweet. And kind. It can't be Beni. It's Beni."

Potter leaned toward the attendant and extended his hand, taking a clipboard from him.

He stood close to Emily, waiting as her tears abated and she began to breathe evenly and then quietly read to her from the papers on the board.

"Benita Ann Steinart. Illinois Driver's license, address on Sheridan, way north. There's a second photo ID for the Chase Mansion. Detective Polski says she was involved somehow in that drug case, the feds trying to tag Cary Chase with dealing. You remember that?"

"Yes," said Emily, "Vaguely. Six, maybe seven months ago? You think that has something to do with this?"

Potter shrugged.

"No way to know. It's a fed operation, we weren't involved, but I heard it had died. She didn't leave a note."

There was a small commotion close behind them. Max was trying to dodge around a uniformed cop who was trying to keep him away from the scene. Max leaned in and said something and the officer quickly stepped out of his way.

"Emmy, what's wrong?"

"She's an old friend, Max. I can't believe this. It doesn't make any sense."

"I'm so sorry," said Max. He put an arm around her shoulder. "Emmy, we gotta get going."

She looked at her watch and shook him off.

"Just a few more minutes, Max."

Emily turned back to Jack Potter.

"Jack, I need tape. Can you tell me what happened here this morning?"

Potter spoke into the mike, his eyes never leaving her.

"Thanks."

"Sorry you had to see that, Emily."

"Me too."

"You take care, okay?"

"Okay."

Max led her to the cab and drove aggressively. When he curbed the cab at the corner of Michigan and Wacker, it was 4:55.

"You take it easy today, Emmy. Shock like this, you need to pay attention."

"Yes, Max. Thanks."

Emily waved at the security guard in the lobby and got into the elevator. She dug a tissue out of the satchel and wiped her face, breathing deeply to relax. She promised herself that after she had gotten the morning's news blocks ready, she could call Ben and talk to him.

In the elevator, Emily grew quickly uncomfortable as her layers of heavy winter outer wear, specifically crafted to fend off razor blade winds and skin cracking cold, collided with the heated interior. It was on a very short list of things which annoyed her about her town. She unwound her scarf and unbuttoned her coat. She paused at the last button, reflecting that she was cranky about a tiny discomfort which Beni would never again experience. She closed her eyes and concentrated on the work she had to do. As the elevator doors opened, she gained some focus. It didn't feel quite real.

When she pushed the doors into the room called the bullpen, everything was normal. The wire service machines were clacking away, the speakers around the room were turned just low enough to carry the live WEL broadcast without intruding. She could see the morning DJ, Sandy Sampson, through the sound proof window on one side of the bullpen. He would build the largest 18 to 34 year old audience in the market later in the morning, but in the 5 o'clock hour he barely spoke, carting up one pop hit after another and cueing his engineer to commercials.

Both her bullpen colleagues were at their desks. The morning anchorman, Dan McIntyre, was staring absently at the small news studio window, sipping hot tea. The assistant news director, Rick Healey, had his feet propped up on his desk. He was dozing but managed to open his eyes enough to watch Emily go to her desk, hoist her satchel onto it and shed her coat.

Healey said, "How come you wear them little skirts, girl? Those fancy blouses? You don't look like any reporter I ever saw."

Emily smiled.

"Rick, here's the problem. I was taught that a lady should dress appropriately when she's going downtown. That means skirts and dresses, no slacks. Much as I'd like to, pardner, I can't wear the pants in this outfit."

Dan McIntyre broke his vacant stare at the window

long enough to glance at Emily.

"Skirt's way too short," he said. "You look cheap. You work for me, you should look more professional, not like some floozy."

"Actually, Dan, I work for WEL. You just happen to be the guy who gets to read superior copy every day." said Emily. "And I'm not sure I need wardrobe advice from a man who starts the day wilted. Most guys shoot for crisp, you know?"

McIntyre's brows knit together for a moment. He looked perplexed. Emily guessed he was groping for how, exactly, clothing could wilt.

"Okay, boys, that's enough. I have work to do here."

McIntyre stared into the studio glass again. Healey put his feet on his desk and began to doze.

Emily dug around in her satchel and found her bagel, setting it next to her coffee container. She rolled a sheet of paper into her typewriter, aligned it and then walked to the wire machines. The streams of paper from all three machines cascaded to the floor; it was piled several layers deep. She started with the city news wire, scrolling through the sheets, scanning and absorbing. She confirmed that the local wire had picked up a front page story from the *Tribune* which she had already flagged as a good lead. She checked to see if there was mention of Beni Steinart's death on the wire, but the story hadn't yet moved.

The national wires, AP and UPI, carried parallel stories at the top and a number of weather related stories from the east coast, where it was snowing moderately. None of the weather stories mentioned Chicago or anything of interest to the plains states where distant listeners tuned in Chicago stations with strong AM signals for crop-related bulletins. Emily found one national story she wanted to use, a good closer.

She returned to her desk and arranged the wire copy in order. Pausing now and then to nibble at the bagel and sip her tepid coffee, Emily started slowly and picked up the rhythm until she and the machine hit a staccato pace. When she was done, she laid the copy on her desk and read it several times; on her last pass, she made a handful of edits with a red pencil.

In her first week on this job, Emily had given Dan McIntyre copy which had supplanted "frame" for "fame." Since McIntyre read what was put in his hands verbatim, he dutifully reported that "Pop star Linda Rondstadt plans to expand her considerable frame with the release of a new album tomorrow."

Emily endured the substantial abuse McIntyre unleashed, kept her peace while Healey shouted at her for about fifteen minutes and quietly accepted mild but firm criticism from WEL's news director, Dean Lyon. It was the last time she turned in faulty copy.

She typed the copy once more and quietly read it to herself aloud. She was not satisfied.

She picked up her phone, dialed a number from memory, identified herself and took notes as her source responded to her questions. When the call was complete, she retyped the package again, adding a bit more to the lead story, and read it aloud once more.

Emily moved to the window facing the broadcast studio and waved at Sandy Sampson's engineer, beckoning him. He nodded, took a handful of music cassettes and passed them over to Sampson, who would insert and play them from his side of the broadcast console.

Emily took the tape from her tape recorder and moved to the editing bay, a sound proofed cubicle tucked into one corner of the large room. She entered and flipped a switch to light the room and activate the "Do Not Enter" sign above the door. Sampson's engineer walked in and took a seat at the editing bay.

She played the interview Jack Potter had given her twice and handed the cassette to the engineer. He fed the tape into the editing machinery and maneuvered the tape back and forth as she indentified the cuts she wanted, paring the interview from 2:21 down to 15 seconds. He cut and spliced the tape and loaded it into a cartridge. Emily had him play it back twice and then glanced at the clock above the editing table. It was 5:54.

At 5:57, Emily walked over to Dan McIntyre's desk, being careful not to make eye contact, and handed him the copy. The delivery launched his ritual.

McIntyre pushed his chair back, stood up and centered his cup of tea in the upper right corner of his desk. He tamped the pages of copy so they were perfectly aligned and placed them in the exact center of the desk. He turned and took four steps to the coat rack by the door, put on his rumpled blazer and walked back to his desk, four paces. He stepped on the same four floor tiles each way. He buttoned his blazer, straightened his shoulders, picked up the copy and executed a military right face to walk to the News Room studio door. Emily opened it for him and followed him in.

Not once did Dan McIntyre look at Emily or anything else. He moved as in a trance, his eyes slightly glazed. Emily had been astounded the first time she'd seen the ritual unfold, not because it was so strange, but because the man did not so much as glance at the copy in his hand. Then, and every morning since, Dan McIntyre read every single piece of copy she prepared for him once and once only, on the air. And every single time, he was perfect.

Emily followed him into the studio and inserted the interview cartridge into its slot on the console. He took his seat, put on a head set, adjusted his mike and stared at the lights on the console.

She closed the door gently as she left and walked to the broadcast speaker nearest her desk to turn it up.

As she sat, Sandy Sampson's voice came over the last bars of Sedaka's *Laughter In The Rain.*

"Okay, team, it's time for some news, weather and traffic with

Chicago's best newsman, Dan McIntyre. Dandy Sandy's gonna go get some joe, be back in a few. You're riding Chicago's El and you know this train is bound for glory. Here's Dan."

Good Morning, Chicago. Dan McIntyre, WEL News.

The City of Chicago established a new record for murders last year. In 1974, nine hundred seventy people including six Chicago police officers died of gunshot wounds in our city. According to a comprehensive survey of all nine hundred seventy murders released today by the Chicago Tribune, the number is significantly higher than the previous three years, each of which saw an increase.

WEL News contacted the Chicago Police Department. A spokesman informs us that senior Department officials are aware of the sharp rise and addressing it with a variety of initiatives. The Department will study the Tribune survey and expects to issue a complete response to it in the next few weeks.

In national news, the U.S. Government will soon auction off gold—and lots of it—for the first time in forty two years. Regulations which prevented the government from selling its own gold stock pile have been lifted and the Treasury Department has announced that it will auction two million ounces of gold in the coming weeks. Individuals and investors will be invited to purchase a four hundred ounce brick of gold bullion for approximately seventy thousand dollars. Despite dire warnings from some, Wall Street leaders, banking officials and the Treasury Department do not believe the sale will have a dramatic impact on the economy.

It's time for WEL traffic. Here's the El's Traffic Reporter Robert Roberts with an up to the minute report. Robert...

...Thanks Robert. In other local news, police are investigating what appears to be the suicide of Benita "Beni" Steinart, whose body was found on the pavement below the eleventh floor room she had rented at the Virginia Hotel near Rush Street. Miss Steinart was the manager and hostess of Chase Mansion, the four story residence and party headquarters millionaire bachelor developer Cary Chase maintains on the near north side.

WEL News was on the scene this morning and we have this report from Chicago Police Detective Jack Potter...

...although Miss Steinart had been indicted by Federal officials

last summer on drug-related charges, Chicago police told WEL that there is no indication that her suicide is related to that case.

I'll be back with sports and weather right after this short break...

...Last night the Chicago Bulls defeated the Kansas City/Omaha Kings, one hundred to eighty-eight. Bob Love led the Bulls with twenty-five points while Nate Thurmond and Chet Walker each contributed twenty.

Now, here's WEL's Chicagoland weather. Bundle up. We'll see a high of no more than thirty five degrees and last night's intermittent sleet and winds will continue through the day, so it will feel even colder. WEL reminds you to drive cautiously when sleet is present. It will be clear and cold across the plains today. Chicago will dip down into the very low twenties tonight, with colder temps in the northern suburbs. I'll be back with more after this...

...Finally, in case you missed it, history was made over the weekend, when the state of Connecticut inaugurated Ella Grasso as its new Governor. Governor Grasso is the first woman ever elected to a governorship in her own right after millions of voters exercised their right to vote and elevated their new Governor, like the Wright Brothers, to pioneer status.

I'm Dan McIntyre and that's WEL News. You're riding the El with Dandy Sandy Sampson and the best music in Chicago. Good Morning, Sandy...

The news block, with commercials, ran just over twelve minutes.

After the second commercial break, while she listened to the Grasso story, Emily swung her chair around to watch through the broadcast studio window as Sampson knelt to adjust the stool in front of his mike and console, raising it about six inches. He climbed up onto the elevated stool and brought his microphone up to his new height. It was a ritual performed with the same religious regularity as McIntyre's and as soon as she noticed it, Emily asked Sampson about it.

"Hey, babe, they pay me big to be big in the morning. Nothin' happens in the 5 hour, but at 6 my people start tuning in, so I make myself bigger."

All Right, Chicago! Dandy Sandy riding the El with you this morning, ready to make your day dazzle. Heads up, team, it's nasty—NASTY—out there. Driving in on the Dan Ryan, it was so icy my truck did a double axel. Ice. Truck. Double axel? Get it? Come on now, keep up with Dandy or the El's gonna leave you behind.

It's birthday time! Dandy Sandy's sending a WEL gift pack and seven hugs and kisses to Huck Margiotta out in Skokie. Huck's seven today. Ol' Huck gets ready for school with me so I'm happy to play this one just for him,—it's by the Tune Weavers and it was a hit way before you were born, Huck, but you're gonna like it. It's called Happy Happy Birthday, Baby...

Happy Birthday, Huck. You get to school today, you tell 'em Dandy Sandy and everybody rides the El with you and me says it's your birthday, you get to be first in line all day.

Gonna keep it rolling now with John Denver's tribute to the joys of being a good Christian lad in the boondocks, Thank God I'm A Country Goy...

Emily chuckled as Dan McIntyre came out of the news booth. He was glaring at her.

"Uppity women! What'd you put that in for? Damn women."

Emily offered him her very brightest smile.

"We are woman, Dan, hear us roar."

He sputtered but said no more. Rick Healey, absorbed in the sports pages, lowered his paper to snarl at her.

He said, "Too many 'rights.'"

Emily shrugged. "It seemed like the right thing to do. So, whaddya think, Rick? She wear pants to the inauguration?"

He didn't respond.

Emily picked up her phone and dialed Ben's office.

"Herberger Whittier Stineford and Bovie."

"Hey," said Emily, "they demote you from junior

partner to receptionist, you might want to mention it to your bride."

"New policy," said Ben. "Before the receptionist gets here, we are directed to answer with the firm's formal name. We are informed that this is good marketing. I am skeptical.

"I just switched off the radio. You knew that Steinart woman, right? High school?"

"I did. Do you have a little time? I need to talk."

"Of course. I'm sorry. You ok? How'd you end up there?"

Emily recounted the horror of the mangled body, the shock of seeing Beni's face, her difficulty getting focused to do her job, her sense of unease. She cried now and then.

Ben offered gentle expressions of compassion and support, but primarily he just listened; she could feel his support as she talked, nearly as strong as physically leaning on him. She rambled, flitting from the bond she and Beni had forged in school to the major fundraising events she had covered at Chase Mansion because Beni always made sure she was on the media lists. Finally, feeling somewhat exhausted, Emily paused.

"Did she leave a note?"

"No, nothing."

"That's odd. Maybe she called somebody?"

"I don't know. I didn't have much time there and I wasn't thinking clearly at all."

"Your report referenced a case involving Cary Chase, a drug case. Do you think there is a connection?"

"Potter and the cops say no. Last time we talked, she didn't say a word about it. Now I think about it, she never talked to me about it at all.

"She was nice, you know? Nice to everybody. Happy all the time. She loved her job. It just doesn't make any sense. I don't understand it."

Her sorrowful tone made him wince.

"Perhaps you would care to join me for lunch? I will

eagerly cancel the predictably monotonous meal I have scheduled with two of the partners. I can walk over, join you in the lobby."

Emily was comforted at the thought. A lunch with the one she trusted and admired most, the one who knew her best of all, would be welcome and it felt good to imagine it. But something else tugged at her with equal force.

"You're the best, pal, but I think I'll take a rain check. We're home for dinner, we can talk then. I think I want to go back to the Virginia, ask a few more questions, see what I can learn."

Ben didn't respond immediately and they both let the pause stretch out. She considered anew her decision to forgo lunch with him. He debated pressing or letting it go in deference to her need to revisit the scene and fully grasp what she had witnessed.

"Dinner, then," Ben said. Emily smiled.

"I'll see you then. But you must call if you need me. There exists no suitable reason to suffer alone. I'm here all day." He chuckled. "'Tis a remarkable departure from my usual routine, to be sure, but there you have it."

Emily grinned. Her husband was a talented and resourceful trial lawyer. He worked in a law firm which spent most of its energy and legal man hours avoiding litigation at all costs.

"They don't let you out because they're afraid you'll never come back, pal. Thanks, though, dinner will be perfect and I'll look forward to it all day. Lamb chops, right?"

"Lamb chops."

"Yum."

"Yes, ma'am."

"You're the best. Love you, pal."

"Not nearly as much as I love you. Good-bye."

Over the next three hours, Emily worked steadily revising the newscast, updating and adjusting for McIntyre's 7, 8 and 9 o'clock broadcasts. The pace was slower than it had been in her first hour, but the work filled the hours and she remained constantly aware of the clock. She rarely needed to check the time; she knew the rhythm of the newsroom and the pace of Sampson's show well enough to know, within a minute, exactly what time it was.

Through the morning, she swapped out the gold story for one from Washington which was timelier. She expanded the sports copy a little. She added a very brief story about a CTA bus accident which had caused a traffic mess on the south side. At 8, the audience heard the first stock exchange numbers and another fresh story from Washington. She made several calls, adding phone-taped interviews with a police department spokesperson responding to the Tribune murder story and, at 9, a CTA representative updating the bus accident.

She left the Beni Steinart story in place. Her call to the U.S. Attorney's Office produced only a promise to have a spokesperson return her call, so she retained the Jack Potter tape. The Grasso story remained as the newscast tag; in his subsequent readings, Dan McIntyre's delivery noticeably lacked energy.

During Sandy Sampson's last hour, Emily cut the morning drive copy down to five minutes and left the copy and the interview carts with the mid-day disk jockey's producer. Mike Mitchell, who had the 10 to 3 slot, would break for McIntyre at five minutes past the hour.

At noon, Mitchell gave way to a full half-hour newscast. News Director Dean Lyon anchored the block, Dan McIntyre sharing the air with him. At least one of two field reporters would call in stories live, one from City Hall more often than not. Lyon would interview occasional newsmakers on air during the broadcast and he also regularly talked with representatives from the US Weather Service and stock market experts.

When Lyon didn't ask her to remain in the bullpen to write, Emily was sent out in the field to provide additional material for the Noon broadcast. Unlike the men who reported live on the air, Emily gathered tape interviews, working them over in the editing bay with a seasoned engineer who arrived for work at 9. She also wrote intro's and exits for Lyon or McIntyre to use with the taped material.

Soon after McIntyre signed off the 9 AM news, the news staff gathered in Dean Lyon's office. Only Rick Healey sat out, remaining in the bullpen on the news desk. Healey rarely did much more than tinker with Emily's copy or shuffle the order in which stories appeared; when a breaking story commanded attention, he would interrupt the meeting to get help from Emily or one of the reporters.

The seating arrangement for the meetings was rigid. Dean Lyon sat in his leather desk chair which he wheeled in front of his desk so he wasn't separated from the group. The two field reporters, Al Coffey and Don Kipper, took the couch, Dan McIntyre sat in a comfortable club chair and Emily, the junior-most member of the staff, sat on a folding metal chair.

* * * *

Dean Lyon had called Emily at the end of her shift in the cop shop and asked that she drop by his office in the next couple of days for an interview.

"Couple my pals around town tell me you're good," he said. "I may have a spot for you if you're interested."

"In news?"

"In news."

"I am definitely interested."

"Wait 'til you hear about it," said Lyon. In the interview, she did.

"I've got an assistant news director, Rick Healey, who's got full union seniority. I can't move him without his permission and he likes morning drive 'cause it lets him play golf or bridge or poker with the guys at his country club. He had his way, we'd rip and read all morning long, straight wire copy. Not good enough.

"Then, I got Dan McIntyre. No doubt, the best set of radio pipes in this town, maybe in the whole damn country. People hear that voice, two things happen. They believe him and they want to hear more."

"I know his work," said Emily. "He certainly has a compelling voice."

"Yeah," said Lyon. "I once ran into a guy grew up with him, told me that Dan's mother said a prayer and lit a candle every single night because she was convinced her son had stolen his voice from an angel, she had to atone for the theft. She may have been right, but there's no doubt that whatever the good Lord gave him for a voice, he held back on other stuff. Voice as big as all outdoors, but the guy's sort of mousey, shy, a little strange."

"I'm not sure I understand," said Emily. "You have a senior news man and an anchor who brings an audience with him. Where's the problem?"

"Two problems. One, Healey has been in the business a long time and he's kind of gliding these days, mostly drawing his check and running up his pension. It comes through in his work, his copy is sludge.

"Two, McIntyre's threatening to quit if I don't get somebody who can give him decent copy. He comes in my office every couple of weeks, tells me he's thinking about leaving. I don't think he'll do it, but I'm tired of having to deal with it."

"So where do I fit in?"

"In a second. There's one more thing you need to know."

"Yes?"

"McIntyre and Healey don't speak to each other. Haven't exchanged a word in at least six months. I don't have the faintest idea why. Don't want to know, either."

"Oh."

"So, here's what I have in mind. I want you to take the morning drive shift, write me great copy. Sandy Sampson is number one in the market, I want morning news as good as Sampson is. On paper, Healey will be your supervisor, but if you give us what we need, I'll make sure he doesn't get in your way. You'll figure out how to handle McIntyre in about two days—he's not very complicated."

"Do I get air time?"

Lyon held up both hands, smiling.

"They told me you're aggressive. What I kept hearing, 'uppity' and 'pushy'."

"I prefer assertive," said Emily.

"Ah. Here's the deal. I've had to juggle and connive to get this slot in the first place. The way management has structured it, it boils down to this. It's a part-time job. It doesn't pay enough to hire a man and it's too important for an intern. I told them that means I have to hire a woman, they didn't like it at all. Had a tough time persuading them, but I did."

Emily forced herself to censor several comments.

"Do I get air time?"

"Not yet. Look, I know it's coming. 'BBM-TV's just moved a gal up, one of their producers, she's co-anchoring their early news block. I hear WIND is going to go with a lady, overnights. Great idea, they're easy listening so it'll be a good sound for them. But our GM thinks rock stations should have guys on the air and the network gets skittish anytime we do anything might mess with our ratings, so WEL isn't there yet."

"When?"

"All I can do is promise I'll do everything I can to get you on the air. You've got a singer's voice, light enough for our audience but still with some weight, you'll be a good fit with our sound. But it's going to take time. I'm gonna have to work the bosses long and hard, but I promise you I will."

"I need to think about this," said Emily. "Can I let you

know in a day or so?"

"Sure," said Lyon. "What it's worth, you pass probation you get in the union, you'll be AFTRA. Good benefits, pension plan, job security. Still technically part-time, but probably some overtime."

"I'll let you know."

"One more thing," said Lyon. "You wouldn't be here if I didn't think you can make this work. I think radio news is perfect for you and you'll be perfect for it. I love radio news. I think you will, too."

She and Ben thrashed it out that evening. They both agreed that the opportunity for newsroom experience was perfect. They concurred that the pay structure was lamentable but agreed that the income mattered less than the opening to news.

It was Lyon's passionate dedication to news which tipped the balance for Emily. Instead of working with guys who didn't want her around in the first place, her new boss cared about the work, not the gender.

"I think he's right," said Emily. "I could learn to love this."

And, in a matter of weeks, she had.

* * * *

"Let's get going," said Lyon. "We'll get to the Noon budget in a second, got a couple of things you need to know.

"First, we're adding a new sponsor, morning and evening drive. Ace Hardware. We'll need to adjust for them, they want spots before and after sports reports."

Don Kipper, who had the Sports beat in addition to hard news, shot a look to Al Coffey.

"See? My stuff sells." he said. Coffey offered a rude salute.

"Knock it off, guys. Second, the suits in the carpeted wing told us yesterday, manager's meeting, they're bringing in a couple of program consultants, guys who work for the network. Going to see if they can't do some tinkering, drive our numbers up a little more."

McIntyre, Coffey and Kipper groaned.

"What's the point? We're number one in the market, selling great."

"That's crazy. What're some guys from New York gonna do for Sampson or Decker, Chicago guys?"

"They gonna mess with our newscasts?"

Lyon held up a hand.

"I know, I know. Nobody here's all that thrilled with the idea, but the network insists and they own and operate the place, after all. They say these consultants—they actually call themselves 'gurus,' you can believe that—have done some pretty impressive work in Boston, Cleveland, Indianapolis."

"Big deal," said Kipper. "Small towns."

"We got no options here, these guys are on their way. I just wanted you to know 'cause the word's going to get out quickly. And the real point is, I've been assured that they will not interfere with the news side at all, so mostly this is just a heads-up.

"Look at it this way. They jack our numbers up, the station makes more money. The station makes more money, news side could get some more resources, maybe even raises. Let's just wait and see, okay? Any questions?"

Lyon paused for a moment.

"Okay, Noon news. Emily, you scooped morning drive with that suicide story, you got anything else we can use, beef it up for Noon?"

"I doubt it," said Emily. "Nothing more in the tape we used this morning."

"Nice work, by the way," said Lyon.

"Thanks. Potter's an easy edit, gives tight short sentences, pauses in between. I suppose there's a chance that I can get something from Tommy Jameson's press staff, see if our hot shot U.S. Attorney has any comment, but when I called earlier, they didn't want any part of it. I'll try again, you like."

"Keep at it, at least until it looks dry, okay?"

"Okay."

"And then let's dig into that CTA mess this morning. Let's get statistics, see how often this stuff happens. Maybe check with businesses in the area, see if they have sidebars?"

"I could check on the driver, find out if there are prior problems. I think I got somebody in my rolodex I can try."

"Good. Do that. One more thing. I want Myles Pritchard, Merrill Lynch, for the stock wrap. Book him and tell him I'm going to ask about this gold sale thing. Give him a heads-up, he isn't caught off guard."

"Sure," said Emily. "You want him 16, 17 after?"

"That'll be fine."

They spent another twenty minutes mapping out the newscast. Al Coffey was sent to City Hall, Don Kipper to the opening of a new Operation PUSH community center. Emily lagged behind when the others left.

"Dean, I'd like to take my lunch away today, if that's okay. I'll wait 'til the Nooner wraps."

"I don't suppose you took your break this morning?"

She colored slightly.

"No. I finished a bagel at my desk. I did go to the coffee machine couple of times."

"Healey didn't say anything?"

"Are you kidding? He barely notices I'm there, other than to snipe at me when I walk in."

"He's losing his touch. Time was, anybody didn't take their break, he'd give 'em a hiding, holler about how hard the union fought. Plus, you're part time, remember? That means you have to take breaks, otherwise management's on me for running up your hours.

"Anyhow, here's what we'll do. You leave right after the 12 'cast, we'll add your break to your lunch, you're done for the day."

"Thanks," said Emily. "There's something I need to do."

Lyon looked at her.

"Something wrong?"

"I knew her. She was my friend."

"Knew her? Oh, lord, you mean the girl worked for Chase, the suicide?"

Emily nodded.

"I had no idea." He hesitated. "Wait. Are you telling me you got that story standing over her body? Damn, Emily, that's some piece of reporting. Listen, you want to leave now? I'll juggle the guys, we'll cover for you."

Emily heard only *standing over her body*. It swirled around and into her until it completely engulfed her.

She began to sob.

Dean Lyon led her to the couch. He seated her, handed her a handkerchief and crossed the room, flicking the lights off as he closed the door and left her alone.

2.

Emily left WEL and caught a bus headed north on Michigan Avenue. She got off near the Water Tower and walked the rest of the way to the Virginia Hotel. The sidewalks and streets were slick with sleet and the wind off the lake was harsh. She got a knit beret and a muffler out of her satchel, turned the high collar on her coat up and wrapped herself up in such a way that only her eyes were exposed as she walked.

Inside the hotel lobby, Emily unwrapped and surveyed the place. The lobby itself was modest and modestly appointed and it wasn't particularly bright or inviting. There was a coffee shop at the far end of a hallway which was next to a bank of three elevators. The coffee shop also had a street entrance. She sat in one of the lobby chairs for a few minutes, watching the flow of guests and hotel staff, and then walked to the lobby desk, holding up her ID card.

"Hi," she said. "I was here earlier this morning, covering the incident. Do you have a moment or two to chat with me?"

The desk clerk went from friendly and happy to be of service to wary and nervous in an instant.

"I don't think I can do that," he said.

"I'm just gathering background, you won't be on the air or anything."

"Doesn't matter," said the clerk. "Can't do it."

"Okay," she said, smiling. "Is there a manager I could talk to?"

"Mr. Banks." He picked up a phone, turning away so she could not here the exchange. "He'll be right out."

A very round gentleman in a suit which didn't quite fit came rolling through a door behind the lobby desk, an enormous smile on his face.

"Hello! Bobby Banks! How can we help you?" He handed her a business card.

"Just a few questions," said Emily, presenting her ID again. "Can you tell me what time Ms. Steinart checked in yesterday?"

A quick grimace scooted across his face.

"*Miss* Steinart checked in at 5:45. Cops asked that, too."

"Just for one night?"

"Yup. Course, she wasn't with us all night, but you already know that."

His amused tone didn't sit well and Emily wanted to chide him. She didn't.

"Any visitors?"

"None that we know of," said Banks. "I asked the night crew about that, cops did too. Far as we know, no visitors."

"I see," said Emily. "Did anyone see her leave after she checked in?"

"No, but we tend to pay a lot more attention to people coming in than guests headed out unless they ask us for directions or something. She didn't."

"What time does the coffee shop close?"

The question surprised Banks.

"Midnight. Why?"

"Well, couldn't somebody come down the hall from the coffee shop and turn right to the elevators? If they used the coffee shop's street entrance, they'd never go through the lobby. So if I knew what room she was in, I could just ride up there, same way a guest would."

"Pretty sharp, aren't you? Yeah, that could happen. Desk staff busy, they might not notice at all."

"And the reverse is true as well, isn't it? Ms. Steinart could have come out of an elevator and gone down that hall and out the coffee shop door. She could have come back the same way."

"I suppose so," said Banks.

"Okay. One more question, Mr. Banks. Did she make any phone calls?"

He looked surprised again.

"Geez, the cops didn't ask about that. I don't have any idea. I'll have to check her bill again. Give me a minute or two."

He went back behind the desk and into an office. Emily went to the coffee shop entry hall and walked a few paces into it. She paused for a moment and then walked back toward the lobby, turning to the bank of elevators. Her eyes on the front desk, she waited until an elevator door opened and stood aside as a couple exited. None of the staff behind the registration desk had looked up to see her. Had she entered the elevator, they would not have known it. Had Beni Steinart gone out and returned using that route, they easily could have missed it.

Emily walked back to the front desk.

"One call," said Mr. Banks. "She made a call, local number."

Aha, thought Emily.

"What time?"

"Right around 8."

"Can you share that number with me? We'd be very interested to know about her last conversation."

"I don't think I can do that," said Banks. He made a

face showing her how sorry he was. "Our guests are entitled to a certain level of privacy, you know?"

"I understand," said Emily. "Very respectful. How about this. If I can find that number another way, would you confirm it for me?"

"You mean, you already know the number, I just say 'that's it'?"

"Exactly."

"I guess I could do that," he said.

"That'll be great," she said. "If you don't mind, may I go up to her room, just have a look around? You can come with, you want to."

"Don't see why not," he said. "You don't need me, door to the room is open, they got that cop tape across it. We asked them not to do that, they promised they'd take it down today. They'd better, 'cause I can't book any rooms on that floor, have guests get off the elevator and find crime tape all over the place. We've already moved two reservations to another floor and a couple of the regulars up there are complaining. We're not exactly at capacity, but long term, that tape isn't good for business."

"I can imagine," said Emily. She promised to be in touch. He pronounced himself only too happy to hear from her.

The elevator interior matched the rest of the hotel, a little worn out, a few years beyond tired. The walls of the elevator were scarred from luggage collisions and the carpet on the floor wasn't quite threadbare, but it was close. There was a scent of strong disinfectant in the car.

When the car reached the 11th floor, the doors groaned a little as they opened. Emily stepped out of the car and looked directly down the hall where she spotted the second room on the right adorned with yellow tape. As she walked to that room, the door across the hall opened just a crack. Emily saw a pair of eyes peering out before the door snapped shut.

The room was exactly as Jack Potter had described it.

There was nothing out of place and the only sign that anybody had occupied it was a crumpled corner of the made bed where, Emily guessed, Beni had sat. Emily pictured that moment, wondering what Beni might have been thinking. Regret? Anger? Fear? At the very least, Emily imagined, her friend must have felt utterly and completely alone—she could not imagine any other state of mind which would lead Beni to do what she had done.

She wandered the room, opening dresser drawers, looking under the bed, lifting the cushions on the two chairs which appeared to be well past an acceptable level of comfort.

She stood a few feet from the window for a long time, sifting through memories and images of Beni. She studied the window and its dressing carefully, but she did not move close enough to look out and down. At her arrival she had paused, and shuddered, at the spot where Beni had landed but she had no desire to see it from on high or to confront the path of the fall to the pavement.

She left the room, walked across the hall and gently tapped on the door which had cracked open when the elevator's groaning doors had announced her arrival.

The door did not open. From behind it, a woman's voice growled.

"Whaddya want?"

"Sorry to bother you, ma'am. I'm with WEL news and I'd like to ask you——"

The door opened on a chain. A woman, not young but not aged either, looked Emily over. The woman was working on what appeared to be two or three sticks of gum.

"You were here early this morning. Down there on the street."

"Yes, I was," said Emily. She held her ID up for inspection. "May I ask you a question or two?"

"Don't see why not," the woman said. "You wanna come in, doll?"

The room was a duplicate of the one Beni had taken. This one was cluttered with clothing and magazines and newspapers. There was a stack of Playbills on one of the bedside tables and an open trunk next to the small closet.

"I'm Mavis, doll. They call you Em?"

"Emily. Do you live here?"

"Between gigs. I don't work like I used to, but I get bit parts, enough to keep my Equity status active, stay in touch with my stage pals. Haven't had a nibble since Thanksgiving, but I got a couple of things pending for spring. Regional theater, but hey, work's work."

"The police told me this morning that they talked to a couple of residents on this floor. Were you one of them?"

She snorted. "Nope. They talked to 1115 down the hall, couple of dancers share it. I'm bein' polite, 'dancers.' They're strippers. One of 'em's got maybe another year before her attractions don't attract, the other's already past her prime, mostly works county fairs. Cops all ga-ga over them, didn't bother to talk to somebody might know what goes on, this floor."

Emily smiled. "Someone like you?"

"Of course, doll. Those two don't pay much attention 'less they've got sugar daddy dates. I keep an eye on things, let roly poly Banks know what needs to be done. Place may be a hotel, but it's still my home, y'know? F'rinstance, I betcha those two pinheads didn't see the guy came to visit that gal pitched herself out."

Emily forced herself to remain calm.

"She had a visitor?"

"Sure she did. 10, maybe 10:15."

Emily's mind raced. Beni had arrived before 6 in the evening. She had made a call around 8 and had a visitor two hours later. Had the visitor done or said something to drive Beni to her death? Had the visitor pushed Beni, murdered her? Had Beni invited her own killer into her room? At the very least, Emily had a lead to what was almost certainly the last person to see Beni Steinart alive, an hour or so before she went out the window.

Her breath came quickly and her pulse grew rapid, so she took a deep breath to calm herself before she moved forward.

"Did you see her visitor?"

"Sorta. Same way I saw you, not quite as good. Caught you coming down the hall. Time I got to the door last night, I was watching Marcus Welby. You like that one?"

Emily shook her head. "I'm never up that late."

"Too bad. Good show. Anyhow, time I got to the door to check, couldn't see him full on like you."

"So it was a man. She let him in?"

"Yup. Sounded sorta like she knew him, knew he was coming, maybe."

"What did he look like?"

"Nice top coat on his arm, pretty handsome suit, shiny shoes. Pretty tall, maybe six feet, y'know?"

Mavis had cleared a chair for her and it was even more uncomfortable than it looked. Emily wanted to get out of it but she didn't want to do anything to interrupt the woman's tale.

"Anything special about him?"

The woman gazed off into the distance for a moment.

"Yeah. Guy had one of those haircuts those Panther fellas like so much."

"The Black Panthers?"

"Yeah, that's them."

"You mean an Afro? All natural, curly, fully grown out?"

"Yeah, an Afro. That's it."

"That's interesting."

Mavis snorted.

"No it isn't. I'll tell you what's interesting. I could see his hands, the back of his neck, got a good look. The guy was as white as you and me, doll. Had that black guy haircut but he was a white guy."

"You're right, that is interesting," said Emily. "Did you

hear anything?"

"Not a peep. They didn't talk much in the doorway, she shut her door, I shut mine. Couldn't hear anything. Didn't hear anything but the TV, then I fell asleep 'til those sirens started wailing, stopped at our front door. I don't remember hearing him leave."

"You're very helpful. Is there anything else you think I should know?"

Again, the woman gazed into the distance.

"Don't suppose it matters, but I saw her when she came in."

"And?"

"Just this. She was a looker. Not those gals down the hall good lookin', I mean really pretty. Dressed nicely, hair and nails all done. She sorta glowed, y'know? I've seen a couple leading ladies had that, like they got a permanent key light, follows 'em around makes 'em look perfect all the damn time. She had it."

"Yes, she did."

"Odd, girl with that goin' for her tosses herself out the window. I had those looks, I'd be stayin' in a place a whole lot classier than this one, I can tell you."

Emily rose to leave, her mind still thrashing around the information she had gathered.

Her hand was on the door knob when one more question occurred to her.

"Did she go out? Before her visitor? Do you know if she went anywhere?"

"Groans and creaks, creaks and groans."

"I don't understand."

"You came off the elevator, the doors groaned when they opened, then the floor in that entryway creaked. It'll happen the other way around, you leave."

Emily thought about it.

"So you only check the hall when you hear the door first."

"You got it, doll. Groan first, somebody from outside's

coming in, I like to see what's up. Creak first, it's somebody already up here, I don't pay it much mind."

"So you wouldn't know if Beni, if Ms. Steinart left her room."

"Didn't say that."

"Okay, now I'm really confused."

"I don't know when she went out. I just know when she came back."

Emily leaned against the door.

"Came back?"

"Yeah. She got off the elevator around 7:30. No, wait, must have been after 7:30. Happy Days was already over. I worked with Marion Ross once, summer stock, she's a peach. Don't like that show all that much but we all gotta support each other, y'know?"

"I suspect you're a great friend to your colleagues," said Emily. "I really appreciate your time and being so cooperative. Thank you. Would it be okay, if I need to, I can come back and talk again? Perhaps get parts of your story on tape?"

"Good press, doll, good press. When they spell your name right, right? Sure, come on back any old time. I like you, girly, you got class."

"Thank you, Mavis. You're quite the pistol yourself."

In the lobby, Emily sat and found a reporters' note pad in her satchel. She filled a page with what she had learned.

5:45, Beni checked in. Sometime after that, Beni went out, returning after 7:30. Emily wrote *out to dinner?* Soon after she returned, Beni made a phone call. Around 10 she had a visitor. And sometime later Beni was dead.

Emily checked her watch and saw it was nearly 4 o'clock and it caused her to focus on how tired she was. Past her twelfth hour awake and on the job for most of those hours, she was ready to stop.

She caught a bus and rode north on Sheridan. She got off at Wellington and walked east to their apartment building. The wind came at her from the lake and she had to lean into it to keep her balance, struggling to make progress. Once in the lobby, she leaned back against the closed door to catch her breath. When she got off the elevator, she didn't have the energy to hoist the satchel onto her shoulder once more, so she dragged it along the carpeted floor, slowing her progress but easing the load.

Ben had built a rectangular platform in the corner of the living room to take advantage of the apartment's most desirable feature, banks of tall windows which consumed most of two walls. The view from the platform covered the vast lake to the east and south and well down the shore to the north. Emily tuned the stereo system to WFMT's classical music, shed her coat, dropped it on the couch and collapsed into the Danish recliner on the platform.

She stared out at the Lake and the traffic on the drive, resisting the temptation to doze off. She drifted back through the day, evaluating, considering, grieving. To distract herself, she looked at the stack of books and magazines on the table by the chair. The table's contents amused her.

Every single book on the table was about Watergate. During the impeachment hearings, Ben listened to every minute he could in his office through the day then came home to watch the same hearings rebroadcast in the evening on PBS. He consumed everything in as many newspapers and newscasts as he could manage every day. Now, he was working his way through the stack of books, frequently referencing one against another.

Ben opened the door and she launched herself from the chair and the platform to greet him. He smiled at her and opened his arms and they held one another in a long, quiet embrace.

"I'm so glad to see you," she said.

"And I you." He smiled. "We can safely omit 'How was your day,' yes?"

She nodded.

"Are you holding up? What can I do?"

"Another hug wouldn't hurt," said Emily. "And I probably need to chatter my way through dinner."

"Hug first," said Ben.

Ben changed quickly and began cooking. Emily set the table and poured wine and they chatted lightly about his day until the meal was ready.

"Not bad," said Ben. "Nice wine, too."

"Even better than I had hoped, pal. The chops are just right. But if you served them straight from the fridge, they'd be just right, too. I'm starving."

"Cooking them is preferable," said Ben. "Healthier, too. Speaking of which, spending the entire day on an emotional roller coaster might be expected to produce a symptom or two. Fatigue, anxiety, confusion, hunger. I believe the professionals refer to this as 'trauma'."

"That describes my day."

"I have observed all the other symptoms," he said. "'Starving' completed the list. So, share."

Emily reported the day, repeating some of what she had shared with Ben earlier. She paused now and then to reflect on her own responses to what had occurred and to grieve anew, but she reported the story with the pace and inflection of a newscast. She was not dispassionate but she remained objective. Her report was comprehensive. Ben did not interrupt her.

"So, yeah," said Emily, "bone tired, a little jumpy and I feel like I'm swimming in circles. In sludge. On the other hand, my husband has driven all traces of starvation from my poor weakened body."

"His pleasure, to be sure. Too soon to take a step or two back? What do you see?"

She thought for a moment and said, "Something's wrong. It's absurd to think that Beni would kill herself. She was vibrant and happy and she loved her work. I can't see why she did this."

"If she did," said Ben.

"You mean the visitor."

He nodded.

"I don't think so. I was in that room, there was absolutely no sign that she had struggled or fought. There were no scuff marks on the windowsill, no torn curtain, no furniture out of place. Plus, she would have screamed and when she did, I guarantee Mavis the actress would have heard it. It was so quiet, Mavis fell asleep in her chair.

"No. Unless she asked her visitor to give her a push, she took her own life. And something extraordinary caused her to do that."

"And what do your instincts tell you?"

"I have no instincts yet. There are too many questions. I don't really know a lot about Tommy Jameson's drug case against Cary Chase or how Beni was involved in that. I don't know if that is tied to this, but it is plausible.

"I don't know who she called or if whomever she called was her visitor or someone else entirely. She left the hotel after she checked in, but to where?"

Ben smiled. "You may think otherwise, but I hear my favorite reporter enumerating nothing but instincts. News instincts, to be precise. Have you asked Dean about following up on the story?"

"He liked that we scooped it this morning and he had me try to work it for the nooner, so he'd probably give me some room. But I'm going to follow this without or without that. Something's wrong."

"I hope and trust that you've not forgotten my central thesis regarding reporters and lawyers?"

Emily grinned. "'The good ones make wrongs right.' I know it like my ABCs."

"Indeed they do," said Ben. "Go watch something silly and decompress before you retire. I'll clean up."

He held up his hand before she spoke.

"No argument is going to overcome my resolve. We both know you've been through an ugly ordeal. Go, relax. Tamper not with my edict."

"You really are the best, aren't you?"

"Jury's still out, but I do strive."

A bit later in the evening, Emily went into the master bedroom closet and selected her attire for the following day. She laid it out on the second bedroom bed. She washed her face, put on her favorite sleeping attire, an ancient and deliciously soft Missouri Tiger tee shirt which was at least two sizes too large for her.

She returned to the living room and snuggled up against Ben on the couch for several minutes during which neither of them spoke. When she began to doze off, she stirred herself, stood and gave her husband a romantic good night kiss.

"Love you, pal," she said.

"Not as much..." he said. "Sleep well."

With the shades down, the curtains drawn and the alarm clock angled so the glow of the dials didn't reach her, Emily pulled the covers above her head and fell asleep before the clock reached 8:30.

3.

*F*or several days Emily worked the story.

She visited all three daily newspapers where she dug through archive files and consumed everything each paper had written about the case involving Beni Steniart. The Tribune's stories, which mirrored the other two papers, were all written by a day shift crime beat reporter Emily knew casually, a fellow she had seen and chatted with now and then when they both covered the same story or event. She dropped by his desk after she'd read his work to ask if he'd left anything out or had an insight he might share.

The reporter didn't have anything to add, "It's all on the page," but he did praise an article Mike Minor at the Chicago Reader had written about the case. Emily read that piece and then spent some time on the phone with Minor, learning what he knew.

She called Jack Potter and he put her in touch with a couple of Chicago narcotics detectives. They didn't know anything about the Federal case, but they were helpful with background about the two men who'd been arrested with Beni.

Eventually, Emily believed she had the basic facts of the case.

Donny Marsh was an efficient, energetic drug dealer. He did a thriving, growing business on the near north side of the city where he maintained a lucrative clientele of affluent liberals. Marsh's extensive reach caught the attention of the FBI. Soon enough, the FBI and the U.S. Attorney's office sought and secured a warrant to tap Donny Marsh's phone.

Among those who communicated regularly with Donny Marsh was Grant Wilson. Although Wilson professed to be a freelance ad sales rep, there was no evidence to support the claim. He was, however, a ready source of pot and cocaine, Donny Marsh being his primary supplier. He did enough business to drive a Corvette, dress stylishly and make sizable donations to his own unique list of charities.

Wilson donated only to charities which held fundraising dinners or parties at Chase Mansion. He did so to gain access to the stylish and exclusive world which swirled around Cary Chase's home, Chicago's sophisticated social epicenter. Grant really liked being one of the select who frequented the Mansion often, but the donations were a business expense. While he recognized that conducting business—cash for drugs—in the Mansion itself would guarantee his permanent expulsion, he didn't hesitate to seek new customers at every event and he rarely failed to find them.

For that reason alone, Grant Wilson made it a point to remain on Beni Steinart's good side. As Cary Chase's executive coordinator at the Mansion, in charge of every event staged there, she had power Grant respected. They chatted often during his regular visits and eventually, Grant asked Beni out. They became friends and occasional casual bedmates.

Grant Wilson and Donny Marsh conducted a series of phone calls planning a trip to Kentucky. The FBI monitored every call. When Marsh told Wilson they would need to rent a car with a "big ass trunk," the FBI organized a surveillance team.

With FBI agents watching and following, Grant Wilson drove a very large Buick while Donny Marsh sat in the back seat with two suitcases. Their first stop was Chase Mansion, where Wilson went in and returned with Beni Steinart on one arm and an overnight bag on the other.

When they got to Paducah, they took two rooms at a motel. The next morning, Donny Marsh drove the Buick to an abandoned barn several miles south of the city where he met a man in a suit and two guys with a panel truck. Marsh exchanged the two suitcases for enough bricks of cocaine to fill most of the trunk. The load made the Buick visibly tail heavy.

The trio spent the rest of the day exploring Paducah. They went to a local bar and ordered drinks and food early in the evening and when it was fully dark they got in the car and headed back home.

When the Buick reached Chicago, the FBI team closed in and arrested all three of them. Donny Marsh, Grant Wilson and Benita Ann Steinart were charged with felony transport and possession of illegal narcotics and a long list of lesser charges.

Emily met with Tim Humphrey, the public defender who had been assigned to Beni's arraignment and bail hearing. Humphrey insisted that they meet in the Federal building's courtroom halls, his work load so demanding that he rarely left that building. The hall was so noisy that they ended up sitting on the steps in a stairwell.

"As soon as I talked to her, I was glad I caught the case," Humphrey told her. "The prosecutors had nothing on her, nothing at all. I knew I could get her off with a minimum of work and there was no question that she was absolutely innocent. I don't get a lot of that."

"You got out on her own recognizance, right?"

"Right. They got, what was it, a hundred fifty grand

bond on Wilson. Prosecutor went on for a while about what a scourge on the city Marsh was and the judge agreed to a million for him.

"I laid out the lack of hard evidence, her solid ties to the community and her full-time job in the city." Humphrey grinned. "I also think I said 'innocent bystander' about nineteen times. Shameful pandering, but it had the virtue of being true. She walked out after the hearing."

"But they didn't drop the charges against her."

"Nope. The Feds had two, three tons of evidence against the two guys. They had the phone taps and the team of agents as primary witnesses, they had the drugs, the cash and the three guys in Paducah. Hell, they even had telescopic photos of the exchange at the barn, with Marsh and the other three so clear they could be sitting right here."

"It's inconceivable that Beni had anything to do a drug deal. Why didn't they just let her go?"

"Well, she was in the car for the whole trip. Doesn't mean guilty but it doesn't look good, either. I knew it was wrong place, wrong time. They're prosecutors so they saw guilty is as guilty does."

"Did they interview her?"

"Sure. I prepped her, although she didn't need it, and she told them exactly what she told me. She had no idea what was going on. Wilson asked her to go last minute and she thought it would be fun. She met Donny Marsh for the first time when she climbed into the Buick. While the exchange was taking place, Grant told her Donny had gone to visit a cousin outside of Paducah. She didn't even know the drugs were in the trunk until the FBI opened it."

"Why didn't the prosecutor believe her?"

"He did."

"Really? Then why—"

"Steinart was in the wiretap transcripts."

"What? How is that possible if she didn't know Marsh

until they took off for Paducah?"

"I didn't say they had her *on* tape, I said *in* the transcripts."

"I don't understand."

"I didn't either until I read them. Turns out Grant Wilson is one disreputable cat. Not only did he leave her wide open for a felony rap, he also bragged about his conquest. Four, five times when they were just shooting the breeze, Wilson tells Marsh he's playing red hot slap and tickle, crows about how great it is, runs on about how he and Cary Chase are so tight 'cause he's at the Mansion all the time, dating the babe runs the place."

"Ick," said Emily, "Stories like that make me happy to be done with dating. But was there anything in the transcripts linking Beni to the drugs or the cash?"

"They swore they gave me every page where she turned up. The feds'll play fast and loose with evidence when they want to, but I don't think they misled me. There were no references to Steinart or Cary Chase in the context of the trip to Kentucky. One of the FBI agents told me they were surprised when she got in the car with those two idiots. They didn't expect that."

"Is there more? That doesn't sound like much of a case to me."

"It wasn't, but I'm not done. Wilson and Marsh hired their own attorneys and as soon as their lawyers talked to the Feds and saw the evidence, they started bargaining. Last thing they wanted was a jury trial.

"So Wilson's guy says Wilson'll testify against Marsh. Wilson offers a guilty plea, depositions, court testimony, whatever the Feds need. He wants his sentence reduced and he wants a guarantee that he will not be sent to the same prison where they lock up Marsh.

"Marsh's lawyer chimes in with a similar proposal, but there's a big twist to it. Marsh claims the entire enterprise was engineered by Cary Chase. Says Chase was going to split the haul down the middle, half and half. Says Chase's money fronted the buy. And, he says, Steinart went on the trip as Chase's liaison, his eyes and ears."

Emily was speechless.

"Yeah," said Humphrey, "that was my reaction, too. I didn't know whether to laugh or spit fire.

"I told the prosecutor I was going to petition the court to provide me with any and all evidence linking either Cary Chase or Benita to the drug deal. Told them I wanted to see bank transactions putting Chase's money in Marsh's hands, said I wanted everything in the transcripts, supported Marsh's allegation. And I told them I'd demand a jury trial just so we could put Grant Wilson on the stand to testify that Donny Marsh was lying his teeth out. Can't recall whether I actually threatened them with a malicious prosecution suit, but it sure crossed my mind.

"The prosecutor told me not to bother, not to waste my time. He said they didn't have anything other than Marsh's cockamamie story, that's the word he used, said Marsh was looking at a lifetime in a cell, he was grasping for straws. Told me to relax, it'll all work out."

"Did it?"

"Not exactly. So now, nobody wants a trial, everybody agrees to the plea deals. Couple of days before the sentencing hearing, the prosecutor tells me they're going to agree to 7 to 10 for Wilson, they cut five off the top end for him, 25 to life for Marsh and time served for my client, which was next to nothing. They asked for a nolo contendre plea from her, didn't even ask for a guilty plea on one of the minor charges."

"So, what happened?"

"It got weird is what happened. We get to court and it goes smooth, everybody playing their part. The two guys offer their pleas and get the sentences as agreed. We get to Steinart and before I can say a word, the prosecutor tells the judge the DA's office wants to delay her sentencing while they re-evaluate. I objected, laid out the facts and the absence of any evidence against her, but the court wouldn't even consider a deal the prosecution hadn't agreed to. The judge deferred to the DA, big surprise, but he told them to be quick about resolving the matter. He didn't think it fair to drag her through much more.

"Wilson and Marsh are doing time as we speak. I called the DA every day for a couple of weeks, then once, twice a week to get it resolved, but nothing happened. She was still in limbo when she died all those months later."

"She wanted to go because she said it would be 'sick' to see a town named Paducah. I remember because I didn't get the 'sick' part and she had to explain it to me. She said it means odd or unique."

"And fun," said Emily.

"Yes. She wanted to have some fun."

Emily and Beni Steinart's mother Lucy were sitting in the living room of a small house in Evanston. Emily had been uncomfortable from the moment Lucy showed her in.

She had known Lucy—it had been Mrs. Steinart back then—because when her high school coterie needed a place to gather they often landed in Beni's large northside Chicago apartment. Mrs. Steinart had been a vivacious hostess. She was always happy to see her daughter's friends, she knew everyone by name, she was quick to break out soft drinks and chips. She would always disappear in the way parents did, out of sight but hovering.

That woman was not in the room with Emily now. Lucy Steinart was bedraggled, her hair dirty, her clothing stained in several places. Her face had no luster, her eyes didn't quite focus and her demeanor was listless. One side of her mouth alternately drooped and twitched. When Emily accepted Lucy's offer of a cup of coffee, the woman came back with two mugs; Lucy's did not contain coffee.

Emily wasn't happy to bring her daughter's death to Lucy's doorstep and she was deeply troubled by the toll that death was taking on Mrs. Steinart, but she wanted more than the press and Beni's attorney had given her and she'd scheduled the visit to that end. As uncomfortable as she was, Emily pressed on.

"When did you talk to her about the trip?"

"The night before they left. We were supposed to have dinner that weekend, so she called to say Grant had invited her on this road trip and she was going. She said she had to see the town with the silliest name she'd ever heard, even funnier than Kennebunkport. But she promised to come for dinner later in the week."

"Did you ever meet Grant?"

"No. She told me he was just a guy she knew. I asked 'cause I thought it was time she married. She wasn't ready, she said, and even if she was Grant wasn't on the list."

It came out "lisht."

"Did she ever say anything about Cary Chase when you talked about the arrest with her?"

Lucy perked up a little.

"No," she said. "But he called me."

"What? Why."

"Wonderful man. Wonderful. He wanted to pay for Emily to have a lawyer, said he'd hire the best in town for her. She turned him down. He called me to see if I could persuade her to change her mind."

"But you didn't. I've talked with her court appointed lawyer."

"She was stubborn as a mule about it. She said it was her mess, she was responsible for it. She thought they were trying to drag Mr. Chase into the case and she knew that was crazy but she wasn't going to do anything to help them. She was afraid that if she took his money, they'd all ask why he was paying for her lawyer if he wasn't involved.

"Besides, she knew she hadn't done anything wrong and she could prove it with that lawyer they gave her, so she didn't need Mr. Chase's help anyhow."

She paused, staring down at her coffee mug.

"We had words about it. I was terrified that she'd end

up in prison if she didn't get a good lawyer and I got pretty loud and angry with her. Wish I hadn't done that now."

Lucy laid her face in both hands, shaking, and Emily felt like an intruder.

"Mrs. Steinart, may I use your bathroom?"

"Lucy. You're grown up now, dear, you can call me Lucy. It's down that hall on the left."

Emily splashed water on her face and spent several quiet moments in the room. She'd done the usual morning shift, worked four different stories for the noon broadcast and then taken a bus and the El to Evanston, walking several blocks to get to the house. It had been a long day even before the anguish of the grieving woman reached her so deeply. She wanted to curl up and lie down on the cold tile floor.

It felt unseemly to her, but Emily knew she had another piece of the story. She had a direct connection between Cary Chase and Beni in the context of the drug case. She understood and admired Beni's refusal to accept Cary Chase's offer of legal assistance. She understood as well why Lucy Steinart had tried to force her daughter to accept that help. Beni was protecting her friend and employer, Lucy protecting her daughter.

When Emily went back to the family room, Lucy Steinart was nodding off in her chair. Emily considered leaving her, just walking out, but she had another question to ask and little appetite for returning to this house ever again.

"Mrs. Steinart, I have just one more question and then I'll be gone, okay?"

Lucy jumped in her chair, a quick blush of embarrassment adding some color to her face temporarily. She sat up and did her best to focus on Emily.

"Yesh, please. I want to help."

"Thank you." said Emily. "Beni made a phone call from her hotel room the night she—the night we lost her. Did she call you?"

Mrs. Steinart registered a moment of shock and then all expression left her face.

"She didn't call me? She called somebody else, but not me?"

Devastated, the woman looked like she might slide from her chair to the floor, as if her bones had turned liquid.

Emily could not press on.

"I'm sorry, ma'am. I didn't mean to upset you. Thank you so much for your time. I can see that losing Beni has been hard for you. If it helps, I'm very sorry about her death. She was a wonderful person. You raised a terrific daughter."

Lucy Steinart's chin lolled on her chest. She appeared to be sound asleep.

"I'll find my way out," said Emily. She reached out and held Lucy Steinart's hand for a moment and went to the phone in the hall to call Uncle Max's cab company.

The cabbie rolled down the passenger window just enough to be heard.

"You Max's girl?"

"Yes."

He reached across his seat and opened the back door for her.

"Hop in. Max says you get kid glove treatment or he pours sugar in my gas tank."

Emily grinned.

"He'd do it, too."

"Damn straight. So where we goin'?"

Emily gave him the address and then said "Can you do me a favor?"

"Any pal of Max's," said the cabbie.

"I'd like to listen to WEL, please."

"You got it."

Emily enjoyed Sandy Sampson's forcefully up-beat play lists and manic approach to his morning show, even though there was more than a little calculation in his work.

She thought Mike Mitchell's more reserved play list, still pop and rock but quieter, and his more subdued style worked well through the middle of the day.

Jon Decker did evening drive on WEL and Emily adored him.

Ben had listened to WEL long before Emily got her job there because he believed "JD the DJ" was a Chicago treasure.

"The gentleman is as cool as Steve McQueen and as smart as Stephen Sondheim," Ben said to all who would listen. "Give him twenty minutes and you'll be thoroughly and hopelessly addicted for the rest of your days. I certainly am."

Emily agreed. Where Sampson had deliberately created a successful morning drive personality, JD was an absolutely natural without a hint of artifice. Jon Decker loved his job because it allowed him to share music he loved even more. He knew more about pop and rock music than any of his peers and he never stopped exploring it all. His affection was so rich and deep that it easily reached his audience.

Jon Decker called that audience "friends" and Emily was convinced that every last one of them believed it because Decker himself did.

In the growing darkness, deeper and gloomier because the sun had not shown all day, Emily settled back in her seat and let the radio supplant the agitated distress she carried from her visit.

In a few minutes, she was sitting up again, leaning forward to better hear the cab's radio.

Friends, I have something special for you. I've been hearing a lot about some guys over in England, got together, formed a band. Spent some time finding their sound, but when they found it—well, you'll see. The band is called Queen.

Last week, I asked one of my friends to get a copy of their hit single from England. Their U.S. label is going to release this in a month or so, but you're going to hear it right now on the El. It's a Chicago radio exclusive with special thanks to BOAC stewardess Suzie Henderson, who flew it in from London just for us. This is "Killer Queen" by Queen...

...Mighty hard to find more high energy rock and roll than that. Slick lyrics, kickin' tune, blazing guitar work and that guy out front, Freddie Mercury, sings with some serious style. I love what he does. The man starts at flamboyant and builds it up from there. He's not just a singer, he's a performer.

Which brings us to today's history lesson, friends, 'cause you can't know where you're goin' if you don't know where you been. Today's lesson is about roots. Freddy Mercury's explosive singing and that I-give-you-everything-I-got-every-time attitude comes straight from the original, another Killer long before Killer Queen.

Freddy Mercury is walking the path blazed by Jerry Lee Lewis. Listen and learn, friends. Here's Great Balls of Fire...

The Killer to Killer Queen—it's all connected. That's today's lesson. Now, now let's check in with WEL traffic...

Over dinner, Ben and Emily chatted about their plans for the weekend, a case Ben was working on and their response to Decker's exclusive. Ben loved it. Emily thought it was okay but agreed that the lead singer was something special.

Most of their recent dinner conversations had included Emily's work on the Steinart story and now Emily steered the conversation to her unhappy visit to Lucy Steinart's house. She shared the discovery that Cary Chase had offered to provide Beni with a high powered lawyer.

"She had Humphrey from the PD's office, did she not?"

"Yes. He's the one walked me through all the courtroom stuff. I liked him."

"He has a superior reputation. I know of at least two firms which have tried to seduce him into private practice. She had good counsel."

"I think she knew that. Chase must have wanted her to

have one of his lawyers a lot if he went to the trouble to solicit her mom to help. But Lucy said she was adamant about not dragging Cary Chase into her mess."

Ben sat back and took a sip of wine, staring out the windows for a moment.

"That raises a question or two," he said.

"Oh?"

"At trail, I've observed, it is never wise to place an overabundance of trust in what one perceives to be the truth."

"I do love how you go on, pal, but I don't understand."

"I'm trying to say that one should look at every possible angle before arriving at a conclusion. We have a vivid example before us.

"Mr. Chase's offer appears to be the gesture of a fellow helping a friend or a boss providing support to an employee. But, suppose that Donny Marsh told the truth. Imagine that somehow Cary Chase set the whole enterprise in motion and that he was more than clever enough to keep himself entirely apart from it at the same time."

Emily stared at him for a moment and then rose from her seat and went to the windows.

After a moment or two, she said "If Chase was behind the drug deal, he'd do anything to make sure that never came out."

"Precisely," said Ben.

"If he thought there was any chance that Beni knew he had a connection to Marsh, he'd have to make sure she couldn't expose that."

"And therefore?"

"He'd hire the best lawyer he could find to make sure Beni never had to testify to anybody about anything."

"The lack of evidence against the man was compelling enough to persuade the DA's office that there was no fruit on the tree," said Ben, "but if Chase was in fact the progenitor of the plan, he would need to be absolutely certain. He would seek to fell the tree. If your friend never got to trial, Chase had no cause for concern because she's the sole connection to him.

"A man of Chase's wealth and stature would invest a lot in maintaining both. The price of a top litigator would be insignificant if it nullified any chance of exposure."

"Sometimes you scare me," said Emily, smiling.

"Alas, the curse of trial practice is the loss of any semblance of trust. In court, I doubt one and all, including my own clients. It may comfort you to know that I make every effort to confine that perspective exclusively to courtrooms."

"It does," said Emily, resuming her seat. "Now I have a question I need to ask you."

"I have been completely, happily and gloriously faithful to you for the entirety of our marriage, my love."

"Not that one, silly, I know the answer to that one. I really need to talk to somebody in Tommy Jameson's office and the press people over there are dodging and ducking. Do you think it would be appropriate to give Greg Good a call, ask for his help?"

Ben considered the question briefly.

"If it is inappropriate, Greg will say so. Of course, he'll be perfectly gracious if he finds it untoward. But it is also entirely possible that he will accede to the request.

"Either way, unless I misread, it will surely do no harm to ask."

"Good," said Emily.

"I believe we've already established that he is the subject here," said Ben.

"What?"

"Good."

"No, I wasn't—." Emily stopped because she saw his wry smile. "You're teasing me."

"Good of you to notice," said Ben.

Emily groaned, stuck her tongue out at her husband and began gathering the dinnerware.

Greg Good had graduated first in his law school class. Ben Winter was second. They were the best of friends.

Ben had taken a job clerking for the 9th District Court of Appeals after graduation. Greg Good accepted a position on the staff of Illinois Attorney General Tommy Jameson.

Good quickly discovered that he was without enthusiasm for trial work or arcane contract disputes. He was, however, intrigued by the politics of the work Tommy Jameson's office did and since Jameson was an elected official with unfettered ambition, politics infused every decision the office made.

It didn't take long for Jameson to realize that Greg Good had rare and welcome political skills and instincts. Good had a quick mind, an innate talent for honing and crafting his words as he spoke and his manners and his gentle southern drawl caused virtually everyone he met to like and trust him. Soon enough, Good was moved out of everyday legal work and named Director of the AG's Communications Office. It was generally conceded that Jameson made no move without consulting, evaluating and calculating with Good. One of the most respected political reporters at the Sun-Times once wrote that Jameson could end up living on Pennsylvania Avenue if he consistently relied on "Good advice."

When the position of U.S. Attorney for the Northern District of Illinois became vacant, Greg Good and Tommy Jameson engineered a quiet campaign to win Jameson the post. They succeeded and Greg moved to Chicago with Jameson as the new DA's chief of staff.

Ben and Emily and Greg and his wife Alicia were very close friends. Ben and Greg found time to chat almost every day and the two couples were frequent dinner companions and occasional movie double dates. When they could work it out, Emily and Alicia shared long lunches.

When Emily called, Greg welcomed her request, noting

that her objective—securing and exposing the story of Beni Steinhart's death—was his own.

"We'd like to put this thing to bed, too," Good said. "Let the poor girl rest in peace."

They met in the Mallers Building and took an elevator to the third floor where a counter service deli, packed to its seams with tables and chairs and a few booths, served an endless line of regulars and visitors who cherished the place despite its odd location.

Emily loved the building. It had staffed elevators, the attendants seated on tiny stools taking floor orders and operating the cars and their doors manually. It contained multiple floors of diamond dealers of every imaginable ethnicity, a sizable contingent of jewelers and a Frye Boot store on the 15th floor. The deli had the best pastrami in the Loop.

She was sampling her pickle when Good said, "So, what do you need?"

"Let's start with this. I know that there were plea deals in place for Grant Wilson and Donny Marsh and that Beni Steinart's attorney had been promised a very good deal, too. But when they all went to court—"

"Our prosecutor delayed Steinart's sentencing."

"Exactly," said Emily. "Why?"

Greg Good took his napkin from his lap and dabbed at some mustard on his lip. At the same time, his eyes swept across all of the tables to his left and right and those behind Emily. He then dropped his napkin to the floor and, standing to pick it up, he swept the tables and booths behind him.

He sat and held Emily's gaze with penetrating intensity.

"We are completely and absolutely off the record. No notes, no tape, no attribution, nothing. Clear?"

Emily held up her hand, palm facing him.

"I promise."

She raised her other hand.

"I double promise."

"You're the only reporter I'd trust with that," Good said. "But just to be perfectly clear, if you use any of this, it'll cost me my job. So when I say I trust you, I'm putting my career in your hands."

"Your job is safe" said Emily. "I swear, it's just you and me."

Greg took a large bite of his sandwich and chewed slowly. Emily could almost hear him parsing his words.

"Tommy Jameson wants to take down Cary Chase," said Greg. "He wants that very badly."

Before she could squelch them, both of Emily's eyebrows shot up.

"I'll try to explain," said Greg. "First, you have to understand that the man is an encyclopedia. He reads everything, he never misses case assessment sessions, litigation planning conferences, senior staff and strategy meetings. He wanders the office checking on people, he reviews staff calendars—nothing gets by him. And he retains it all.

"Once, we were standing outside the break room when a secretary walked up to the coffee machine. She hadn't been with us more than a week. As a joke, I bet him he didn't know how she took her coffee. He said 'artificial creamer, one and a half packets of sugar.' That's exactly what she put in the cup. Cost me five bucks."

"Impressive," said Emily.

"Yes. So here's the point. The minute he heard that the FBI was on the trail of a guy with a connection to Cary Chase, he took over. The whole investigation, the arrests, the plea negotiations, all of it. When they pulled that Buick over, the first thing the agent in charge did was radio Jameson. Tommy personally confirmed that Steinart was one of the three in the car."

"That's when he announced an investigation."

Greg sighed.

"Against my firm objections," he said. "I thought it was premature and the case against Chase was already looking weak, but he wouldn't hear it. I'm telling you, he was on this like Jimmy Walker on 'Dyn-O-Mite!'"

Emily gave him a blank look. She had heard others use the phrase, but it had no meaning for her.

"Sorry," said Greg. "I forget you keep those horrible hours, no time for prime time, right? Kid on this show, Good Times, hollers that about sixteen times in half an hour."

"Ah, got it," said Emily. "Can you tell me why he's so hot to get Chase?"

"I think so, sort of. Tommy was raised in a religious family. They went to church every Sunday, he stills attends that church and the congregation is rock solid conservative. He's spent his life learning to be agin sin and it's a great big part of who he is now. When he isn't careful, it can be a real blind spot. This is probably one of those times.

"Tommy Jameson thinks Cary Chase is a sinner of the highest order. He talks about debauchery, lechery and licentiousness at Chase Mansion. He's convinced that everybody who goes to a party there sleeps with everybody else. He calls it a sin palace. I've actually heard him say 'den of iniquity.' When we argued about the press conference, he told me he would be ashamed for the rest of his life if he didn't smite the devil down."

Emily laughed. Greg Good shook his head sharply.

"Don't. This is serious. He was on a crusade and nothing we tried would stop him. The prosecutors told him over and over again that there just wasn't any evidence connecting Chase to Marsh or Wilson. No paper trail, no phone contacts, no financial transactions. He sent the FBI team out three times to find something, anything, and every time they came back empty. He was not happy and he let them know he wasn't happy. The agents were pretty well ready to shoot him by then, but he didn't care."

Emily considered it all and said, "I think I see what happened. Beni was the only possible link between Chase and the drug deal, so Jameson refused to close that door."

"Yes. The plea deals were all in place and at the last minute he told the prosecutor to back away from the Steinart deal. The prosecutor objected. I objected. Jameson ordered. It happened."

Good spoke with a level of intensity which Emily had not seen before. There was an unpleasant undercurrent in his tone and Emily thought there was a note of sadness as well.

"So, what did he do?"

"As far as I know, he didn't do a damn thing. We kept asking him to let it go, to let *her* go, but he kept saying he wasn't done yet."

"So Beni died thinking she was, what? A criminal? A pawn? Helpless?"

"I don't know about that. I do know justice wasn't very well served and it sure as hell wasn't fair to her. She deserved better."

There was icy anger in his eyes. He looked away and then came back.

"Are you busy later?"

"No. Why?"

"You can see for yourself. There's a minister, church not far from U. Chicago, who's on the warpath about rock and roll. He thinks it's the devil's work and he wants most of it banned. He's hosting a panel discussion this afternoon in his church's assembly hall. Some guy who's an expert on the Buckley Report will be there—"

"Buckley Report?"

"State Senator in New York, James Buckley, William F's brother. A while back, he wrote a report which concluded that the rise in drug use in the U.S. is caused by rock songs which celebrate getting high."

Emily giggled.

"Seriously?"

"Seriously. But here's the point. Tommy's going to be there too."

"On the panel? He's a U.S. Attorney, how can he do that?"

"He's there to offer advice as an attorney who's an active member of his own church, representing an allied congregation. For balance, the minister has somebody from the ACLU on the panel, but Tommy's technically there as a private citizen."

"That's weak," said Emily.

"I agree," said Greg, "and I told him so. But, as I say, he places his sense of morality above all else. He told me he had to do this, heavy emphasis on had. Point is, you can go see for yourself."

Emily sat in the back of the hall. She'd left her satchel at the office, so she had no press badge, no equipment to record or take notes. She fancied herself just another interested citizen, although there were but a handful of white faces among the hundred or so people assembled.

The event host began with a somewhat muted and brief sermon about sin. He cited adultery, disrespect for elders and the ravages of drug use in particular and tied each of those directly to lyrics he quoted. When he found an unacceptable sexual reference in "I found my thrill on Blueberry Hill," Emily suppressed a giggle, wondering what the minister might say upon learning that the good Christian Pat Boone had recorded that song soon after Fats Domino made it a hit.

The Buckley Report expert cited chapter and verse as well, using lyrics from dozens of songs to portray contemporary music as one unending ode to the glories of adultery and addiction.

The ACLU lawyer quietly asserted the view that art is speech, fully protected by the First Amendment. He also expressed his skepticism about the ability to tie drug usage or adolescent sex to songs of the radio, but he did so without rancor.

The others had remained at their places at the table on the stage, but Tommy Jameson rose to speak. He paced as he spoke, gesturing in swoops and waves as he made his points.

Jameson assured everyone that he was not speaking in his capacity as their U.S. Attorney and he would not comment on legal theories about censoring music. Instead, he said, he wanted to talk about rights and responsibilities.

"It may well be true that these artists have rights," said Jameson, "but the exercise of those rights carries a responsibility. Those who create popular music have a responsibility to enlighten, to celebrate our precious values, to lead those who seek out this music to a sober and responsible way of life, a life of fidelity and faith. The failure to do so may or may not be illegal, but it is certainly immoral."

Jameson spoke of the "satanic seduction" of virtually all the music young people consumed on the radio every day. He castigated stations catering to younger audiences as "irresponsible demons." He questioned the Federal Communication Commission, an agency he thought to be in the grip of "spineless sinners." When he was done, a few in the audience rose to their feet and others shouted "Amen!"

Yet for all of that, Emily felt the man was restraining himself, holding back. On several occasions his cadence and his energy rose, taking on an urgent, driving rhythm. Each time, Jameson caught himself, deliberately slowing the pace, dampening his passion. She wondered what might result if he shook off the restraints and gave in to his zeal; she imagined it would be something to behold.

When Jameson returned to his seat, Emily slipped out of the hall and left the building. As Greg Good had predicted, she had seen the at least some of Jameson's zealotry. She found it impressive and powerful.

4.

"*W*ell, there's no doubt you know how to run down a story," said Dean Lyon. "How'd you find the time to get all this?"

"I spent a Saturday in archives at the Sun-Times and the Daily News. The rest I did on my lunch hour or after hours during the week."

"Impressive. So, where do you think it all leads?"

They were sitting in Dean Lyon's office. Emily had taken the club chair Dan McIntyre claimed in news staff meetings, an act of rebellion she rather enjoyed. It was Friday afternoon. Typically, she would have left work as soon as the Noon news wrapped. Instead, she had remained because the entire program staff, those in front of and behind the WEL microphones, had been summoned to a meeting at 3. She had taken a long lunch and scheduled her meeting with Lyon for 2.

"I think it leads to Jameson. If this was some sort of vendetta, if he used his office and its power to serve his own glory mission, that's news."

Dean Lyon shook his head.

"Nope. Doesn't fly. Look at what you really have. Tommy Terrific has been notorious for as long as he's been around for headline grabbing, he'll show up at a dog pound opening if he thinks cameras will be there. I got twenty bucks says he saw Cary Chase's name and began composing headlines on the spot. The hungriest politician in Illinois wanted to be on the front page? That's not news, it's an everyday fact of life."

"But he left Beni out in the cold, dangling. That's an abuse of power."

"Might be, but you'll never get him on it. He's too slick, for one thing. I can already hear that guy, what's his name, Good, saying that she wasn't damaged in any way, she wasn't in jail or even fined, she was just waiting for a final resolution which was sure to be in her favor. Not news."

Emily had to concentrate to avoid flinching at the mention of Greg Good's name. She also briefly lamented her agreement not to tape their discussion, because she was certain that Good's passionate analysis of his boss's actions would make the point more strongly than she.

"Well," she said, "I still think there's something there."

"Not worth our time. But that's not all you have."

"No, it isn't. The events the night she died come next. Who did she call? Where did she go? Who was her visitor?"

"Right," said Lyon, "that's where I'd go too. How?"

"The hotel staff on the shift that night might have something. I haven't checked with the coffee shop, but she may have been in there."

"All we know, she may have had dinner there and gone right back to her room."

"Maybe. Then there's the visitor. Mavis the actress described him and he's sort of unique. I don't quite know how to go about it, but finding him could lead to something valuable."

"They have a door man at the Virginia?"

"No, I already thought of that—maybe somebody on

the street or in the lobby saw him too. Or somebody saw her leave. I'll go back and see what else I can find."

"What else?"

The question unsettled Emily. She had evaluated all the leads several times over lunch before their meeting. She had tried to anticipate what Dean Lyon would ask and say to each thread and she decided that more investigation at the hotel was her best bet. She had laid out the Jameson vendetta angle because she thought it had a little merit, but she relied in the main on the hotel and Beni's last night. Dean had agreed with her and now she had nothing else.

"I think that's our best bet, the Virginia," she said.

"That's it?"

Something in his tone set off an alarm.

"Pretty sure," she said, letting it hang as a question.

"Come on, kiddo, work it out. There's a big piece missing."

"Donny Marsh?"

"Nah, I don't think so. Guy trying to bargain his way out of a life sentence is gonna say whatever he thinks the prosecutor wants to hear. And you say there's no evidence to support his story about Chase. Almost certainly nothing there."

Emily dug into her satchel and pulled out her reporter's notepad, flipping pages, searching for anything and, embarrassed, stalling.

"Emily. Who's missing? Who hasn't said a word?"

"Oh, damn," said Emily. "Cary Chase."

Lyon smiled and nodded.

"Chicago's most famous bachelor, top ten richest in town every year, has that mansion every living soul in town wants to get invited to. He's on top of the world, Jameson says he's being investigated for drug dealing and he's silent? Chase's confidante, the woman he trusts to manage his house and his social life, gets arrested and we don't hear from him? She kills herself and he *still* doesn't say anything.

"You don't have him quoted anywhere, right?"

Very quietly, Emily said "No. No quotes."

"He's the gold medal, kiddo. You get him, WEL's gonna shine all over town."

Emily clenched her fists and used her left to pound the arm of the club chair sharply.

"Damnit, Dean," she said, "I didn't see that. Not at all. There are days, I wonder what the hell I think I'm doing."

"You're being a reporter, Emily, asking questions. You just hadn't gotten to that one yet. You would have sooner or later."

"But I didn't get there. You did."

"Look here, lady. You've done a great job on this and you can do more. Find out about that night. Go after Chase."

"I will," she said, and then looked away, a grimace crossing her face.

"What?"

"Not so long ago, I would have called Beni and she'd have talked to Chase for me, probably convinced him to talk to me then and there."

"That's sad," he said. "But I suspect you can find a way to make it happen anyhow."

"We'll see," she said.

"Atta girl."

"Thanks, Dean. Thanks."

"Just doing my job, kiddo." He checked his watch. "Let's get out there now, meeting's in about five minutes."

The bullpen was as full as Emily had ever seen it. All the station's producers, engineers, news staff and air talent were there. Sandy Sampson, rarely seen after 11 or 11:30 in the morning, was slumped in a chair wearing sunglasses. Emily wasn't sure he was awake. Mike Mitchell and his producer were engaged in an animated conversation. The overnight dj, Dave Gershwin, was there; Emily had seen the man in person exactly once.

Jon Decker was on the air, the studio speakers quietly

broadcasting the opening of his afternoon gig. That confused Emily because JD was also, unmistakably, in the bullpen with everybody else. Decker, well over six feet tall, was wearing faded red jeans over ornate cowboy boots, a starched sequined cowboy shirt, a tooled leather vest and, at a jaunty angle, a black British bowler. She skirted around the room to the main studio window and saw a reel to reel tape machine feeding into the broadcast console. When she looked back at Decker, slouched against the editing bay door, he winked at her and grinned.

WEL's General Manager, Sam Butler, walked into the room. He was virtually indistinguishable from the dozen or so men who worked in the advertising department because until his promotion he had been one of them. He was gregarious and energetic and he worked the room as soon as he entered, wandering among the group glad-handing and grinning. He didn't acknowledge Emily, but Emily suspected the slight was because she was standing next to JD.

The two men did not get along, Decker the unruly kid to Butler's school principal. Most recently, Butler had taken an angry call from Queen's label and their lawyers, furious that their embargo on the Queen release had been violated. Butler embraced and then expanded on their anger when he spoke to Decker about it; most who had been in the WEL offices at the time, including those at the far ends of the entire floor the station occupied, heard the exchange.

While Butler was still being everybody's best friend, two men came through the bullpen doors. The first was a very large man, well over six feet, extremely rotund and heavy. He wore a dark suit which featured a flowing coat cut much like a monk's cassock. He wore his hair in an exaggerated, slightly overlong Beatle cut but unlike those mop tops, he had a sizable and perfectly round bald spot in the center of his scalp.

His companion was the big man's antithesis. He was

small and wiry and he moved like an eager puppy, dancing and prancing behind his colleague. His hair and a full beard, three competing shades of light brown, were tightly curled. Emily wondered if she was the only one in the room who had an urge to pat the man on the head.

Sam Butler gave up his tour and headed for the far end of the room where the two men had settled. As he joined them and turned to face the group, Jon Decker uncoiled from his slouch.

"My friends," Decker said, "I give you Nip and Tuck."

Butler shot a paint-singeing look. Everyone in the room saw it and stopped laughing, but Emily was a click behind them and the distinctive giggle from the only woman in the room hung in the silence. Butler shifted his angry glare to her and she put on a serious face.

Butler welcomed everyone and introduced the two men, but it was too late. Nobody remembered the names they heard that afternoon. The two men were Nip and Tuck for the duration of their stay at WEL.

The big man did most of the talking, the little one nodding enthusiastically and fidgeting endlessly. They were from New York, they had worked in several radio markets on several of WEL's network sister stations and now they had arrived in Chicago to "rev up" the station's ratings and to "protect WEL" from its enemies.

The presentation was filled with language Emily found difficult to understand. Tuck talked about "the synergy of culture" and "audience compatible programming" and "market driven initiatives" and "audience survey integration." Every now and then, Sam Butler would nod sagely, although he looked slightly unnerved by the little man beside him who wouldn't stand still.

Emily did understand Tuck's discussion of WEL's competition. He was correct that a growing contingent of FM stations was aggressively experimenting with formats and playlists which traditional AM stations either could or would not try. Tuck talked about FM rock station program directors who were creating formats well removed from the traditional classical music playlists which had been FM's staple. Many of those were expanding well beyond the pop and rock hits released as singles which AM stations, including WEL, broadcast. These upstarts were playing more album cuts and artists and songs which didn't fit the typical Billboard Top Hits formats. The landscape was shifting, Tuck said, and WEL had to move ahead of the shift.

When Tuck was done, Sam Butler took over and informed the group that he was excited to have fresh ideas at the station and that he knew everyone in the room would be cooperative and supportive as the two consultants went about their business. He didn't ask for questions, but when he paused, Sandy Sampson jumped into the opening.

"So, Sam, what exactly is it these guys are gonna do?"

"Sandy, they're here to help us make our market share even larger than it is, to put us even further ahead of our competition."

"Yeah, yeah," said Sampson, "I got all that. But what are they going to *do*?"

For the first time, Nip spoke.

"We're going to listen to what we have, look at what the rest of the market is doing and make some recommendations. We know you're number one in the market, but we think you can be more than that."

Sampson chuckled. "What's better than number one?"

"A higher number one," said Nip.

Butler closed the meeting by repeating his directive for full cooperation, staring directly at Jon Decker as he did. Smiling just a little, Decker met his stare and held it until Butler led Nip and Tuck out of the bullpen.

Most of those in the room lingered, buzzing.

Emily prepared to leave, collecting a couple of items from her desk and organizing her satchel. While she was getting ready, she watched as Jon Decker headed for the broadcast studio, leaning over to discuss something with his producer. As he passed the bullpen broadcast speaker nearest the room's double doors, he reached up and turned the volume control up a lot.

Decker went into the studio and waited for The Carpenter's *Please Mr. Postman* to finish. When it did, he hit the stop button on the tape machine, cued the engineer and leaned into his mic. He gave a live station ID, a time check and then cued a commercial break.

By the time the commercials ended, Decker had swung the mic boom around so he was facing the bullpen. Standing, he looked through the window at the staff with one hand in the air giving his engineer a stop sign.

Happy Friday, friends. JD the DJ here to remind you that there's nothing but fun between here and stormy Monday. And on this fine Friday, I want to dedicate a song to some very special friends. This one's from Paper Lace and it's for the gang here at the El.

Decker offered a slightly twisted grin as he cued his engineer. As the speaker broadcast *The Night Chicago Died* into the bullpen and down the WEL halls, Jon Decker removed his bowler and placed it over his heart.

5.

On Friday nights, Emily didn't have to get to sleep by 8, 8:30 at the latest. The end of the work day on Friday marked the beginning of her brief weekly return to the real world's clock and she cherished it. However tired she was, she always found a way to set the fatigue aside and enjoy life on her own timetable. On most Friday nights, her weekends began at Ricardo's, a restaurant which was literally below the Wrigley Building just west of Michigan Avenue. Ricardo's was almost exactly equidistant from the Tribune and Daily News offices, walking distance from both.

On Friday nights, print and electronic reporters, photographers, freelance writers, radio and TV producers, news anchors, publicists, ad agency creative staff and ad sales reps all met and drank at Ricardo's fanciful bar, an enormous artist's palette turned on its side. Sportswriters talked politics, political writers talked sports, print reporters swapped stories, celebrity columnists mingled with beat reporters, movie critics shared drinks with political operatives.

The conversations were smart, fluid and passionate and Emily loved all of it. On the rare occasions when the spirited and spirits driven gathering didn't generate a strong second wind, the other standing feature of her Fridays at Ricardo's did. Whatever else they had planned for the night or weekend, Emily and Ben always met at Ricardo's.

Emily left her coat and canvas satchel at the coat check and stood on the raised entry steps to survey the crowd around the bar. She knew at least half the people in the room by name and another dozen or more as faces among the press, acquaintances if not friends.

She took in the crowd at the bar first and then checked the booths which ringed the room. When she spotted The Rules Committee in a back booth, she worked her way through the crowd to join them.

There were no men in the booth. The women, each with at least one drink at hand, were all professional colleagues and they welcomed Emily heartily. Mary Massey had been a producer with the local CBS affiliate's TV news department until, quite recently, she had been introduced as the co-anchor of the station's first evening news block at 4:00. Linda Marshall was the business reporter at one of Chicago's larger radio stations. Lois Lipton covered Illinois courts for the Tribune. Abby Evans was a feature writer and music critic for the Chicago Reader. Marcy Marcus produced most of the day part programming at an FM rock station which had generated a lot of talk around town for its adventurous and eclectic playlist.

They all shared a bond. Each was the first female to fill their respective jobs. They had discovered one another through work and one of them—none could remember who it had been—had suggested that they all meet to share stories and support; Ricardo's was the only logical meeting place. Their first meeting was delightful, reassuring and so warmly supportive that each of them was thrilled to be part of it.

During a discussion at that first meeting about the ways in which their male bosses consistently treated them as outsiders, one of the women said there should be a manual for other women trying to break through to male only jobs.

"It won't work," Emily had said. "It's impossible to know what they'll do next. When we *think* we've figured it out, they change the game. There aren't any rules at all."

"Well, then," said Lois Lipton, "let's make some up."

It took time, but they eventually realized that there really weren't any rules to guide them. While they were slightly frustrated at their lack of progress, they were more than satisfied knowing that, however tough their work might be, they were not alone.

"Maybe," said Emily one evening, "the only rule we need is the one we use all the time. Maybe the only rule which works is 'Break the Rules.'"

Linda Marshall rapped a spoon on the table and called for a vote. The women all laughed, but a motion to adopt the rule drew unanimous support. So did their resolve to continue, with or without a mission, and The Rules Committee had been meeting weekly ever since.

When Emily joined them, Mary Massey was sharing an encounter from earlier in the day. Mary had dressed as she normally did for her anchor shift. She wore a tailored blazer over a blue blouse which accented her eyes and her blond hair. Her boss, the news director, was in the studio and four minutes before they were to go on the air, he walked up to her and said, "You can't wear blue jeans on the air."

Just as Massey had done, the table burst out in laughter.

"You sit at a desk," said Lois Lipton, "Nobody can see your waist, never mind anything lower."

"He was joking, right?" said Abby Evans. "Lord knows, he's got me in stitches."

Massey said the director had been completely serious. In less than 3 and a half minutes, she had returned to her office, grabbed an on-air suit she kept at work "just in case," changed and made it back to her anchor desk in time to welcome her audience.

During the first commercial break, her boss came onto the set and smiled.

"Much better, Mary. Next time, let's get rid of the sneakers, shall we?"

A round of drinks arrived at the table. Mary held up her hand and said, "Wait. There's more.

"First, the skirt from my backup suit didn't match the blazer or the blouse at all, not even close. A full-blown fashion nightmare. *That* didn't bother anyone at all.

"Plus, I'm co-anchoring with Skip Boone, right? Skip Boone, who never buttons the top button on his shirt. Skip Boone, who wears his ties permanently loosened, even on the air. And, get this, Skip Boone, sitting right next to me, was wearing blue jeans."

Groans and laughter followed and then the discussion moved forward. When a lull appeared, Emily jumped in.

"I need to get to Cary Chase and I don't have a solid inside contact. I can go through the front office but they'll just run me over to the PR people. I need Chase, one on one. Do y'all have anybody I can try?"

Most said that they covered Chase only when he sought the coverage, at groundbreakings, business news conferences or charity events.

Linda Marshall said that she had a cooperative contact in the Chase Enterprises communications office and offered to call Emily with a name and number on Monday.

Lois Lipton said, "You might try Joe Burton."

"Who's he?"

"Joe Burton's the lawyer who represents all the cab companies in town. Every time some taxi scam gets reported or a cab's involved in an accident or a crime, Burton's the guy who represents the cab industry. Somebody takes a cabbie to court, it's a sure bet the lawyer representing him will be from Joe Burton's staff. The City wants a new regulation governing cabs, Joe Burton's all over City Hall knocking it down."

"But what does that—"

"Patience, girl, patience. Joe Burton is very quiet about it, but he also works for Cary Chase. Burton's the Executive Director and chief legal counsel for the Chase Enterprise Charitable Foundation. He and Cary Chase are close friends, have been for years. Cary Chase listens to Joseph Burton. If Burton says take the interview, Chase'll probably take the interview."

"That's super," said Emily. "I'll chase that down on Monday."

"No pun intended?"

"What pun? Oh, 'chase.' I get it."

The conversation shifted again and continued for an hour or more. They were merrily discussing the hilariously ill-fitting toupee which a nationally known Sun-Times reporter had recently adopted when Emily spotted Ben coming through the front door.

He checked his coat and a package and headed for the bar. He swept the room as he moved and spotted Emily and The Rules Committee, waving to get her attention. The wave was unnecessary; Emily hadn't taken her eyes off him from the moment he entered the place.

Emily excused herself and made her way to the bar.

"Hi, sailor," she said, "you in town long?"

"All weekend, ma'am. You shore are a beauty, you are. I mean, Golly!"

"Buy me a drink?"

"Shucks, it'd be my pure pleasure, ma'am."

He grinned and leaned over to kiss her lightly.

Emily frowned.

"Let's not get fresh here."

"Too forward?" said Ben.

"No. Too early in the evening."

"Aha."

"Aha indeed, my handsome friend."

They had no specific plans, so they sipped their drinks and ran through a list of places to go for dinner, finally settling on a small cafe near Lincoln Park. They collected their coats and gear and caught a cab.

"What's that?" asked Emily, pointing to the package Ben had retrieved with his coat.

"A treasure, I hope. A colleague of mine in New York works in a firm which represents several reputable publishing houses. One of those is circulating advance copies of a new book called 'How The Good Guys Finally Won.' It's by Jimmy Breslin."

"Fine writer," said Emily. "What's it about?"

Ben didn't blush, but there was a hint of chagrin in his answer.

"Watergate."

"Really? Another one? How many does that make?"

"I fear I have lost count. Let us agree on more than several. Before I lose track of it, do we have anything scheduled, next Friday?"

"Other than drinks at Ricardo's? I don't think so, but I'm not sure. Why?"

"The firm has purchased a table at ACLU's annual dinner. It will, no doubt, be tedious, rife with maudlin speeches and the presentation of awards nobody will remember. Still, it is a most noble cause. The partners have all decided not to attend."

"Uh-oh. You've been tagged to represent the firm, haven't you?"

"With my lady by my side, I most desperately hope. Much as I love the organization, such an affair would be well nigh intolerable without you."

"Who else?"

"The partners are going to fill the table with clients or colleagues they believe will enjoy the evening. Ten at the table, I'm told, thee and me and an octopus of strangers."

"Gee, that sounds like more fun than just about anything else we could come up with."

"Doesn't it just? Still, we'll be together and I promise—nay, I swear by all that matters—that we will be seated side by side."

"That's good enough for me," said Emily.

Over dinner, Emily shared her update and strategy session with Dean Lyon and then recounted the entire session in the bullpen.

"Did these two fellows, this Nip and Tuck, happen to mention plans for the news department?"

"Nope. When we first heard they were coming, Dean promised us they'd leave the news side alone. They didn't mention news and neither did Butler."

Ben snorted. "I remain skeptical, but time will tell. The entire undertaking leaves me unsettled. It probably would have done so in any event, but JD the DJ's response seems rather an ominous storm warning, does it not?"

"At first, I thought it was funny," said Emily, "but when he removed his hat it seemed a little like a funeral."

"One hopes his vision is faulty," said Ben, "even as one fears otherwise."

Riding to their apartment, Emily set her satchel aside so she could sit close to Ben.

"Hey, pal. Care to make out?"

Ben grinned and nodded.

When her formal shift ended on Monday at about 1 o'clock in the afternoon, Emily remained at her desk, tethered to a telephone.

She called Chase Enterprises and requested an interview with Cary Chase. The receptionist who took the call initially laughed aloud at the request and immediately routed the call to a Marketing office secretary. The secretary was cordial but insistent that Mr. Chase was not granting interviews at this time. When Emily persisted, she was referred to Penny Public Relations.

When she called the agency she was transferred to its principal, Donna Penny, who told her that Mr. Chase was not available to the press, that he had not given any interviews of any kind for quite some time and had made it clear that he had no plans to do so.

"I'd really like to ask him about Beni Steinart's suicide," said Emily. "I can only imagine that it has had a significant impact on him and on the management of the Mansion."

"I'm sure it has," said the agent, "but if that's what you're after, I can absolutely guarantee that he will not speak with you. There is absolutely no chance of it. None."

"Could you at least convey my request to him?"

"It won't do any good."

"Still," said Emily.

"OK, but there's a catch. I'll tell him what you want, but you have to promise me that you won't be calling me every twenty minutes about it."

Emily hesitated.

"One call, just to follow up?"

"No calls. If he says yes, you'll be the second to know. Otherwise, no pestering. Deal?

"Deal."

Emily called Joe Burton's law offices, identified herself and asked to speak with Burton about a matter involving Cary Chase.

"He's not here," the receptionist said. "If you give me a number where he can reach you, I'll give him the message."

"I'd appreciate that," said Emily. "It's a matter of some urgency."

"I see. Well, then, I'll make extra sure he sees the message. Is that okay?"

"Yes, thank you."

"Okay. Listen, I don't want to be rude or anything, but can I ask you a favor?"

"It can't hurt to ask," said Emily, thinking any leverage she could garner might get her beyond the brick walls she faced at the moment.

"I just love that Jon Decker, JD the DJ? He's funny and

so smart with his history lessons and all. I'm not supposed to have a radio at my desk, but when it's quiet here, I sometimes get to listen to him before I close the office down."

"Do you want to make a song request? I can pass it along?"

"Gee, that would be great, but what I'd really like is a photo, maybe autographed?"

"I think we can arrange that. What would you like it to say?"

"Honestly? You can do this for me? Wow, let me think. How about 'To Joan, my biggest fan.'"

"Sure," said Emily. "I'll see what I can do. Thanks for letting Mr. Burton know I'd like to speak with him."

"Oh, I'll be real sure to do that."

Before she left her desk, Emily found Decker in the WEL lounge. He laughed at the exchange she described and signed the 8x10 glossy she'd pulled from the files, adding 'Love!' to the inscription. She put it into an envelope with a brief thank you note and her business card and dropped it in the outgoing mail box at the station's front desk.

Although the sky was dark, it was only about 4 in the afternoon when Emily left WEL. She bundled up and walked down Michigan Avenue, window shopping and ducking into a favorite shop or two along the way to get warm for a few minutes. Along the way, she encountered two people she knew.

An associate at Herberger Whitter Stineford and Bovie she had met at some office gathering hailed her and spent a few minutes telling her how grand it was to work with Ben. Emily thought he was being overly enthusiastic, but she was cordial.

A block or so later, a Chicago publicist who worked with Hollywood studios promoting stars and their latest films corralled her, urging her to interview an actor whose name she did not recognize about a movie she didn't know existed. She listened attentively and took his business card but made no promises.

In the final few blocks before she got to the hotel, Emily reflected on a city large enough to be second in the nation could also be a village, the Loop or Michigan Avenue its unofficial town squares. She doubted that such encounters were common in New York and she suspected the only way residents in Los Angeles met one another was on freeways as they crawled side by side.

The young man behind the counter at the Virginia Hotel coffee shop wore an apron tied at this waist, a plain white uniform supply service shirt and a paper cap which sported the hotel's name on the crown. The shirt was not fully buttoned, exposing a Loyola University tee shirt. A stack of text books, one open, and a notebook sat on a shelf near the cash register. The kid looked up from his book when she took a seat at the counter and ambled over.

"Good evening, ma'am. What can I get you?"

"Just a Coke for now, please."

"Fresh from the fountain. Coming right up."

While he drew her soda from the tap, Emily pulled her news staff ID and a 4 x 5 photo from her satchel.

"Just the Coke? You want a burger? Tuna salad? We got a grilled cheese, bacon and tomato. It's pretty good."

"Not right now, thanks, but I'd like to ask you a few questions if that's okay."

He looked at her identification.

"No kidding? The El, that's Dandy Sandy's station. Cool. Whaddya wanna know?"

"How long have you worked here?"

"Since school started, last September. Well, August. I came back early 'cause they needed help right away and I needed the job real bad. So, what, about 5 months, I guess."

Emily slid the photo across the counter.

"Do you recognize her?"

He looked, frowned and shook his head. Then he

looked again.

"Wait. She's that girl, jumped out the window here, right?"

Emily opened her notepad.

"Yes, it's the same woman. How do you know that?"

"She was here. Same night she jumped. Right after I came on, I think, early in the shift. She was knock-out pretty, I mean Wow, you know? She had a Coke too, I didn't charge her."

"She didn't eat anything?"

"Nope. Mostly we do coffee and soft drinks in the evening, sometimes a sales guy'll drop in, order a club sandwich, maybe a slice of pie ala. I'm not complaining, mind you. Gives me more time to study."

"How was she? Nice? Upset about something? Crying?"

"She was real quiet. I remember 'cause like I say, she was a beauty and I thought, can't hurt to flirt, you know? But she was really sort of far off, like she wasn't quite here. She didn't sit still much either, seemed nervous. Then she was gone. Maybe fifteen minutes, sitting just down there."

"Did you see her leave?"

"You bet." He blushed. "I don't want to shock you or anything, but I wanted to see that girl move. I watched her walk out. Man, she was somthin'. Stone cold fox."

"Which way did she go out?"

He pointed to the street entrance.

"That way."

"Not through the lobby?"

"Nope. Right out that door."

"Then what?"

He shrugged.

"Beats me. The door closed, I stopped watching."

"Did she wave down a cab? Maybe got in a car, waiting for her? Did she walk down the street, one way or the other?"

He shrugged again.

"I really didn't see a thing after she left."

"Do you remember anything else?"

"Don't think so. 'Cept, I was real sorry when I heard she was the one on the pavement that night. Real sorry."

"Yes," said Emily. "So was I."

She paid for the Coke, left a generous tip and went out the same door Beni had used. She stood on the sidewalk, searching for a cab stand or a bus stop and saw neither. The street was quiet, lined mostly with low rise apartment buildings, small store fronts and a couple of office buildings. There was not much traffic and the only people she saw were two middle aged couples, speaking French, who walked past her and turned the corner. There was nothing else of interest so she followed the tourists, enjoying the lilt of their language. When they turned into the hotel's front entrance, so did she.

There were two clerks behind the front desk. The first saw her ID badge and walked away. The other was polite enough to ask if he could help and caught a venomous glare from his colleague. When Emily asked if Beni had asked the front desk to call a cab for her, the fellow smiled.

"Can't help you with that. I just started here couple weeks ago. I wasn't around back then."

"Was your colleague here then?"

"He sure wasn't. You notice he's sorta cranky? That's 'cause they moved him from day shift to nights. He's not exactly thrilled about it."

"Is there anybody around who worked nights last month? Maintenance man, night security guard?"

"Um, we don't have security here. There's a maintenance guy on call, but he's not here unless we call him."

The clerk glanced over at his colleague, busy trying to understand and assist the French foursome. He leaned forward, lowering his voice.

"Truth is, there's a whole lot of turnover here. The manager's been around forever, they say, but the rest of us are pretty new. Other hotels pay better, draw clients who know how to tip. This place is mostly a stop between better jobs. I'm on the prowl myself. Sorry."

Emily thanked him and turned away, then turned back.

"Do you happen to know if Mavis, the actress with a room on eleven, is here?"

The clerk smiled.

"She's got work. I can't remember, Boston, maybe? There's a note right here, says her mail is being held at the Post Office but we should keep an eye out for anything slips through."

He checked the note.

"She didn't give us a return date."

Emily walked back to Michigan Avenue and caught a bus. By the time she arrived at the apartment, she was completely discouraged.

"Nothing," she told Ben over dinner. "Not a single lead, all dead ends. Nothing."

6.

*A*bout half an hour after she got to work the next morning, Nip and Tuck came into the bullpen. Tuck took a seat against a wall, watching the room and the studio window as he sipped coffee. Nip didn't sit. Instead, he moved to the other side of the room from his partner, near the editing bay door, and paced back and forth.

Rick Healey noticed the two men in the room and did his best to appear to ignore them. Still, while he continued reading the sports pages, he did so with his feet on the floor, not propped up on his desk. Emily saw him look over his shoulder at least twice to glance at Nip; both times, Healey returned to his reading shaking his head.

Dan McIntyre's desk was closest to the spot where Tuck sat and it clearly made him nervous. He tried his best to maintain his usual empty gaze at the newscast studio window, but he couldn't stop turning around to confirm Tuck's continuing presence.

Emily thought it odd the two didn't speak or otherwise acknowledge anyone else in the room and, while she focused on her work, she couldn't ignore their presence.

When she finished the 6 AM news copy, she walked it over to McIntyre and watched his pre-broadcast routine carefully. When he went to get his suit coat he still stepped on only four tiles but they were not the same four he normally used. He veered off course to be as removed from Tuck as possible.

When she saw that, Tuck's intrusion on the news team's morning pace and rhythm annoyed her. She worried that McIntyre might be thrown enough to actually make a mistake reading his copy and she felt a pang at the thought. She resolved that if it happened, she would ask Tuck to move. Or leave.

She needn't have worried.

Good Morning Chicago. I'm Dan McIntyre and this is WEL news.

President Gerald Ford told a group of oil industry executives at a conference in Texas yesterday that gas will be rationed in America quote over my dead body close quote. The President met with the executives to assure them that the nation's current petroleum supply problems will be addressed quickly and forcefully. Rumors of rationing measures such as alternate day gas purchasing have persisted in Washington. The President's remark was taken as a sign that the administration is not considering any of those options.

In local news, election finance statements issued this morning reveal that Alderman Bill Singer has raised just over $255,000 in his bid to unseat Mayor Richard J. Daley. Alderman Singer told supporters at a rally yesterday that his drive to bring change to the city is generating more contributions that even he had hoped for.

Mayor Daley staged his own campaign rally yesterday in a Baptist church on the south side where 50 Chicago ministers gathered to endorse his honor's re-election bid. Political observers expect the Mayor to continue rallying his base among the city's African-American communities and in union halls as he seeks another term.

In other local news, Elijah Muhammad, the leader of the Nation of Islam remains in critical condition following a recent heart attack which doctors describe as quote severe unquote. Mr. Muhammad, whose family is at his side, is expected to remain hospitalized for several days.

We'll have sports and weather on the El right after a brief break and Robert Roberts' report on traffic this morning...

Thanks, Robert. The Chicago Bulls lost to the Philadelphia 76ers last night, one oh nine to ninety seven. While they briefly held the lead in the first half, the Bulls' four game winning streak was snapped as the Sixers pulled away to the twelve point final margin.

On the ice, the Los Angeles Kings bested the Chicago Blackhawks, two one.

Here's today's weather. There is no relief in sight from the cold snap gripping the city. Our high today will again remain below freezing with temps no higher than thirty degrees. Cloudy skies and a chance of snow flurries will remain throughout the day. Tonight's lows will be in the mid to low twenties across Chicago land. I'll be back with a final story after these messages...

History was made yesterday when Great Britain's powerful Conservative Party elected Margaret Thatcher as its leader. Mrs. Thatcher is the first woman to lead her party and when next Parliamentary elections take place, she is expected to stand as a candidate for Prime Minister.

I'm Dan McIntyre, that's the news from the El. Now, here's Dandy Sandy Sampson. It's all yours, Sandy.

McIntyre glared at Emily when he came out of the studio, but he hastily checked to see if Tuck was still in his seat and, confirming that, didn't say a word.

Rick Healey beckoned Emily to his desk.

"Nobody gives a damn about some broad in England, girlie. Drop that one from the 7."

"Rick, it's history in the making. Sooner or later, she'll be England's first female Prime Minister. Seems to me that's news. How about this? I'll leave it in, but we'll ask Dean when he gets here. You both agree, I'll take it down."

Healey hesitated, calculating his odds of winning the argument if Dean Lyon became involved. He concluded, as Emily already had, that Lyon would support Emily's choice.

"Fine. Leave it. But I think still think it oughta go."

Good Morning Chicago! Dandy Sandy here to make your day dazzle. Let's get you up and running with Linda Rondstadt's hot new single, which also happens to be a tribute to my first wife: You're No Good...

Okay, team, birthday time! I'm sending a WEL gift pack and a couple of tickets to a Blackhawks game to one of Dandy Sandy's best buddies, Kathy Adams out in Schaumberg. Your package is on the way along with birthday greetings from the whole gang here at the El. And just for you, Kathy, the Beatles are here to rock your morning because You Say It's Your Birthday!"

For the first time, Tuck stirred in his chair. He took a small note pad from his monkish coat and jotted something in it. He then waved at Nip who came bounding across the room. Tuck opened the doors and both men left. Neither of them had said a word to anyone during their visit. Emily wasn't sure whether they were being mysterious or just rude.

The news staff came out of their morning planning meeting just as Sandy Sampson ended his shift, giving way to Mike Mitchell. As Mitchell adjusted the mic and positioned himself at the broadcast console, Nip and Tuck came into the room and resumed their earlier posts.

Emily took up her satchel, bundled up and walked from WEL to City Hall. She had been assigned to capture audio at a news conference where Mayor Daley was scheduled to introduce a dozen Democratic big wigs from Washington, all in town to endorse the Mayor's re-election.

She was walking down the hall to the press room when the Mayor and his entourage exited an elevator and joined her. The Mayor spotted her immediately and turned to his colleagues.

"Hey, guys! It's the little lady reporter. Hey, little lady! Come over here and say 'good morning' to me."

Emily, blushing, turned to find the Mayor immediately behind her. As he swept forward, he threw an arm around her waist.

"Little lady, I'm always glad to see you. You here to cover all my friends from D.C?"

Emily nodded, hurrying to stay beside him.

"Great, just great. Walk in there with me, okay?"

His arm still around her waist, the Mayor surged forward toward the press room door smiling at everyone he passed, calling out to many by name. Waving with his left hand, he began to tilt slightly until his girth, his rapid pace and his firm grip lifted Emily off the floor. When an aide pulled the press room doors open to admit the Mayor, he entered carrying Emily on his hip.

"Excuse me, your honor."

"Little lady?"

"Sir, could you please put me down?"

Laughing heartily, the Mayor dropped her.

When all the luminaries had praised the Mayor and the Mayor thanked them, a press aide moved to the podium to conduct a Q & A session. Everyone, including several of Chicago's most seasoned City Hall reporters and a contingent of Washington reporters covering one or more of the assembled visitors, began shouting and waving to get the aide's attention. The Mayor came to the podium and elbowed his aide aside.

"Hold on there, Chip. I want the little lady to go first. Little lady, what's on your mind?"

"Your honor, do you have any reaction to Alderman Singer's recent campaign fund figures? He reports raising quite a bit of money. Are you concerned about that?"

"Ha! See, guys? The little lady knows her business. Well, let me say this. Dese guys come and dese guys go, but da Mayor is here to stay. Dese guys can raise all the cash dey want, but da people know what's best for da fair city a Chicaga and you can't buy dat."

The Mayor's quote, with the reference to Emily edited

out, aired as the lead story on WEL's Noon News. The NBC affiliate's local evening newscast aired video of the Mayor's response and it turned up in two of the three daily papers.

Later, she was sitting at her desk listening to the half-hour Noon newscast when one of the office staff walked up and handed her a pink telephone message. It said "Call Linda Marshall."

Under R in her rolodex, where Emily filed every business card she collected at Ricardo's, she found Marshall's number.

"I'm sorry I lost track of this," said Linda, "I promised you a connection to Cary Chase."

"Thanks, Linda. I'll take anything I can get at this point. I'm just not getting anywhere and I'm afraid Dean's going to kill the story. As things stand, I'm not sure I can argue with him."

"Well, maybe this will help. My first job out of college, I was in marketing at the Art Institute. I shared an office with Kirsten Bonner. We both moved on pretty quickly. She went to a PR firm and then to work for Cary Chase, been with him ever since. The communications office there handles mostly investor relations and b-to-b marketing. It's not a big staff, but she's senior in the office and she's very close to him. Try giving her a call. Use my name."

"That's great. Really, thanks so much for this. First round's on me on Friday."

"If it gets you what you need, every round's on you."

"Linda, if this works out I'll buy you drinks *and* dinner. Thanks again."

Emily dialed Chase Enterprises and asked for Kirstin Bonner.

"This is Kirstin."

Emily identified herself and offered the reference from Linda Marshall.

"How's Linda doing?"

"Quite well. You know she's been at WBBM radio doing regular on-air business reports, but now they've got her covering day-to-day news, too. I see her frequently, she loves her work and she's happy."

"That's good. We were both bored to tears at the Institute. Nothing to do with the place, it's as grand as they get, but we were at the bottom of the heap and it was pretty tedious work. We both moved on and up from there."

"That's why I'm calling you. You may be in a position to help me. I would like to interview Cary Chase about Beni Steinart's death."

There was a long pause. Emily was considering saying something more when Bonner finally spoke.

"I can't talk to you from here. Can we meet somewhere? I haven't taken my lunch break yet."

Emily suppressed an urge to cheer aloud.

"How about the Tea Room at Marshall Fields? It's walking distance from both of us."

"I love that place," said Kirstin. "Half an hour?"

"I'll leave now. First one there holds a table. Thank you." Emily was already on her feet, organizing her satchel.

"I may thank you before we're done," said Kirstin. "See you soon."

Ladies who lunched in the elegant surroundings of the Marshall Fields Tea Room were invariably well-dressed and well-coifed. Kirstin Bonner fit right in. A striking brunette in a smartly tailored suit, she strode across the room to Emily's table with considerable authority, a woman at once comfortable and confident. Emily liked her before a word was spoken.

As soon as their tea and a plate of finger sandwiches arrived, Emily provided enough background to persuade her companion that she was not seeking a salacious or sensational story but the news behind such an unexpected and inexplicable suicide.

"You said you might thank me after we talked," said

Emily. "What did you mean?"

"Cary Chase has changed. I am worried about him. Extremely worried. I am hoping that I can help you get him to talk about it, to, I don't know, to try to heal. He's not in good shape, I can tell you that."

"Is his empire in jeopardy?"

Kirstin laughed. "Hardly. That's part of what's going on. He is in his office before any of us arrive and he stays until the last of us has left. All he does is work."

"But he's famous for his energy, all that drive. How is this different?"

"Well, for one thing, he used to get in around 9 or 9:30 because he always had breakfast meetings. Friends, business, charity work. I don't think he's had one of those breakfasts since she died.

"But the real difference is much more troublesome. He used to revel in the work. The details, the contracts, the planning, even getting through the bureaucracy, he loved it all. That's all gone. He's going through the motions, but there's no heart in it, no fun, no joy. He's lost some weight, too. Did you know he's not living at Chase Mansion anymore?"

"No," said Emily. "I hadn't heard that. That's surprising."

"It's true. He's got a suite at a hotel near the office. It's being billed as an office expense and we're not a very big staff, so we all know about it. But nobody will say anything because he won't. Have you ever been on the top floor?"

"Of the mansion? No. I covered lots of events there, I've seen the pool and playrooms in the basement and the bars and banquet hall and that industrial kitchen on the first floor. Beni showed me the second floor once, with the screening room and the billiards tables, the music room. I know there are guest rooms on the third floor. But the residence? Beni knew it was his home, she never let anybody up there."

Kirstin smiled. "Last year, he hosted the staff holiday

party at the Mansion and it wasn't downstairs. He invited us all to his home. It is magnificent. It isn't the bachelor pad everybody imagines at all. It's tasteful and comfortable and genuinely warm. He was so proud of it and so happy to share it with us. It was a special evening in a special place.

"Now he won't set foot in it."

Bonner's gaze drifted away. She took a sip of tea and exhaled heavily.

"They were very close. He trusted her, he nurtured her. He told me once that the luckiest thing he ever did was hire her. She's the one who suggested he open the mansion up to charitable events. He talked to her every day. This is tearing him up. He's not Cary Chase anymore. He looks like Cary, but he's been hollowed out."

Emily waited, allowing Kirstin to gather herself.

"Can you arrange an interview for me?"

"No. I can't even be your source, or at least not by name. I just thought if you knew a little more, it might help you reach him."

"Any thoughts on the best way to do that?"

"Joseph Burton. When Cary needs to meet people, he goes to them or he uses our conference room. But Joseph Burton goes straight into Cary's office for meetings, he's the only one who does that. Beni was the only other one—she'd walk right in and he'd drop whatever for her."

"Do they meet often, Burton and Chase?"

"They met almost every day, sometimes twice, right after Beni died. Burton still comes by every couple of days. So yes, they meet often. I think Burton is the only way to get to Cary. But I can't help with that, either. I honestly think that if Cary knew I was talking to you, he'd never trust me again."

Emily stirred her tea absently for a minute or two.

"How about this? I'll tell Burton I've heard from close business colleagues who believe Chase's life is falling apart. I won't use your name, but I will use the part about the

Mansion. That'll tell him I'm getting solid information, maybe surprise him enough or scare him enough to at least talk to me. Can you live with that? If I don't use names, you should be safe."

Kirstin didn't hesitate. "Yes, do that. If you or Joseph can make Cary face up to what's happened to him, I'll take my chances."

"Is there anything else you can tell me?"

"I had another reason to talk to you."

"Yes?"

"Beni. She was a really nice gal and we all liked working with her. I don't understand what happened, why she did what she did and I need to. We all do. She was in the office a lot and she was a friend to everyone. Maybe if you can make sense of it, we'll be able to find a way to accept the loss."

"I'm not sure I can ever accept it," said Emily, "she was my friend, too. But I know what you mean. I need to know, too. I'm running into brick walls everywhere I go, at least until today. I'm not even entirely sure what I'm after. Revenge? Some measure of justice? But I can't give it up, at least not yet. Maybe I'm just hoping for answers. I'd settle for that."

"Me too," said Kirstin. "That and having my boss back."

"You've been extremely helpful, Kirstin. I can't thank you enough."

"Sure you can. Find out what happened and tell the story. That's the thanks I want."

The two women exchanged business cards. Kirstin wrote her direct line on the back of her card, telling Emily to use it rather than calling the main number. When the bill arrived, Kirstin snatched it up and extracted a credit card from her purse. She grinned when she laid it on the table.

"Chase Enterprises corporate card," she said. "If they ask me about it, I'll have to lie."

Emily thought for a second or two.

"Tell them Robert Redford was in town and he insisted on dining with you once more for old time sake. You agreed, but only if he let you pick up the check."

Kirstin's laugh was rich and musical.

"If push comes to shove, I'll give it a try."

When she got back to WEL, Emily stopped in at the Marketing office and took copies of publicity photos of Sandy Sampson and Mike Mitchell. The office had a rubber stamp of Sampson's signature and Emily used it, just below her own scrawled "For Joan." Mike Mitchell had just handed the studio to Jon Decker, so Emily was able to get him to sign his own publicity shot.

Nip and Tuck assumed their chosen locations as Decker came on the air. Emily still felt ill-at-ease with the two interlopers, but their presence through the day had grown sort of ordinary.

She sat at her typewriter and composed a note to Joseph Burton. She regretted that he had not responded to her earlier telephone request, but now she had become aware of Cary Chase's current and surprising living arrangements and the dramatic changes in his behavior. She sought Burton's knowledge of the events surrounding Beni's death and asked for his help in understanding Cary Chase's role in and response to that death and its relationship to Mr. Chase's recent aberrant behavior.

After some editing, she typed the note anew on WEL letterhead and signed it. She wrote *Mr. Joseph Burton CONFIDENTIAL* on a WEL envelope and sealed it, dropping it in her satchel.

She was about to leave when Jon Decker's broadcast stopped her.

Friends, it's time for our history lesson, but this one's history in the making. Way back in '67, a teenager named Janis Ian wrote and performed a hit song. It was about interracial dating so it was kinda controversial. It was called Society's Child and I don't know about you, but I thought that song was a fine piece of writing. Still do. Give it a listen...

...Sweet and subtle, right? So, a couple of days ago one of my pals over at Columbia Records dropped by and gave me a demo copy of a new album Janis Ian's going to release later this year. I'm going to share a cut with you, it's going to be a hit, no question about it and you're going to hear it for the first time ever right here on the El. From Janis Ian, here is At Seventeen...

As she listened, Emily watched Decker, his earphones atop a bright green driving cap, gently conducting the song, his hands floating. His face showed pure delight.

Poetry, friends. Now, give a listen to a couple of messages from the folks who bring you the fine music you hear on the El...

Emily headed for the bullpen doors. As she walked past him, Tuck was writing furiously in his little notebook. Although she did her best, Emily couldn't see what he wrote.

Joan Ashley sat behind a handsome, low-slung receptionist's desk in the lobby of Joseph Burton Law's offices. The waiting area was small and Joan was engaged in a call when Emily approached. There was a board behind her which charted the comings and goings of the staff; Emily counted about twelve attorneys not including Burton himself.

"May I help you?"

"Hello, Joan. I'm Emily, from WEL News."

"Oh." She looked embarrassed. "I gave him your message, honest. He didn't seem happy about it."

"I'm sure you did. It's okay. And you're right, he hasn't responded. I thought I'd stop by and renew the request in person. I don't suppose he's here?"

"Nope. He's at City Hall, I think. When he left he said he'd be gone for the day."

"Ah, well then, I've got another favor to ask, if it's okay. I hope Mr. Burton gets this."

She slid the WEL envelope across the low desk.

Joan picked it up and moved it to an In Box at one end

of her desk.

"That's his mail. When he comes in, I take it out of his box and hand it to him. He's expected tomorrow morning. I'll put yours on top."

"Perfect," said Emily. "I thought you might like to add these to your collection."

She handed Joan the two shots of Sampson and Mitchell. Joan took her time examining both of them, her delight open and obvious.

"Wow, that's great. Look. Here."

Joan pulled open the top desk drawer on her right. Jon Decker's signed photo was the only item in the drawer, protected in a clear plastic sleeve.

Emily smiled and thanked her for her assistance. Joan repeated her joy at having the "whole EL gang" with her at her desk. They shook hands and Emily left.

She got home in time to hear the last segment of Jon Decker's show.

Just about time for me to leave you, friends, but before I go, I have three in a row for you...

Decker played "Chantilly Lace" "Peggy Sue" and "La Bamba" without interruption.

We miss you all, guys. Our music hasn't been the same since we lost you.

So, that's it for me today, friends. I'll be back to share the joy with you tomorrow. Until then, as always, I ask only one thing of you—Shine On, Chicago.

Emily switched off the stereo. She spent a minute or two at the windows watching the traffic and the lake beyond, then moved to the kitchen to begin organizing for dinner. The dining area table was set and the stew they had made over the weekend was warming aromatically when Ben opened the door.

Ben started the dinner conversation eagerly seeking to confirm that Emily had heard the Janis Ian song Jon Decker had played. They discussed it and then Emily told him about Decker's last set. Ben had not heard it.

"The man has a great soul," said Ben. "Buddy, Big Bopper, Richie. Classy. And sad. Mr. Decker's right. I muse occasionally about what Richie Valens would be doing with his music now. Buddy Holly, too."

Eventually, they came around to Emily's meeting with Kirstin Bonner and Ben listened intently while Emily reported what she had learned.

"She's one really smart lady, Ben. I trust her. Based on what she told me, Cary Chase went over a cliff the day Beni died and he's been falling ever since. I know they were close. He trusted her with his house, she greatly admired him. But still...it sounds like he's deeply depressed."

"You have already determined that there are two possible explanations, I assume?"

"Yes."

"He is distraught beyond all reason at the loss of a trusted friend and loyal confidante.

Or—"

"He is wracked with guilt." Emily winced as she said it.

"Or perhaps a combination of the two, but that still leaves open the most unsettling of the options. If he's guilt ridden, of what does he believe he is guilty?

"Despair or guilt, it seems more than reasonable to assume uncovering the answer opens the door to all the questions you have."

"Yes," said Emily, "it does."

7.

Ben's Monday morning note reminded Emily that they were hosting the firm's table at the ACLU dinner on Friday evening. He added another thought.

"I sincerely hope you are soon assigned to cover Mayor Daley again. I image it is great fun to ride the Mayor-go-round."

Emily scrawled "Incorrigible!" just as Max was pulling into the driveway.

"Hiya, Emmy. Good weekend?"

"Great, Max. We spent the entire day yesterday at home, noshing and reading and napping."

"You watch the game?"

"Nope. No TV."

"Didn't miss much. The bagels weren't ready yet, just day-old this morning. Got you a blueberry muffin instead. That okay? It isn't, I can pull over at a doughnut shop I know, not far from the station. We got time."

Emily opened the bag and sniffed.

"Straight to the station, Max. This smells delicious."

"So, your cousin, well, Ben's cousin, Ronny, you

remember? Tall guy, pretty hefty, great big loud voice."

"He's got a couple of kids, right?"

"Why I bring him up, in fact. Had dinner with 'em last night. The older kid, Ronny Junior, listens to your station all the time, says all his gang does. He wanted to know, you still workin' there? I told him of course, asked him he needed anything, maybe a poster or a photo or something. He didn't want none of that."

"Max, I have to go through these papers, okay? Can you get to the point?"

"Yeah, sorry. Junior wants to know how come, you work at the El in the news department coverin' the Mayor and all, how come he never hears you?"

Emily sank into her seat, her head rolling back until she was staring at the cab's roof. She let a sigh escape.

"Tell him it's the way things are at some stations, Max. Tell him he doesn't want to hear me half as much as I want to be heard. Now leave me alone."

She focused on the newspapers for the rest of the ride, but the question kept coming at her, slapping up against her thoughts and distracting her from her routine. When Max pulled up at the station and wished her a good day, she thanked him and closed the cab door gently. On the sidewalk, she drew a deep breath and let it out very slowly. She drew herself up to her full height, set her chin forward and took determined strides to the door.

She set a personal record for prepping the 6 AM news, polishing it to her highest standards with more than ten minutes to spare.

As she was getting ready for the morning news staff meeting after the 9 AM newscast, Emily noticed a buzz in the hallways outside the office. It was a quiet, persistent drone, too soft to be clear but loud enough to be noticed. The noise was odd, somehow out of character with the normal office hum. Before she got out of her chair to see what was going on, Sam Butler's secretary pushed open the bullpen doors carrying several loose sheets of paper and a tape dispenser.

The secretary propped one door open with her foot while she taped one of the sheets to it. The door open, Emily identified the buzz. From the bullpen at one end of the floor to the other end of the building, everyone at WEL was talking quietly, hushed conversations swirling through the station. Emily had a sudden sense of anxiety as she and the others in the room quickly gathered around the notice on their door.

It was a schedule of meetings, one after the other through the day, three days hence. In order, the Advertising and Marketing staff, the general administration staff and the air talent and their support staff were "instructed" to attend meetings with General Manager Sam Butler and Nip and Tuck. The news department was folded into the air talent meeting, the last session scheduled.

Those who would attend the earlier meetings were admonished to refrain from discussing the contents of the meeting until everyone had been informed of "momentous news for the WEL family."

In the morning news meeting, Dean Lyon addressed the memo before anyone in the room could bring it up.

"I want you all to know what I told you earlier still holds. There are some changes coming but they will not reach into our operation. We are to be business as usual."

Don Kipper leaned forward in his chair.

"What changes?"

"Don, I can't answer that. This is Butler's show and he's giving out the info the way he wants to. I've been told—all of us in management have been told—to shut up until Thursday's meetings."

Al Coffey shot his boss a look.

"But you know what's going on, right? Come on, Dean. If we're not involved, what's it matter if we know ahead of time?"

Lyon bristled just a little.

"Al, don't. I can't tell you a thing and I won't tell you a thing. I don't want to be pressed on this. Got it?"

Coffey nodded.

"Okay. Let's get to it, then. Emily, anything from the AM 'casts we want to roll over to Noon?"

It was a typical morning meeting. They worked through the day's assignments and guest selections for the Noon broadcast, sharing ideas and evaluating stories. They did some planning for a special report on Cook County's foster care system which was in turmoil following several well publicized instances of abuse. They functioned as they usually did, as a team.

Yet, Emily sensed that something was not right. Dean Lyon seemed distracted and his energy was low. She guessed that whatever Dean knew about the pending changes was not sitting well. Her first instinct was to hang back after the meeting to ask if her boss needed to talk. Instead, she decided to take his brusque response to Al Coffey as a signal and left with the others.

The last to leave, she turned at the door to say something to Dean and saw him, his shoulders drooping, staring out the window at a cold grey sky.

Before she started working her assignments for the day, Emily walked out to the front desk to check for messages. There were none. Joseph Burton had not responded to her note. She reminded herself that it was still early in the day, but she also began to wonder what, if anything, she could do if he continued to avoid her.

Her Monday assignment took her to Evanston to an announcement from that town's Mayor about a planned shopping mall development. She enjoyed the ride on the El, but Evanston was in the path of harsh winds coming off the lake and the winds cut through her as she made her way to the site of the announcement.

The Mayor and the developer were boring; the renderings of the new mall looked just like a new mall, neither interesting nor innovative. Neither speaker had much energy or flair. Emily left knowing that extracting a quote she could put on the air would be difficult if not impossible.

She returned to find her message box empty. She called Joan Ashley to confirm that Joseph Burton had in fact come to the office that morning and the young woman told her that she had put Emily's note in his hand personally.

"Is he in? Can you connect me to him?"

"Not today. He's here, but he's in a pre-trial meeting. It's just down the hall and it's really loud in there. He's doing a lot of shouting. He won't take any calls and, what I'm hearing, you don't want to get in his way today anyhow."

After the Noon news broadcast, Emily called the Virginia Hotel and asked to speak to Bobby Banks, the manager.

No, he hadn't learned anything more about "that girl's death" and no, he really could not give Emily the number Beni had dialed from her room but he reaffirmed his promise to confirm the number if she found it. And no, he had no contact information for Mavis the actress; he didn't even know where she was.

Emily knew that she could spend some time making calls and find Mavis' agent, but she didn't really have a specific question to ask so she concluded the hunt wasn't worth it.

She called Beni's mother, hoping that a chat might reveal some new recollection, a memory or something new about the day Beni died. There was no answer.

She called Jack Potter at CPD and left a message seeking anything else he might have heard. Potter left a message after she had left for the day: "No news. CPD has closed the file."

Ben had to work late so she dined at home alone. The apartment was less comfortable without him and the television far less entertaining.

Max had picked up a nasty cold, so on Tuesday and Wednesday two different substitutes drove Emily to the station. The first forgot to pick up the papers so they had to stop while she ran into an all-night convenience store. The second had the papers but he was wearing heavy cologne which infused the entire cab and reminded Emily of high school. For relief, she cracked the back window open and the frigid air quickly turned the back seat into a refrigerator shelf.

Max returned on Thursday morning still not feeling well and crabby about it. Emily concentrated on the papers for most of the ride and the meager traffic for the rest of it.

As she left the cab Emily said, "You should be drinking lots of orange juice, Max. Vitamin C'll be good for that cold."

"Hate it," said Max.

When the news planning meeting ended, Dean Lyon asked Emily to stay for a moment.

"You still chasing down the Steinart story?"

"Yes," said Emily. She'd been anticipating the question all week, even as she hoped the topic wouldn't come up.

"Anything?"

"No, but I'm convinced that I can get to Chase if I can get to Joseph Burton. So far, Burton's not responding to me at all."

"You putting a lot of time into this?"

"Yes and no. Yes, I'm still working it. No, I'm not using company time to do it—I've been working after hours and on my breaks, but not on the clock."

Lyon frowned.

"Appreciate that, Emily, but I think it's time to set it aside, don't you?"

She wanted to say "No!" but did not.

"For now, I'd like you to concentrate on the special about foster kids and abuse we outlined on Monday. We need a bunch of interviews for it, I want our best interviewer doing them. That'd be you."

"Thanks," said Emily, "I could use a pat on the back right now. I'll get on the foster kids piece today."

"Thanks. It's important. It's a good story, too."

"But—"

"Of course, 'but.' What?"

"If I hear from Joseph Burton, I can get back on that story, right?"

"Depends on what you hear, but yes, if he gives you something useful, we can evaluate it and see where we are."

It was the best she could hope for and she knew it.

She dove into her assignment and spent most of the morning interviewing foster parents, their lawyers and several emancipated foster kids. She got excellent sound from most of them and worked with the sound engineer to edit and prepare several cuts. It was exciting work and she genuinely enjoyed the editing process, finding just the right quotes so the audience would hear the story so clearly that it came alive.

Her work was colored by the nagging thought that she had lost a chance at a very good story and frustration that she hadn't gotten it. And in the bargain she had failed Beni.

The air staff assembled in the bullpen. Everyone was edgy. Jon Decker was clad from head to toe in black. Dean Lyon wouldn't make eye contact with Sam Butler. Sandy Sampson was so tense that he was unconsciously tapping one foot on the floor with force and without cessation. The morning and mid-day program producers sat side by side and looked as if they expected to be lined up before a firing squad. The news crew all stood against the studio windows, most appearing less troubled than curious.

When Sam Butler arrived he didn't glad hand his way around the group. He moved straight to one end of the large room and waited, looking frazzled and very fatigued.

Tuck, also looking tired, entered first. Nip, at full

strength, was right behind his partner and as peppy as ever. While his companion took a seat, Nip set up an easel and placed a large poster board on it. The poster itself was concealed by a draped cloth cover.

Sam Butler stepped forward.

"We will be inaugurating changes in our programming in two weeks. We'll be running a tease ad campaign starting next week to introduce the new WEL to our audience and everyone else. Our advertising crew will spend the next several days meeting with key advertisers to bring them up to date. We're offering a very attractive package as part of the launch.

"I want you to know that I am fully behind these changes and that is why I have authorized them. I believe that they will make us stronger and healthier. I also want to tell you that our parent company, including the network's President and programming executives, have reviewed our plan and they are just as enthusiastic about these changes as I am.

"All change is hard at first, but once you have heard what the new WEL is going to be, I'm sure you'll agree that this will be good for us, entertaining for our audience and—most important—good for our bottom line.

"Our consultants have spent a lot of time and talent on these changes. Please give them your full attention and—as I've said before—we expect you to fully embrace and support the changes they will outline."

Tuck stepped forward.

"We are going to bring WEL to the forefront of popular music and we are going to take Chicago into a bold new era of radio.

"Starting two weeks from yesterday, we will introduce a brand new WEL playlist. To keep our sound dynamic, we will be changing the list every two weeks. There will be some new guidelines about how we use the list and I'll get to them in just a second.

"First, I want to share with you the new WEL music

line-up."

Tuck moved to the easel. Nip took the opposite side and together, with a flourish, they pulled the drape from the poster.

The poster contained the current top twenty-five Billboard hits.

"That's right," said Nip, "WEL is going to be all hits all the time."

The stunned silence lasted for almost a minute until, almost as one, the gathering unleashed a cacophony of groans, angry epithets, shouted questions and expressions of disbelief.

Nip let the tremor continue and when it subsided he stepped away from the easel.

"This isn't just a list, people. This is a gold mine. We're going to give our audience exactly what they want to hear. They're telling us with their wallets what they want to hear.

"And we're going to give it to them in a brand new format."

Another round of groans and angry murmurs swept around the room.

"As you can see, this list is color coded. The top ten songs are red, the next ten are blue, the last five green. We're going to use color coded music cartridges—we're having them made especially for this format—so you'll always know which section of the list you're using."

"This is a joke, right?"

Jon Decker's deep bass voice, at full timbre, nearly caused the windows to rattle.

"It is not. We have devised a system. Here's how it works. Every other song on the air must be red, top ten. The songs which are not red will alternate, blue, blue, green, but always with a red in between."

Sandy Sampson stood up, his fists clenched.

"Do you know the first damn thing about radio? You're telling me that several times every morning I'm going to play Olivia Newton-John's 'Have You Never Been

Mellow?' It's 18 on that list. It's junk. Even if it isn't, it sure as hell doesn't belong on morning drive. My job is to wake them up and get them going, not put them back to sleep."

Sampson started moving toward Nip. Jon Decker took a couple of quick steps, extending a long arm to restrain him.

"You may not get it quite yet," said Nip, "but there is creativity here. You air personalities get to pick which songs you want from each category, so you're free to mix and match within the system. But there's something else to make it even better."

"Somebody save us." said Decker.

"And it's great news! We're going to play more music in longer sets. Every other hour, we're going to have a block of 10 in a row. In the alternate hours, we'll be playing 15 in a row."

"This is a nightmare," said Decker.

"It's also insulting," said Mike Mitchell.

Sam Butler stepped forward.

"Listen, guys, I know this is dramatic, but bear with us, please. For one thing, you haven't heard the entire plan yet."

Decker's face was cold, his voice cloaked in fury as he glared at his boss.

"Sam, you're taking the joy away. We play only top 25, we rob the audience of new voices. We ignore music history. If we play extended music blocks, we have to create commercial blocks, too. That's simple math, but here's what's worse.

"As soon as they figure out the format, our people will leave the minute they hear the first ad in a block 'cause they'll know there's a batch more coming. That's not exactly what advertisers hope for, is it?"

"Jon—"

"I'm not done, Sam. You're leaving us with no more than a couple of minutes to visit with our audience. You're going to scrub all the personality off the station. And now you tell us there's more?"

"Calm down, Jon, please. Let's at least let these gentlemen finish their presentation."

"By all means," said Decker. "Do go on."

Butler stepped back and Nip moved forward.

"At the same time we energize the playlist, we're going to give the station a brand new identity. When we launch the playlist, we will not longer be WEL or 'the El.'

"We will be Hits 980. It's the new station ID, perfect for what we're doing."

That caused another explosion. Shouted questions came at Nip, Tuck and Butler from all directions and while Tuck didn't say a word, both his colleagues tried to answer whichever question they heard first. The result was noisy and impossible to follow.

In the chaos, Jon Decker and his crew slipped out of the room and into the studio. There was pre-taped programming on the air and as soon as Decker and his producer and engineer were in place, Decker signaled and they cut off Frankie Valli's *My Eyes Adored You* in mid-chorus.

Hey, friends, that's enough from the top of the charts for now. Instead, how about a trip back to the days when rock and roll was just getting started. It's important to stay in touch with our roots, right? Matter of fact, it's so important that I'm gonna give you a real treat. Friends, for the first time ever on the El, here are ten in a row.

The first song was an early Elvis hit, then Chuck Berry, then the Everly Brothers. While those played, Decker and his producer scrambled around the studio and into the music library gathering more. When the set was done, they had played ten top 10 hits in a row, every one of them no less than a decade old.

There you go, friends—living history riding along with us on the El this afternoon. Don't you just love it?

On Friday morning, Sandy Sampson came out of the studio as soon as Emily arrived. During a commercial break, he told her that if she wanted to add some time to the newscast, it would be fine with him.

"You wanna go an extra five, six, seven minutes, it's okay with me, kiddo."

Although she did expand the sports report by an extra 30 seconds, Emily stuck to the traditional morning news time frame.

When the news ended, Sandy Sampson immediately cued a song and followed it with another before he spoke a word.

Good morning. This is Sandy Sampson on WEL. Here's more music for you.

He cued another song.

Sampson remained eerily subdued through the morning. When his shift ended, he walked straight out the doors of the bullpen and left the building. When Mike Mitchell took over, his producer came into the studio wearing a black crepe armband.

In the sales office, all the reps who weren't already out on the streets were hammering away on their phones, working their clients. The small marketing staff was also hard at it, taking and making calls. Everywhere else, the mood was somber and conversations muted.

The news team went about its business. The guys all wanted to discuss the new format, but Dean Lyon shut it down. When her shift ended, Emily packed up to leave. Dean caught up with her in the lobby.

"Hey. I just got finished listening to the foster care material you put together. It's fine work, Emily, really good. You're getting better and better."

She smiled and thanked him. "How are you feeling about all this?"

He hesitated.

"It's not what I'd want, but I think these guys have one thing right. The AM dial is going to change a lot. I'm not sure how, but there's no doubt it's coming. If we're going to survive, we have to change and Nip and Tuck see that."

"But we're doing so well, Dean. We're on top."

"For now. We're losing ground to FM. The new guy over at Boss 1500, what's his name, Donny Monaco, he mostly takes calls and insults people. Barely any music at all."

"I've heard him. He's rude. And mean."

"And he's chipping away at our audience, moving up on us every quarter. Look, Sam Butler reads the numbers, the network reads the numbers. They can see what's happening. That's why these consultants are here."

Emily thought for a moment.

"If you're right, if they're right, radio's never going to be the same."

"But it never is, Emily. There was a time when the hottest thing on radio was Jack Benny. Burns and Allen, Bob Hope, Edgar Bergen, the Bickersons, Helen Trent in the middle of the day, all long gone. It's never the same, at least not for long.

"Anyhow, we should be glad they haven't come after us. News is still news and we still have an obligation to inform our listeners, right?"

Emily smiled. "Aye, Aye, Sir!"

"You have a good weekend, okay?"

"I'll do my best," said Emily. "You, too."

"See you Monday."

The bus ride to her neighborhood in the early afternoon mid-day was pleasant. The bus wasn't rush hour packed and the sun broke out along the way, so Emily got to watch Lincoln Park, snow coated, sparkle.

She flipped on the stereo while she grabbed a bite to eat and decided what to wear to the evening's event. Mike Mitchell seemed a little off his usual pace but Jon Decker was at full speed, playing his own selections and sharing his observations about them and having fun doing it.

Emily called Ben's office to leave a message with his secretary that she was on her way and took a cab to the hotel where the dinner was held. The hall outside the banquet room was lined with registration tables and Emily checked in, confirming with the volunteer that Ben was already in the room. She knew more than a few of those in the room and stopped to chat with them. She went out of her way to find ACLU's Executive Director, thanking him for his cooperation when she called for comments or interviews and congratulating him on the success of the evening.

Ben was standing in front of his place at the table and the chair next to his had been propped forward, held for her. They hugged and he whispered that he had news for her. Before he could continue a very tall, very thin woman in a simply smashing dress took his arm.

"A word, Benjamin. Now."

Ben seemed a bit nonplussed. He gave Emily a look of apology as the woman all but dragged him aside.

Emily introduced herself to the rest of the table. There were three couples, two firm clients and a Herberger Whittier legal secretary and her date, winners of the office raffle for tickets. The single woman at table was a young associate in her first year with the firm. Emily took a glass of wine and joined the conversation.

She watched the room amid the table chatter and her gaze soon landed on a striking man moving from table to table among the guests. He was tall and very handsomely dressed, his expensive suit well cut, his shirt fresh, his tie smartly knotted; he sported a silk pocket square. He appeared to know somebody at every table in the room and he had smiles and warm greetings for all of them.

As he angled and danced among the tables he drew closer and Emily noticed his hair. It was tightly curled, jet black with a few tiny hints of silver. It was expertly cut, high, wide and bushy. Emily thought it looked like a carefully manicured Brillo pad and she suppressed a giggle.

She was wondering who, if anyone, the man knew at their table when he approached and greeted Ben enthusiastically, intruding on the tall thin woman with a smile.

"Sorry, Linda," he said, "my turn."

As she moved away, the woman said, "I'm quite serious, Benjamin. I need you."

The tall fellow threw an arm over Ben's shoulder.

"Great of you to bail me out, Ben. Don't know how, but as I said, we overbooked our own table. I sat on the ACLU Board for a couple of years, so I couldn't possibly miss this, but we ended up with eleven at a table for ten. You saved me. I owe you one."

Ben waved him off. "As I told you, we had a last minute drop out, so it worked out quite nicely. And, of course, it is an honor to have you dine with us."

Ben took a step back and laid his hand on Emily's shoulder.

"I don't believe you have met my wife. She works at WEL. Emily, allow me to introduce Joseph Burton."

8.

Emily had trouble breathing. Ben waited and Joseph Burton smiled politely. She could not speak. She was barely able to keep up with the thoughts crashing in on her.

Why had Ben not told her? The event had been on their calendar for at least a week. She had told him of her efforts to reach Burton repeatedly. Had Ben arranged this moment, as a surprise no less, creating events to secure what she had not been able to do on her own? Or had Burton orchestrated the encounter and, if he had, why?

She struggled to find the right reaction to Burton. Her first instinct was a forceful demand that Burton acknowledge her efforts to contact him, but it seemed unsuitable to the setting and probably impolite. Yet, the man was at arm's length and she could not—would not—let the opportunity go.

Another thought cascaded in on her. She heard Mavis describing Beni's visitor, a tall, well-dressed man who had a "black guy haircut but he was a white guy." Burton's Brillo hair suddenly became vitally important. Had Cary Chase's best friend and most trusted advisor been the last to see Beni alive?

Ben said, "Emily?"

She snapped back, still reeling.

She took a sip of wine and rose. Ben took her arm as she did and she looked straight into his eyes. He showed nothing but affectionate concern and it settled her a little.

She turned to Joseph Burton and took his hand.

"A pleasure to meet you, sir."

"I had not expected this, but I'm glad to meet you, too."

He stepped around Ben and pulled her chair back so they could face one another.

"I owe you an apology. I've spent quite a bit of time considering the interview you've requested, but I neglected to let you know that it was in fact under consideration."

Emily started to say something and he waved her off.

"I certainly could not respond before I discussed the matter with Cary. It took several days before we could arrange our schedules to discuss it properly and, again, I should have contacted you. In any event, we are in accord.

"We're prepared to give you the interview you seek. Would sometime next week be acceptable to you? In my office?"

"We? Will someone else join us?"

He smiled.

"I meant that Cary and I are agreed that I should grant the interview. Let's get that done and see where we stand."

Emily nodded. Joseph Burton wrote a private number on his business card and handed it to her. He promised he would arrange his schedule to fit hers.

Emily took the card and thanked him. He returned to his seat and she turned to Ben.

"OK, pal. Hallway. Now."

She worked her way to the doors in the back of the hall, Ben following closely behind. In the broad corridor, she turned away from the registration tables and its few straggling latecomers to find a quieter space. She turned to face Ben. He spoke before she could.

"I tried to tell you, Emily, I swear. But circumstances collided. Another of our first year associates was supposed to sit with us, but she absented herself when flu struck. We searched high and low but none in the office were free, so I alerted the event planners that we had a seat available.

"Late today, Joseph Burton called ACLU when he discovered his staff had overbooked his own table. They told him about our vacancy and he called me. By then, you were on your way here and I couldn't reach you until you arrived.

"Of course I planned to tell you the minute you got to the table, but then Linda Hirsh accosted me and then Burton showed up. I am chagrined. I regret the shock this must have given you. I'm sorry, pal. I beg your forgiveness."

Emily smiled, any thought of a conflict over Ben's unsolicited intervention in her work gone. She went up on her tip toes to give him a kiss on the cheek.

Ben smiled and took her arm. "As the table's putative hosts, I think it appropriate that we return to attend to our guests."

Emily planted her feet.

"Hold on, there, my handsome friend. Not so fast. Exactly who is this Hirsh woman and what is it that she needs from you?"

He grinned.

"Ah. Her designs are noble and chaste. Ms. Hirsh chairs ACLU's Legal Committee. She is recruiting volunteer counsel. She asked if I would be willing to work on an occasional pro bono case on their behalf. I told her I would be honored, but the partners in the firm must first accede to such an arrangement."

"Oh, yeah? Well, she better watch her step. 'Benjamin' indeed. You, sir, are spoken for."

"Happily so, ma'am, happily so."

As the festivities and table conversation swirled around her, Emily drifted in and out constantly. She worked over the fact that Burton needed Chase's approval before he agreed to the interview. And she assumed that, if they had discussed the interview, they must have reviewed and perhaps rehearsed what Burton would tell her.

She studied Burton as he responded to the podium speakers and chatted with the table. She found him charming and smart, but she sensed he was also calculating and sly. She listened attentively to his casual chatter, assessing his speech patterns, watching his facial expressions and his eyes. She caught herself staring at his Afro more than once.

When the event ended, Joseph Burton made his farewells to the table and rose, moving to Emily's seat to bid her good evening personally. After they spoke briefly, he turned to extend a hearty greeting to a couple at the next table.

She had picked at the tepid banquet food until the table was bussed; most of her meal remained on her plate when they took it away. Holding Ben's arm as they left, Emily demanded a visit to the Billy Goat Tavern where, ravenous, she wolfed down two cheeseburgers of her own and the last two bites of Ben's.

"Good weekend, Emmy?"

"Terrific, Max. And you sound a whole lot better. That cold letting go?"

"Mostly gone, thanks. So, terrific?"

Emily told him about her pending interview with Joseph Burton. She told him she thought she might finally get some answers about Beni's death.

"I know him. Burton."

"What? How?"

"Well, not personal, but I met him in the barn a couple times. Nice guy."

"Details, Max. I need details."

122

"He's the lawyer for the taxi association, you know that, right? Pretty much runs the whole show."

"I know."

"So, he likes to stay in touch, top to bottom. Now and then, he shows up at our barn when the shifts are rolling over. Brings doughnuts or pizza, schmoozes folks, checks on how we're doin', like that."

"You trust him?"

"Geez, Emmy, what a question. Seems pretty straight up to me. They say he's real good at his job, so you gotta figure he's got some savvy, knows how to play the game, but a con artist? Nah, I don't think so."

"Good to know. Thanks, Max."

"This interview, it's going on the air?"

"I won't know until I have it, but it might."

He grinned at her in the mirror. "You going on the air with it?"

"I should have you negotiate for me, Max."

"Bet your—, oops. Sorry, Emmy."

"It's okay, but if you don't start paying attention to the road, I'm going to kick your ass."

Max laughed and started weaving in and out of lanes expertly; he dropped her at WEL five minutes early.

Rick Healey didn't like Emily's patterned stockings.

"You look like somebody splattered stuff on your legs, girl. Whatever happened to those ones make you look like you got a little tan?"

Dan McIntyre turned and stared at her legs for a moment.

"Tsk."

Emily threw one leg onto the side of Healey's desk and carefully adjusted the stocking along her ankle and calf.

"You boys get a good look? Can I go to work now, or do you need to check my bra, too?"

McIntyre blushed and turned away.

"You got some mouth on you, girl," said Healey.

"Just trying to balance your witty sophistication, Rick.

By the way, those socks are tacky."

Healey had one leg propped up on a corner of his desk, revealing a pair of white socks under his dark brown oxfords.

"White, Rick? Really? Whatever happened to those ones make you look like you got a little style?"

While she went to the wire copy machines and started reviewing the news, Rick Healey reached out and tugged his trouser cuff down so it almost covered his sock.

Dean Lyon wandered into the bullpen while McIntyre was delivering the nine o'clock morning news. He stopped at Rick Healey's desk to chat for a moment or two and then headed for the editing bay. Emily waved him to her desk.

"I got Joseph Burton. I'm hoping to schedule an interview for tomorrow or Wednesday. We may be back on track with the Steinart story."

"We have more to do on the foster care series."

"I know. I'm working on it this morning. I've got two more phoners set up and I can edit them before lunch if I'm not on the street. You should have the last of my part today."

"That's the first priority. Get that done, the Burton interview can come after. You have any idea why all of a sudden he wants to talk?"

"My girlish charms? He says he talked with Chase about it. I think it's because I've been hounding them, but if Kirsten Bonner's right, maybe Chase needs to get whatever's eating at him off his chest."

"Maybe he'll confess. Seriously, be alert to a set up, okay? These guys are in the big leagues, they don't make a move they haven't checked from every angle. Maybe they're ready to talk 'cause they want to use us, move their own agenda forward."

"I've considered that," said Emily. "And I agree it's possible. I'll be on guard. But even if they've got their own story to sell, one of them is talking and he's going to talk to us. That's a lot better than where we were last week."

"Can't argue with that. Okay, see where it goes and we'll talk next steps. Good luck."

"Thanks."

As Lyon walked away, Rick Healey made a show of digging into one of his desk drawers. He had been eavesdropping on their conversation from its inception and Emily had noticed him doing so. His effort to appear as if he had not been listening was useless, but it was also so juvenile that it made Emily smile.

When she completed and edited her interview with the Director of Services for the county's foster care program, Emily went straight to Dean Lyon's office. She popped the cassette into a player and cranked up the volume.

"*We are working to regain control of the system and its participants*? She said that? On the record? She knew you were taping, right?"

"Of course."

"Wow. She admits they have no control over their own department. You think she understands what she said?"

Emily nodded emphatically.

"I think it was deliberate. You heard her. She sincerely wants to give these kids safety, security and a future, but she doesn't have the resources to protect them. We're doing this special because it's been one grim headline after another, right? 'Foster Child Abused.' 'Foster Twins Die In Stove Fire.'

"I think she's trying to shame her higher-ups into a bigger budget so she can do more."

"If you say so. Still, it's one hell of an admission. We're still putting this thing together but my guess for now, that piece of tape is the lead. 'Foster Care System Out Of Control.' Powerful. Fine work, Emily. Damn fine."

As soon as her official work day ended, Emily called the Virginia Hotel.

"Hello," said Bobby Banks. "You are persistent, I must say."

"It's my job, Mr. Banks. I'm calling to confirm that phone number with you. Did Ms. Steinart call one of these numbers from her room?"

Emily read him Joseph Burton's main office and private line numbers.

"Give me a second," said Banks.

"Sorry, wrong number. Boy, I've always wanted to say that!"

"You're certain?"

"Positive. Neither of them is even close."

"Okay. Thanks anyhow."

"You're welcome."

She had expected confirmation, assuming that if Burton was Beni's visitor, Beni had called him to arrange the visit. She had not. It wasn't what she'd hoped to hear and she was disappointed.

Her next call was more productive.

Joseph Burton himself answered his private line and she suggested an interview early on the following afternoon. He put her on hold.

"Sorry," he said. "Had to bump a meeting with one of my staff, but we're all set. Tomorrow, two o'clock is fine."

"I'll be there."

"Mr. Burton, I believe you were the last person to see Beni Steinhart alive. Is that true?"

They sat on opposite sides of a handsome coffee table. Joseph Burton had offered Emily a seat on a low leather couch in his minimalist, stylish office but she took a matching chair instead. The choice was calculated; his seat on the couch was lower than hers. Her recorder and a microphone on a short tripod were centered on the table between them.

"As far as I know, it is true. They told me you're good."

"I also know that she made a phone call, but not to you. And shortly after she checked in, she left—"

Burton stopped her.

"I'm going to tell you exactly what happened that evening. I believe all of your questions will be answered, but please don't hesitate to interrupt me if you need to.

"Beni had the day off. She spent the morning taking busses to Old Orchard and back, exchanging a couple of Christmas gifts. The weather was lousy, but she'd exchanged a different book for The Seven Percent Solution so when she got back she curled up with it.

"At about 3 o'clock, she got a call from the U.S. Attorney's Office. She was told to attend a meeting in the Federal Building at 6:30 that evening. She was told the purpose of the meeting was to dispose of all the charges against her."

Emily made a note or two as he talked. She also double checked to be sure the tape machine was doing its job. Burton continued, his manner relaxed and his presentation crisp and clear.

Beni had been given specific entry instructions because the meeting was to take place after official Federal Building business hours. She was told to walk down a ramp into the underground garage; the entrance ramp would be gated at that hour but the exit lane would be guarded only by a swinging arm which she could easily walk around.

Once in the garage, Beni was told to take an elevator to the appropriate floor as close to 6:30 as she could make it. She would be met in the office lobby and escorted to the meeting.

As soon as the call ended Beni called her public defender Tim Humphrey. He was on vacation and unavailable. She thought about calling back to postpone the meeting until she could talk to Humphrey, but the meeting promised exactly what she had wanted ever since the Marsh and Wilson mess had begun.

It was too enticing. Convinced that she was going to be free, rid of all the stress and embarrassment and anguish which colored her life all day every day, Beni Steinart set her book aside and got organized to go to the meeting.

She didn't have a car, so Beni deliberated between using cabs or public transit with its potential delays and waiting times in open air kiosks buffeted by wind and sleet. She was more than aggravated because she'd have to make the same trip three times in about twelve hours, to and from the downtown evening meeting and then back again for work the next morning.

She called the Virginia Hotel, much closer to downtown and just a few blocks from Chase Mansion, and booked a room for that night.

She arrived at the hotel and dropped her overnight bag in her room. She had a Coke and then caught a cab to the Federal Building, arriving just a minute or so after her appointed time. She followed the garage instructions and when the elevator doors opened, she was ushered into an office with its own private entrance.

Beni was presented with two choices.

She was told that all of the charges against her could disappear completely or she could spend 25 years in prison. She was told there was only one way to guarantee the first and avoid the second.

Beni was asked to provide information which would enable the U.S. Attorney's Office to bring charges against Cary Chase in the Wilson-Marsh drug deal. That information would cause all charges against her to be dropped. If she didn't provide it, the US Attorney's office would return to court and recommend the prison term.

Beni was devastated. She could not provide any such information because it did not exist. Prison terrified her.

She fought back. She insisted that she had never known the purpose of the trip until the arrest took place. She said she never discussed the trip with Cary Chase. She said that Grant Wilson and Donny Marsh never mentioned Cary Chase during their road trip. She said that as far as she knew, Cary Chase had no relationship with either of the two drug dealers.

She was told that story was unacceptable. She was

urged to reconsider.

She was encouraged to grasp at any straw which could link Chase to the convicted dealers. What about Wilson's frequent appearances at fundraising events at the Mansion? Perhaps there was something in the fact that she had been picked up at the Mansion? Had she ever seen any of the private records Chase kept in his fourth floor home at the Mansion?

The suggestions and the force with which they were delivered led Beni to conclude she was being asked to lie.

She could testify falsely, betraying and destroying the most important man in her life, her boss, her good friend, her mentor. Or she could lose a quarter century of her life.

The cassette in Emily's recorder popped open and she held up a hand so Burton would pause while she flipped the cassette and restarted the recording. Joseph Burton ignored the signal.

"You understand you can't use any of this," he said.

Emily was stunned.

"Why not? If I can't use it why am I here at all?"

"To gather information about your story. The problem is hearsay, double hearsay to be precise. I was not in that meeting and Beni didn't share most of what I've just told you with me. I heard it all from another source."

Emily stared at him for a moment.

"She called Cary Chase."

Burton nodded.

"That's right. She told him what Jameson had done and he called me. He asked me to go see her at the hotel and I agreed. I'll tell you what happened when I visited her and you can certainly use that, it's not hearsay. But the best you can get on the meeting is a second hand account from somebody who wasn't there either."

"Cary Chase."

"Cary Chase. We'll talk about that a little later."

Emily punched the record button on her machine.

"So, tell me about your conversation with Beni that

night."

"I will," said Burton. "But first there's one more thing you have to know.

"When she got off the elevator for the meeting, there was only one person in the lobby. That same person was the only one in the meeting with her. The only person Beni saw or spoke with from the moment she entered the building until the moment she left was Tommy Jameson."

9.

"The U. S. Attorney for the Northern District of Illinois threatened to put an innocent woman in prison if she didn't lie about her boss. I'd say that's news."

Burton nodded, frowning.

"It won't be news for long."

Emily considered that and then smiled.

"Jameson will deny it," she said.

"Of course he will," said Burton. "The only other person who can bear witness to what happened in that meeting is dead. I have no doubt that Jameson planned it that way. Even if she hadn't committed suicide, it would still be her word against his."

"And she'd lose, 'cause he's Tommy Terrific," said Emily. "I need to confirm what you've told me. When Beni left the hotel after she checked in, she went to the Federal Building to meet with Tommy Jameson. Nobody else saw her or participated in the meeting. When she got back to the hotel, she called Cary Chase. Chase called you and you were the visitor who went to her room a few hours before she died."

Burton said, "Exactly."

"So, what happened in your meeting with her?"

Burton's face turned sorrowful.

"We were really angry, Cary and me. He was roaring mad when he told me about the meeting and it made me even angrier. It's an unconscionable abuse of power, classic bullying. It betrays everything his office is supposed to stand for. Justice? Rule of law? Hardly.

"We both wanted to take him on, we both wanted to protect her. We decided to call Jameson's bluff, get him in court and go right at him. I told Cary I'd handle the case myself. We agreed that I'd visit her and tell her what we wanted to do.

"Cary was deeply concerned about Beni's state of mind, said she sounded completely lost and frightened. Whatever he heard, it scared him."

"He was right," said Emily. "But you were on her side, you were going to help her, protect her. Didn't she trust you?"

He was no longer relaxed on the couch. He was sitting straight up on the edge, his eyes intensely sad.

"I've thought about this ever since and I'm still not sure I know the answer. I told her we'd do anything and everything for her. Cary said he'd spend whatever it took, I told her that. I said I'd handle the case with Humphrey without fee. I told her she would never see the inside of a prison. Ever."

"And?"

Burton sighed.

"She was grateful, but she couldn't see a way out. She was determined to protect Cary. She said Jameson wanted Cary so badly that he didn't care if she lied, so she figured he'd twist any help Cary gave her, from me or anybody else, into something sinister. And she didn't want to go back to court anyhow because she was convinced that when she did, she'd go straight to prison.

"She was terrified. She said Jameson was a bully—that's

the word she used—and he scared her and she was certain he'd crush her if it came to that. I argued with her, told her once we got things lined up, she was going to safe. I promised her we could fix it."

Tears began to form in Burton's eyes.

"She kept saying she was so tired of it all, so worn out. You knew her, she was enthusiastic and energetic and confident, but Jameson had spooked all that out of her. A week or so ago, I realized that when I saw her that night, she was defeated. That's a word I'd never think to use about Beni, but it's what she was. Defeated.

"I tried everything. I shouted, I argued, I tried reason and logic, I told her we cared for her and wanted to help her. I kept at it for almost an hour. I failed."

He continued to cry gently. Emily gave him a moment.

"How did she seem when you left?"

"She was exhausted. She was despondent, forlorn. I wanted her to rest, to take some time to consider what Cary and I could do for her. I told her to come home with me and spend the night in the spare bedroom at our place, but she said she wouldn't go anywhere else in that horrid weather, said she'd be fine at the hotel for one night. I made her promise to call me first thing in the morning, as soon as she got to the Mansion. She gave me her word. She promised. She was hugging herself when I went out the door. She gave me a smile and a little wave. It simply did not enter my mind that she was going to do what she did. I should have stayed, thought of something else, done something else. I should have saved her."

Emily leaned forward and stopped the recording.

They remained silent for several minutes. Burton gathered himself slowly and rose to refill his coffee cup. Emily made some notes, digesting what she had learned.

When Burton resumed his seat, she leaned forward to start the recorder.

"Don't bother," said Burton. "I've given you everything I have, there's no need to record the next part."

"What next part?"

"The real story is the Jameson meeting and what he said. The rest, about my meeting with her, isn't as important."

"I disagree. I mean, I understand you weren't in the meeting with Jameson, but you were the last person to talk with her. I think that belongs in the story."

He nodded. "I promised you an interview and you can use anything on the tape. But you need Cary Chase. He's the only the one who heard about the meeting from Beni herself. He's got a lot of clout and when he wants to make news, nobody's better at it. He's ready to make news about this. The only thing left to do is make that happen."

Burton rose and walked to his desk. He picked up the phone and dialed.

"Cary? Joseph. We just finished. She's sharp and she knows what she's doing."

He paused and listened.

"Okay."

Burton turned to Emily.

"He's tied up today and tomorrow, but anytime later this week is fine. He'll be available whenever you call. Here's his private line."

He picked up a business card from his desk and handed it to her. He had written Cary Chase's number on the back of it. As she put it in her pocket, Emily realized that he had not written the number while she stood there. It had been written before the interview began. She wasn't comfortable thinking that they had predetermined the outcome of the interview, but she had no choice.

"Thank you. I'll call him day after tomorrow. Can I get back to you? I may have more questions."

"Sure," said Burton, reaching out to shake her hand. "I'll do whatever I can to help."

"I may need it," she said. "Thanks again. I can't speak for the station, but if I get my way, we'll air this story."

"Good," said Burton, "that's what we all want."

Emily went back to WEL. As she settled in at her desk, she couldn't ignore the banner hanging above the doors to the bullpen. It was gaudy, bright yellow with bold red lettering. It said:

8 DAYS TO HITS 980!!!

Nip and Tuck had put the thing up. Every morning Nip scurried in and lowered the number. The sales staff were all energy and enthusiasm about the new format. Everybody else viewed it with equal measures of anxiety and anger, but nobody had defaced the banner.

As Mike Mitchell cued his closing set, Emily gazed at the banner and considered how the three daytime jockeys were reacting to what was coming.

As on the morning after the new format was announced, Sandy Sampson remained only slightly more entertaining than silence. He rarely engaged in patter and when he did, it was listless and flat. The regular features he himself had enjoyed fell short; his morning birthday greeting remained, but without an accompanying song. Sam Butler had called Sampson into his office to discuss Sandy's work, but since there were no new ratings at hand, Sandy was still number one in the market. Butler was mostly gruff and bluff and the discussion, loud enough to carry down halls and around corners, had no impact on Sandy's on-air demeanor.

Mike Mitchell had maintained his typical broadcast for a few days, but then he began slowly to adapt his show. He leaned more heavily on the top 25 and he added sets of five or six hits in a row. While the music cassettes were not yet color-coded, Mitchell began using the pattern the colors would represent, a top ten hit every other time. He also began to reduce gradually his own air time, expanding the music sets and diminishing the patter between them. On the air, he was the same Mike Mitchell he had always been, casual, easy-going, warm and calm. There was just ever less of him as the countdown moved on.

Jon Decker continued his program as he always had, using the entire music library. He quickly and eagerly embraced longer music blocks, but his sets had nothing to do with the top 25.

Instead, Decker devoted one block of uninterrupted songs to pop singers who had passed away, another to songwriters with multiple hits. His long sets saluted the music of Memphis and New Orleans and Detroit; over several sets one afternoon, he created a ranging, rich history of doo-wop. He remained as energetic and as infectiously joyful as ever.

Emily ended her reverie and rummaged through her satchel to find her notebook. She flipped the pages back until she found her original notes from her first visit to the Virginia Hotel. Pen in hand, she scanned those early notes, checking off each in turn. She knew where Beni had gone. She knew who Beni called. She had found the white guy with the Afro and then she had interviewed Beni's only visitor. She slapped the notebook on her thigh, satisfied with the work.

The satisfaction gave way to anxiety. Her one and only story about Beni's death had aired the morning after Beni died. The story was old news, growing ever more stale. Emily had new raw material and more in the offing, but she felt a sense of urgency to get and use that material. She was close to an important news story and her desire to report that story all but burned. She was so intent on moving forward that she felt suddenly energized. She left the station and walked at a steady, forward leaning pace down Michigan Avenue, switching the satchel from shoulder to the other along the way. When she got to the Drake Hotel she caught a bus and rode home.

Ben had pre-made the evening meal and Emily had the table set and dinner at the ready when he arrived home. His tossed his tie and suit coat on the couch and wrapped an arm around Emily's waist; together, they walked to the bank of windows. They watched the evening traffic along Lake Shore Drive, gently embracing and sipping wine. As the dinner aromas snuck into the living room, they stood quietly entwined for several minutes.

"Hungry?" said Ben quietly.

"Starving," said Emily.

Later in the meal, Ben asked about the Burton interview. Emily told him what she had learned.

Ben said, "Conventional wisdom and every single political pro and operative in Illinois have all but anointed Tommy Jameson as the next Governor of Illinois. If this story is true, he'll be lucky to get nominated. Explosive, to say the least. There is, of course, another possibility."

Emily nodded and said, "Their story is a lie. It can't be authenticated by anyone except Jameson, who won't dream of verifying it. And it tilts everything in their favor. If I air the story, the focus shifts from Chase to Jameson. Burton served notice that he's going to put Jameson on trial for what happened to Beni. Anything Jameson does after that looks like vendetta, which is exactly what Chase and Burton are saying."

Ben gazed out the window for a minute or two and then spoke.

"I concur. It is but one of two compelling reasons for them to concoct such a sly story. If Cary Chase was indeed involved in the cocaine deal, they have fashioned a plausible defense. Burton will use you and every newsroom in town to get the image of an innocent girl protecting her innocent boss into the public consciousness. He'll play on public sympathy, he'll turn Jameson into a demon. Long before he ever gets to court—by no means a certainty— the whole world will weep for Beni, support Cary and hate Jameson. It is to their great advantage when you deliver their message."

"Well, you and Dean have turned me into a permanent skeptic about this, so I'm being extra cautious. What's the second reason?"

"Chase sent Burton to the Virginia to murder Beni. Nobody believed Donny Marsh, but what if Jameson had something else?"

"You mean, what if he had Beni? The meeting is real, but instead of holding her ground, Beni offered Jameson what he wanted. She had so much guilt she called Chase to warn him, maybe ask for forgiveness, understanding? Chase would conclude that she's going to take him down. He has to get rid of that threat."

Ben's jaw flexed. "So he called his best friend and most trusted ally and the problem went away. It is a grim prospect."

Emily stood and went to the windows. Ben waited, sipping the last of his wine.

"It doesn't work," she said, turning to face Ben.

"Tell me."

"First, you weren't in the room with Joseph Burton. If he was lying to me, he is the best actor ever to take on a role. His grief and his anger were painful to see, his tears were heartfelt. I have no reason to believe he was lying."

"Second?"

"Even more convincing, I think. If Chase was in on the drug deal and Burton killed Beni, why on earth would they want a reporter looking at any of it? They have to know I'm going to investigate their claims. At the very least, I can't air this story without getting a response from Jameson. If one or both of them are guilty of something—anything—why would they want Jameson to focus on them even more?"

"I cannot argue with the first, of course. Your instincts are a significant asset in your portfolio and I know them to be well tuned. As to the second, you must admit they have created a story which is nearly impossible to prove. When Jameson denies their accusation, what do they have to refute him? And more to the point, what do *you* have?"

"I have plans and schemes. I think there are ways to give their story greater credence even if it can't be positively verified and I am going to exhaust them all. Once I get close enough, I have an ace in the hole."

Ben stared at his wife, holding her gaze.

"Tommy Jameson."

Emily smiled. "Tommy Jameson. If Greg Good told me the truth, Jameson is more than capable of doing exactly what Beni told Chase he did. If he's the obsessed zealot Greg describes and I can shore up Chase and Burton's story, I think Jameson will want to defend himself, to remind us that he's a righteous crusader. I'll be waiting when he does."

Ben held up both hands, palms out as if fending off an attack.

"He'll have to be deft and agile and he'd be well advised to have reinforcements at the ready. I sense that the time has come for those in your way to seek cover."

With a glint in her eye, Emily curtsied and lifted her glass to her husband. Then she drained it.

10.

*D*ean Lyon asked Emily to get to the morning planning meeting five or ten minutes early. She arrived twenty minutes early so she could fill him in on her interview with Burton and the pending interview with Cary Chase.

"I'll be damned," said Lyon, "I know you don't give up easily, but I was pretty sure this one had run dry. It's not ready to air yet, but if Chase gives us something strong, it might be enough 'cause he's such a prominent figure in town. If he's willing to accuse Jameson on the record, we might be able to go with that. It'll be one potent story if it holds up."

"I'm going to work other angles. Going with Chase alone is your decision, but I want to find other facts to support his charge. I've got leads to follow. "

"Anything supports their story and doesn't come directly from them would make your boss more comfortable," said Lyon, smiling. "Go get it. Anyhow, here's why I wanted to speak to you before we meet. We're going to make a short-term adjustment in the morning news block. You'll need to focus your work in a different way, just for a couple of weeks."

"I don't like the sound of this."

"Of course you don't. Here's the deal. The news block won't change. Ten, twelve minutes if we need it, not counting spots—but we're going to do more stories."

"I really don't like the sound of this."

"Yeah. Sam Butler thought it up. Nip and Tuck love it. The idea is, our news will be more compatible with the new format if it comes faster and there's more of it, just like the music. Butler wants the news to sound like it belongs on Hits 980."

"Dean, really? Top 25 news? You promised. You said they wouldn't come near us. I'm afraid to ask, how many more stories?"

"You typically do four to six, right?"

"Not counting traffic. With sports, it can run to eight, nine."

"Let's try to double that."

Emily stood perfectly still and struggled for control. When she felt it was safe to speak, she forced herself to do so very quietly.

"We're going to shrink the war in 'Nam down to ten seconds? Turn the Governor's race into a box score? That's not news, Dean, that's headlines. It's irresponsible."

"Please, Emily. I fought them hard on this. If I hadn't, they probably would have made it permanent. As it is, we're just doing this during the two week launch phase and then it's back to normal."

"Why am I not comforted by that?"

"I have Butler's word. I made him shake on it."

She snorted.

"Golly, Dean, that's just swell. He promised no changes at all, but today there are changes. His promises are as permanent as a snow flake. So, let me guess, the half-hour Noon News will become a three minute express?"

"No. They haven't touched it. It's morning drive they're worried about. Mornings build the audience we need through the day until evening rush. You know this, it's why we brought you in to write morning news. They want to make sure the new identity is strong and they want morning news to contribute."

"Does Healey know about this? And, lord, can McIntyre even do this? He's so deliberate, his delivery is careful and controlled. He's not exactly a rapid fire bang-bang guy, Dean. I know he won't like it. This could be a disaster."

"Healey doesn't like it. He had me get a promise, no changes in hours or benefits. I've asked Dan to meet with me this morning. I'll make it as smooth as I can for him. One way I'm going to keep him calm, Emily, is tell him he'll still have great copy to work with. You hear me? He's going to need you to get through this. Understood?"

He looked at her across the top of his glasses.

"Understood. But I want it on record, Dean. I object."

"Objection noted. Coffee?"

"Lace it for me? Shot of that good bourbon you keep in the desk?"

"Tempting, isn't it? Probably not a good idea."

After the news planning meeting, Emily made two phone calls.

She called Tim Humphrey's office and left a message asking that he return her call at his earliest convenience.

Then she called Joseph Burton. His private line didn't pick up and after a number of rings, it transferred to Joan Ashley.

"Mr. Burton's office, how may I help you?"

"Hi, Joan, it's Emily from WEL."

"Hey! What can I do you for?"

"Is Mr. Burton in the office?"

"He is. He's in a meeting with the team going to court tomorrow on a bumper thumper, kicked off a whiplash claim."

"Could you tell him I'm on the line and it's important?"

"I don't think he wants to be—"

"I think if you tell him it's me, it'll be okay. Please?"

"I will, but if he yells at me, you owe me one."

"Thanks."

In two minutes, Joseph Burton greeted her.

"How can I help you?"

"Good morning, sir. I have a request."

"Shoot."

"We can't put Beni Steinart in Tommy Jameson's office unless he admits to it."

"Right."

"But we can put her in his building on the day and at the time the she said the meeting took place."

"How?"

"The weather was absolutely miserable that night, it was raining ice. She had already stood outside waiting for busses in the cold and wet and it made her late getting to the hotel. She had to get to the Federal Building by 6:30, right?"

"That's right," said Burton, a question hanging on it.

"So she took a cab."

There was a momentary pause.

"You want the cab driver."

"Two of them would be even better. The one who dropped her off and the one who took her back to the Virginia. We prove she went and returned that night, the story is stronger."

"It may take some time."

"Sooner is better, but it's really important, especially if Jameson denies the meeting ever took place."

"Why would she take cabs to and from the Federal Building after hours if not for that meeting?"

"Exactly. The drivers can put her in the building. I need to find them."

"I'll do whatever I can."

"Thanks."

"Sure. Gotta run." He hung up.

Emily cradled the phone.

"Ha!"

Rick Healey flipped his Sports section down and looked at her over it.

"You got something to cheer about, girl?"

"Just savoring a moment of reportorial bliss."

"You working a story?"

"Beni Steinart, you remember?"

"The babe tossed herself out the window, right? Cary Chase's madam."

Emily bristled.

"That's just ugly, Rick. She was a talented and skillful executive. All that Chase Mansion orgy nonsense is just that, nonsense. And she certainly didn't deserve to die."

"Suicide. Big deal. What's the story?"

"Ah, my friend, you'll just have to wait and see."

"You put a lot of hours into this thing?"

The question caught her off guard.

"Why?"

"No reason, just wondering."

"Some. Enough to get the story right."

"Huh." He resumed reading.

She hoped Tim Humphrey could confirm that Beni Steinart had in fact called him right after she was summoned to Jameson's office. It wasn't much on its own, but it would help substantiate Chase and Burton's account if Beni tried to talk to Humphrey on the same day she went to the meeting.

The more important initiative, however, was Joseph Burton's assignment. If they could locate the cab driver, he could verify Beni's trip to the Federal Building at an odd hour under unusual circumstances.

What Emily liked most about the cab strategy, however, was below the surface. She was all but convinced that Burton and Chase would not have made up a story they knew would be challenged and investigated. But she had an obligation to double check.

She enlisted Joseph Burton's help in the investigation

as a test. He hadn't hesitated, dodged or argued and Emily noted that with relief.

She remained fully aware that Burton and Chase might be using her to disguise their involvement in the drug case or Beni's death. By making Burton an ally, she realized she might also create an opening for him. He could easily find at least one cabbie who would say whatever Burton directed him to say, furthering the cover up.

Just to be safe, she had a plan for that, too.

When Cary Chase met and ushered Emily into his office, the first thing she did was stifle a gasp. Kirstin Bonner was sitting in a corner on an Eames chair.

"Emily, this is Ms. Bonner. She is the senior member of my communications staff. I thought it would be wise to have a third party who can confirm what takes place here."

Emily, recovered, walked over and extended her hand.

"Good to meet you," she said.

"My pleasure," said Bonner.

Emily turned to Chase.

"I'll be recording the interview, you know. The tape will be raw, verbatim. I'm not sure I see the need—"

"Really?" Chase raised an eyebrow. "We're going to talk about a meeting to which there aren't any witnesses. Under the circumstances, I'm inclined not to take any chances. She stays."

It wasn't a fight Emily wanted to make.

"Fine," she said. "Let's get started."

Chase directed her to a chair on the opposite side of his desk. When she pulled the cumbersome recorder out of her bag, he cleared space for it. She tested the microphone and confirmed that she had fresh tape in the recorder. When she was ready, he moved around his desk and sat.

As soon as he met her in the lobby, Emily believed Kirstin's evaluation. Chicago's bon vivant, the attractive, likeable source of so much of the city's energy and vision, looked terrible and sounded worse. He was haggard and

146

drawn, he hadn't shaved in several days and there was a small coffee stain on his shirt. His voice was ragged and had little spark.

"Mr. Chase, why do you think Beni Steinart took her own life?"

Color rose in his face and his body was all but jolted as his energy surged.

"U.S. Attorney Tommy Jameson gave her a choice between perjury and prison and she could not live with either. He is responsible for Beni Steinart's death."

"Why?"

"She worked for me. No more than that, but it ended her life. There was and to this day there is no evidence whatsoever to suggest that I had anything to do with Grant Wilson and Donny Marsh and their dealings in cocaine. There is no evidence whatsoever to suggest the Beni Steinart was involved either, other than being in the wrong place at the wrong time.

"But Mr. Jameson is a fanatic. He believes that I am evil. He bullied and threatened Beni to join his crusade against me. He trampled justice and fairness and the facts before him because he is convinced that I am his sworn enemy the devil. To prove it, he did everything but throw Beni Steinart out the window to her death.

"Had she worked for your station or Carson Pirie Scott or the sanitation department, none of this would have happened. Jameson hounded her to death because she was my most valued associate, my confidante. In that sense, I'm responsible for her death, too, and it has been agony."

Chase's eyes blazed. His fists were clenched and twice he pounded the arm of his chair so forcefully that Emily thought he might break the chair or his own hand. The pulse in his neck was throbbing violently.

His delivery was sharp and tight, nearly edit-proof. She was momentarily tempted to shut down the recorder and run back to the station to get what she had on the air. She also resisted an impulse to glance at Kirstin to gauge her reaction.

Instead, she went through a series of questions which elicited from Cary Chase the full details of his conversation with Beni. Now in first person, the story tracked what Joseph Burton had already provided—the unusual time and entry, Jameson's threats and efforts to turn Beni against her boss.

Emily heard no variation from what Joseph Burton had told her. She also noticed that Chase's version was very much his own; he wasn't merely repeating a rote version of a story, he was unleashing an unpracticed and unbridled stream of conscious.

Through it all, Cary Chase was sharp, focused, crisp and, Emily thought, deliberately quotable. It was the polished work of someone who knew and understood how to communicate news and she admired his skill.

"Mr. Chase, did you have any contact with Donny Marsh?"

"I never met the man."

"Do you know Grant Wilson?"

"I am told that he was a frequent guest at various charitable fetes we hosted at the Mansion, but I do not recall meeting him. Ms. Steinart once mentioned that she was dating the fellow. When I asked, she said it wasn't serious."

"Did you direct Beni Steinart to accompany Grant Wilson and Donny Marsh to Paducah?"

"Absolutely not."

"Did you send Joseph Burton to Beni Steinart's hotel room on the night she died?"

"I'm not sure 'send' is quite right but yes, we agreed. I called Joseph and shared Beni's account with him and we both worked out our plan to protect her. When we spoke on the phone, she sounded so scared and sad I was worried about her, greatly concerned. Joseph and I agreed that she should hear our plans in person so he went to see her on my behalf as well as his own."

"Mr. Chase, why have you just come forward with this story? Beni Steinart died weeks ago."

Chase stared at her and then lowered his head. He spoke very quietly.

"My grief consumed me." He paused to draw a full breath.

"I could not cope with her death. I lost so much I cannot measure it. I hurt so much I could not stand it. There were moments when I lost my own will to live, because I had an indirect hand in her death. I still cannot set foot in my own home because she will be there, everywhere. I am not yet strong enough to bear that."

Chase raised his head and folded his hands on his desk. He stared directly at Emily.

"My grief has now been overpowered by something else. I believe Tommy Jameson hounded Beni Steinart to her death. He must answer for his actions and I will not relent until that has happened. I could not speak before. Now, I must."

Emily broke his stare to glance down at her recorder. It was running smoothly. She had it all.

"Thank you, Mr. Chase. I want you to know that Beni was a friend of mine and that I cherished that friendship. I am being extremely careful to set that aside as I work on this story, but my professional objectivity doesn't mean I can't share your grief. I do."

"Thank you. May I ask a favor?"

"Please."

"That part about maybe losing my will to live. If you don't have to use that, I would prefer that it remain private. I am in business, after all. I am ready to return to it."

He paused, smiling, and turned to face Kirstin.

"I believe my senior communications counselor would advise against announcing to those I do business with that I don't want to live. It might make them skittish. Yes?"

Kirstin smiled and nodded vigorously.

Emily said, "We agreed that I could use anything from the interview, but I appreciate your concern and I understand Ms. Bonner's counsel to you. That's the best I can do."

"Fair enough."

Cary Chase stood and for a moment Emily thought he was actually taller. He certainly looked more at ease. When he came around the desk to shake her hand, there was energy in his step. Some of the tension along his jaw line had eased.

Kirstin joined them beside the desk and extended her hand to Emily. When they shook, Kirstin held firmly, deliberately meeting Emily's eyes. Emily saw gratitude and relief.

"You did a good job," said Kirstin. "Thank you."

"I'll walk you to the door," said Chase. "Kirstin, can you stay, please? We should spend some time discussing all the fires I probably need to put out."

Kirstin beamed. "Yes, sir!"

"OK, here's my first question," said Dean Lyon. "Are they talking to anybody else?"

Emily blushed. "I don't think so."

"You didn't get an exclusive? You do know what you've got here, right? This is a home run, lady. You put it out of the park, you broke somebody's living room window on Waveland. Please tell me nobody else is on this."

"I can't," she said. "Give me five minutes."

She called Joseph Burton and got Joan Ashley instead. She told Joan she needed to hear from Burton immediately and gave her Dean's direct line.

She called Kirstin Bonner.

"Hi. Boy, did you turn him loose! He's down getting a shave now, but—"

"I don't have time right now. I need to know if you all have talked with other reporters or plan to."

Bonner laughed.

"Hardly. Cary wasn't sure he should talk to you, never mind anybody else. That's why they sent you to Joseph first. When Joseph said you were ok, Cary agreed. They aren't talking to anybody else because they don't trust anybody else. Cary says he trusts you, but he's nervous, too."

"Thank you. If anybody else from the media contacts you about this story, would you let me know?"

"Sure, but it's not going to happen. Nobody cares except you."

"I have to run, Kirstin. I'll call you when things settle down, we can have lunch, grab a drink."

"That'd be fun. Let's do it."

She walked into Dean Lyon's office with her thumb up.

"Chase is exclusive with us. Burton will call to confirm that he is too, but he and Chase are hand and glove, so Chase's word is probably good enough. The story is ours."

The phone rang.

"I bet that's Burton," said Emily. "You want me to get it?"

Lyon picked up his phone, punched a button and handed it to Emily.

"Mr. Lyon's office. May I help you?"

"Emily? That you?"

"Hi, Mr. Burton. Yeah, I'm in his office. Listen, we've got this speaker box thing for the phone, can I hook it up so we both can talk to you?"

"Sure."

"Okay. Dean Lyon, WEL News Director, this is Joseph Burton. Joseph, my boss would like assurances that the story I'm working is exclusive to us."

"Are you kidding? Actually, it's exclusive to *her*, Mr. Lyon. I wouldn't give this story to anybody else on a prayer or a bet. Mr. Chase and I are confident that she will do the story justice and we know she is diligent and professional. That's all we need or want. As long as she delivers that, we aren't talking to anyone else. Period. That cover it for you?"

"Amply, sir. Thank you."

"Holler if you need anything else, Emily. A good afternoon and evening to you both."

Lyon cradled the phone. "Lesson learned?"

"Lesson learned. I was so intent on getting the story, I never thought to ask. Didn't even think about it until you brought it up. Pretty dumb, huh?"

"Nope. Not perfect, but it's an understandable miss. I probably woulda lost track myself, something this big staring me in the face."

"Well, it won't happen again. Anyhow, I haven't edited Burton's tape yet, but he's got some good stuff, too. He certainly backs up what Chase says."

"Of course he does. If he didn't, that would be even bigger news. So where are you on shoring this up?"

She told him about the search for cab drivers and her calls to Tim Humphrey.

"Jameson is going to go after Chase and Burton with guns blazing, but he'll fire off some rounds at us, too. It won't be pretty. Right now, all we've got is Chase's word for the whole thing. It's dicey enough, I'm gonna to let it sit over night. Now we know it's exclusive, we can afford to do that. I want to give this a lot of thought. Plus, maybe you'll hear from Pomfret—"

"Humphrey."

"Yeah, whatisname. You hear from him or find a cabbie, the decision gets a whole lot easier. We go with it pronto."

"Not without Jameson. If we're going to air I have to contact his communications guy, Greg Good, and get a statement or some tape from them. We have to include their side or at least make the offer to air it."

And, Emily thought, I couldn't live with myself if we blindsided Greg on this story in particular. I owe him.

"Of course, we get Jameson's response. My guess, it'll

make the story even more explosive. So, we'll hold while you give them a reasonable deadline. We can send Kipper or Coffey over to get a statement, they want to give us tape."

"Don't you dare. They want to give us tape, I go get it. Nobody else."

"Of course. Didn't think. Sorry. There's one more thing."

"I bet I can guess."

"You're guessing I have to put this in front of Butler, you win. We're about to kick off a new format and the news department has a ticking bomb on its hands. I gotta tell our GM what we've got."

"I'd rather lose the bet. I know you have to do this. One thing, though."

"Yeah?"

"If this story turns up someplace else after you talk with Butler, I will personally come after him with weapons and criminal intent. Tell him I said so."

"He leaks this to somebody else, he'll be dead on the floor before you get to him."

"Then I'll need to see the body. Have a nice evening."

"You too, kiddo."

11.

Emily invited Kirstin Bonner to join her for the Friday night meeting of The Rules Committee at Ricardo's. Bonner dove in as if she'd been part of the group forever, engaging first in a spirited reunion with Linda Marshall. Emily sat back in the booth savoring her wine and the rapid raucous repartee.

Mary Massey had worked with Kirstin as a producer coordinating a live remote interview with Cary Chase. The anchors were snug in their studio while Cary stood in an enormous deep pit prepared for a tall, handsome new Chase condominium complex. Recent weather had left thinly iced puddles everywhere and before the work crew on the site laid out a plywood slab for Chase, he had soaked his shoes, socks, and pant cuffs through and through. Kirstin and Mary admired his determination as he gave a sharp, if slightly accelerated, interview. When the interview ended, a workman brought Chase a hugely oversized pair of galoshes. While Mary and Kirstin laughed until they cried, Cary Chase happily splashed around in the puddles like a seven year old.

The table spent some time discussing Chase and his business, his Mansion and his status as the city's most eligible bachelor.

"If I happened to be in a relationship at the moment, which as we all know I am not," said Lois Lipton, "I'd dump him in a hot minute just to have dinner with Cary Chase. He is one attractive man."

"He's as nice as he is good looking," said Kirstin.

"And that Mansion," said Massey. "I'd love to see his bachelor pad."

"Including the ceilings," said Lipton, grinning. The table roared and raised glasses.

Kirstin shot a glance at Emily, who winked at their shared secret—Chase didn't live there anymore.

"His home is special," said Kirstin. "Really beautiful. So tell me, Lois, why's such a bright attractive young lady without a guy? Or several of them?"

Lois grimaced and sighed.

"Bad choices. Lots of bad choices."

"We all know about that," said Kirstin.

"A toast to bad choices and the men behind them," said Abby Evans, laughing. They all raised their glasses.

"Not you, Emily," said Marcy. "You got one of the good ones, you can't toast bad choices."

"Oh, I had my share and more, believe me" said Emily. "But it's true that when I got lucky, I had the good sense to know it."

"Her Ben's another one I'd be available for right now," said Lois. Two others nodded.

"As if I'd ever let him go," said Emily.

Ten minutes later, Ben walked up to the table. He was greeted with a collection of knowing smiles which made him a bit uncomfortable. Emily introduced him to Kirstin and while they chatted briefly she slid out of the booth and joined Ben in the crowded aisle.

"Grand to see you all," said Ben, saluting them. "Nice to meet you, Ms. Bonner."

"Have a good evening," said Marshall.

"And take good care of our girl," said Massey.

"My pleasure, to be sure," said Ben.

"See you all next week," said Emily, waving.

"Thanks for inviting me, Emily" said Kirstin.

"Happy to. No invitation needed from now on, we're here every Friday—I sense unanimity that the committee's membership has expanded by one."

They all agreed with a toast and as the conversation resumed, Emily turned to Ben.

He said, "Dinner and a movie?"

"Oxford Pub after?"

"Done and done."

"I love Fridays," said Emily, "nearly as much as I love you."

Max had a new cab. It was a Ford, smaller than the Checker he'd always driven, but the back seat was in much better condition and there was still enough room for her satchel, the newspapers and a bagel and coffee.

"Don't like it yet," said Max. "Seat's good up here and the meter's a little closer, don't have to stretch for it, that's nice. But it doesn't feel right, you know?"

"It's a comfortable ride," said Emily. They were pulling onto Lake Shore Drive at Belmont. "It have any pick up?"

"Does okay," said Max, smiling. He gripped the wheel at ten and two and firmly accelerated. Emily steadied her coffee cup as the cab leapt forward.

"Don't be doing that in snow, Max."

"Yeah, well, that's the thing. That Checker, I knew exactly how she drove in all kindsa weather. This thing, I can't be sure."

"Confidence comes with experience," said Emily. "You'll be loving it in two weeks."

"If you say so, Em. Better get to your papers, we're movin' right along today."

The bull pen was alive with activity. Two producers

were racing around while Nip and Tuck were in a corner, engaged in a heated discussion. Rick Healey was directing traffic, visibly agitated. Dan McIntyre wasn't at his desk. It was such a departure from the routine that Emily felt a burst of anxiety.

"What is going on, Rick?"

"Glad you're here, Emily. Sampson's a no show. Didn't call anybody, didn't leave a note or anything. At 4:45, he's not here like he always is, I called Butler to tell him. He was not happy. While he called around to get a replacement, he had me air nothing but tunes and ads. Half an hour, give or take, Emily, we had nobody on the air. Nobody. It's embarrassing."

Emily looked past Healey to the studio. Mike Marshall was at the microphone. In the confusion, she hadn't noticed that one of the producers running amok was Mike's.

Healey nodded toward the studio. "Mike's floundering. He's never done morning drive and he sounds like a rookie. Butler made the producers come in to help, but they're mostly just trying to look useful. Like, Mike doesn't know where the library is, couldn't possibly find music carts on his own, right?

"Plus, Dan's not doing well. Look. He's over there."

Emily followed Healey's eyes to the corner of the room opposite Nip and Tuck. Dan McIntyre had squeezed himself tightly into the corner; he almost disappeared. He was staring at the floor, shifting from one foot to the other.

"I'll talk to him, see what I can do," said Emily. "Could you rip the national and regional copy off the wires for me? City News, too? Just drop 'em on my desk?"

"Sure," said Healey. "You want sports?"

Emily thought for a moment.

"The way Dan looks, I may be a while. Could you write sports for me, Rick? Please?"

"Think I remember how, might be fun," said Healey.

"How long?"

"Take sixty, more or less. You run over, we'll cut a little from traffic."

"Okay."

"Thanks."

She walked across the room and stood beside Dan McIntyre.

"Pretty hectic isn't it, Dan?"

He nodded.

"I don't like it. You?"

He shook his head vigorously.

"It's just for today, though. They'll figure out what to do and everything will be back to normal tomorrow. That's good, right?"

McIntyre didn't move.

"Dan, we'll be okay. I'll get your copy ready and then you'll give it that pro delivery of yours and it'll be okay. We'll just ignore all this other stuff. Does that sound like a plan?"

He still didn't respond. Emily watched Healey spin a sheet of paper into his typewriter while she tried to figure out what to do.

"I have an idea. While I'm getting your copy together, why don't you wait in the news studio instead of out here? Nobody will bother you in there and it's sound proof, you won't even hear anything. I'll bring your copy to you in there. If you get your blazer off the hook now, you'll be all ready to do the six o'clock."

He frowned for a moment and then moved, hesitantly at first, to his desk. He paused, gathered himself and marched to the coat rack and back again, using the correct tiles. By the time he reached the news studio door, he was adjusting his tie and striding with confidence.

Emily opened the door for him and he went straight to his position. He took his seat, settled in, folded his hands and stared at the console. Emily paused for a second and saw a small shudder ripple across his shoulders. It was followed by the rise and fall of a very deep breath. As he relaxed into his chair, she pulled the sound-proof door shut.

The banner over the bull pen door said: **4 Days to Hits 980.**

On his way to a bathroom during his break, Mike Mitchell stopped at Emily's desk.

"How do you do it?"

"Do what, Mike?"

"This. These hours. It's insane. I'm so bleary I barely know what I'm doing. I'm about to pour my sixth cup of coffee and I'm still not awake. Has a jock ever actually fallen asleep on the air? That'd be embarrassing, huh? I'm so blurry I think I might do that, doze off in the middle of a song. And my tongue feels like a doormat."

"What time did they call you?"

"Couple minutes before five, I think. Not sure. I was dead to the world."

"That's not much notice. Plus, you're not in shape. You do it every day, you get used to it. Almost."

"Not me. You got to bed, what, 7:30?"

"More or less."

"And you're up 3:30 or so, right?"

"Right."

"I don't care what you say, nobody can get used to that. It's just too strange."

"Life off the clock isn't for everyone, I guess."

"It sure isn't for me. Couldn't pay me enough, do this every day."

"You want a tip?"

"I guess."

"Back down on the coffee. You'll wake up any minute now. I'm telling you, another cup will have you wide awake into the middle of tomorrow. If you have to come back tomorrow morning, you'll need to get some sleep."

"Bite your tongue. Don't even say that out loud." He glanced over at Nip and Tuck, who had grown calmer.

"Geez, I hope they didn't hear you."

Mitchell dashed off and returned just in time to say good morning right after Dan McIntyre closed out the news. He had been flawless as usual, but he still looked a little frightened when he came out of the news studio and sat at his desk.

"I'm going to tell Sam we're airing the story, but only when we have confirmation. I can't justify going with Chase alone—it's just too risky. If he's led us down the path, we'll never recover. Have you heard from Hamster?"

"Are you doing that on purpose, Dean? It's Humphrey. No, but he's on my call list today."

"We need him. I don't even need tape from him, just confirmation of a call from Steinart on the day Chase says the meeting happened."

"That or the cabbies. I can call Burton, press him."

"Press him? You think he's stalling? That makes me nervous."

"No. Relax, Dean. He said it might take time. I believe he'll deliver if he can."

"Well, anyhow, I want it to air if we can make it work, so I have to tell Butler."

"Good luck."

Dean grimaced. "What you wanna bet, he asks Nip and Tuck to help him with this?"

"I thought about that when I saw them here this morning. I'm guessing the only question is, are they there when you walk in or does he stop you to bring them in? They'll be there."

Emily called Tim Humphrey's office and got nowhere. She debated pestering Burton and decided to wait, at least until later in the day.

Her only assignment for the Noon news was a phone interview with a popular member of the White Sox who had given his name to a new restaurant in the Loop. She had to fight through the restaurant's publicist, an insistent and intrusive woman who kept trying to feed Emily the questions she should ask. When she finally got to the new restaurateur and asked him to explain why he wanted to be downtown, his response was tightly deliberate and controlled. When she asked about features on the menu, she got another careful response and it dawned on her that he was reading his answers. When she asked him if some of his teammates would join him at the grand opening, he read her a list. When she thanked him for his time, he responded in kind but she was pretty certain he had done so on his own.

Emily played the tape for Lyon and they agreed to use no part of it. She wrote a brief story using parts of his answers, although she did make a change—from "lots and lots of beer and mixed drinks" to "full bar"—just to annoy the publicist.

When her shift ended, Emily decided to walk over to the Federal Building and roam the courtroom halls to see if she could find Tim Humphrey.

Before she left, she stopped at Rick Healey's desk to thank him for his help earlier in the day. He responded graciously.

"So, I'm headed over to the Federal Building, may be there for an hour or so. It looks like everything here has settled down, but if you need me, maybe call the court press office and see if they can find me?"

"You working over there?"

"Trying to chase down a piece of the Steinart puzzle."

"You're off the clock, you know."

"Of course. Still need to chase this guy down, though. It's worth it."

"Okay. Probably won't need you today. They're keeping Mitchell in the slot tomorrow. Still haven't heard from Sampson, but Butler says even if Sampson shows, he's not going on the air. He's drawn at least a one day suspension for this. Plus, Nip and Tuck say Mike's the one has the best feel for the new format, so they're happy he's stepping in."

"Mike must be delighted."

Healey grinned. "He demanded more money. A lot more. They didn't even flinch. He looked stunned, but he couldn't say no. I don't think he's up to the hours, managing the clock the way we do. Boy's not like you and me, honey."

"Takes a special breed," said Emily.

"Very special, I'd say."

"Rick?"

"Yeah?"

"I am not your honey."

He grinned again.

"My mistake. Sorry, sweetheart."

"Impossible, Rick. Just impossible."

The hall outside the courtrooms was no less chaotic and noisy than it had been when Emily first interviewed Tim Humphrey in the stairwell. Defense lawyers and prosecutors were huddled in groups working deals, bail bondsmen were milling, drifting in and out of court rooms checking on their investments. Families sat glumly waiting for something to happen; a handful of toddlers were being kept under vague control by anxious mothers and grandmothers.

Emily spotted an attorney she had seen in Burton's offices and approached her.

"Hi, you're with the Burton firm, aren't you?"

"Oh, you're the reporter. Joan Ashley's pal from the rock station, right?"

"That's me. I'm trying to run down Tim Humphrey, with the PD's office. Do you know him? Have you seen him?"

"I don't know him. But they're doing arraignments in 1208 today, that's where the PD's usually wait if they don't have cases on the calendar. You could try there."

"I will. Thanks."

The courtroom was almost as loud as the hallway and no less hectic. The proceedings were being conducted at a breakneck pace, one defendant after another facing their charges, answering a pro forma question or two from the court, hearing bail set and moving on. The attorneys on both sides spoke in shorthand which outsiders, including Emily, could not fathom. She shut out the noise and swept the room; about half the people in it were in motion.

On her second pass, she spotted Tim Humphrey. He was seated, but he was so tall that his head rose above the others on the bench where he sat. She dodged around the shifting crowd and slid into a seat directly behind him.

"Mr. Humphrey?"

"Yeah?"

"I'm Emily—"

"Yeah. Hi. You been calling me."

"I have. I need your help with something."

He had swiveled around so he could see her and it was not comfortable.

"Hallway," he said. "Can't talk in here."

They found an empty space between the restrooms. Humphrey dropped to one knee and opened his briefcase.

"I'm trying to confirm that Beni Steinart called you—"

"Here."

He held up a small pink slip of paper. It was a phone message form with one small hole in its center.

"I got one of those long knitting needle things, like a spike sits on its end? You get your messages, you make the calls, you slide the message down the spike."

Emily looked at it.

TO: THumphrey

FROM: BSteinart

RE: Meet with Jameson?

There was a check in the "URGENT" box.

The lines for date and time had scrawled entries. The message had been taken on the day and at the time Cary Chase had specified.

"I've been meaning to call you," said Humphrey. "By the time we got back from our holiday, I knew Beni was dead so I just spiked the message. I planned to file a motion to get the charges against her dropped, clear her name, but I got so many other cases, real people looking at real time, it just sort of got pushed aside. I feel bad about that. Anyhow, I found that message slip."

"This is extremely helpful," said Emily. She pulled the recorder out of her satchel. "This isn't going on the air, but I need to ask you a question or two."

"Okay."

"Can you tell me where and when you got this phone message, please."

"It was part of a pile of messages I picked up when I got back from vacation, little over a week after New Year's. When we're not at our desks, the switchboard takes messages like this one. The stuff we deal with is life and death, at least to our clients, so we make sure the gals who answer the phones get the details exactly right. I have full confidence that this message is accurate."

"That was my next question. You did not return the call, right?"

"No. There was no one to call back, she was gone."

"Did you also have a message from the U.S. Attorney's Office on the same day?"

"No. Why?"

"If Jameson's office didn't inform you of the meeting, ask you to be there to represent Ms. Steinart, that's part of the story."

"It didn't happen."

"You sound certain."

"I am. If an AUSDA calls a PD who isn't available and the call's about a live case, a court date or hearing or negotiation or whatever, the call gets transferred to the catch desk. We have a clerk, she's got a law degree, coordinates calendars so she can schedule whatever the prosecutor needs and make sure our clients are always represented.

"If somebody called me about a settlement meeting in Beni's case, the catch desk would have sent a colleague or scheduled it for me. And they would have sent me a memo about it. None of that happened. If Jameson or his people set up a meeting with my client, the PD's office didn't know about it. I certainly didn't know about it."

"That's all I need," said Emily, killing the microphone.

"Greg, hi, it's Emily."

"Hi! How are you? How's Ben? I've been so busy, we haven't talked, me and Ben. Everything okay? We need to get together, the four of us. That why you calling? Alicia has the social calendar, doesn't trust me to remember things."

"We should get together soon, but this isn't a social call, Greg."

"Hmm," he said, "sounds serious."

"Greg, are you sitting down?"

"At my desk."

"Good."

Emily gave him a facts-only account of the charges Cary Chase had leveled against Tommy Jameson. She said that she had solid confirmation that Beni Steinart had called her attorney to seek his counsel several hours before she went to Jameson's office alone.

"Are you out of your mind?"

"Greg—"

"No, seriously. This is outrageous. Tommy knows better, for one thing and for another—what's that date again?"

"January 6."

"Right. Hold on just a sec...our secretaries coordinate his calendar with mine and vice versa, so I have his...nope, one more page...here it is. What time did this alleged meeting take place?"

"6:30 PM."

"No. It didn't happen. Our office had been assigned to develop new fraud prosecution guidelines for pyramid schemes. Our fraud team did all the drafting, but the final product was going to be sent to D.C. and adopted as the DOJ standard."

"What does that have to do with—"

"I'm telling you. The team put together a presentation on the whole package when it was ready. The presentation was after hours that night, January 6. The whole top tier of the office was there. It's on Tommy's calendar, he was there, too.

"Are you sure? Did you see him in that meeting?"

"I wasn't there. Calendar says—and I remember this— there were a couple of candidates for a junior prosecutor slot in town. Tommy liked one of them, but he asked me to take the other one to dinner, see if maybe I saw something Tommy might have missed."

"Can someone else confirm that? That he was there?"

"Of course. Emily, this is nuts. I'm telling you, Tommy didn't harass that poor girl and he didn't threaten her. And he sure as hell didn't have anything to do with her death— she did that on her own. Chase has you chasing ghosts."

"I believe him," said Emily.

"You're making a mistake. You're really going to air this nonsense?"

"It's not my decision, but my boss is considering it seriously. Unless you can tell me to a certainty that the District Attorney didn't have a meeting with Beni Steinart that night, we think the story is viable."

"Wow. You have any idea how he's going to react, have you thought about that? Emily, he's going to come after you and the station like a guided missile. I won't be able to protect you. You could lose your job. You really want to take that chance?"

"Beni deserves to have the truth come out."

"I'll try once more 'cause it's you, Emily, and we're friends. I can assure you that the U.S. Attorney will categorically and emphatically deny all the charges because they are false. I strongly suspect that our office will consider a defamation action against Cary Chase. I would not be surprised if we also carefully weigh our options to bring action against WEL, too.

"Do you still want to air the story?"

Emily's grip on the phone was so tight that her hand began to ache, so she switched hands. In doing so, she discovered that her entire body was so tense that movement felt alien.

She closed her eyes and drew a deep breath.

"As I say, Greg, it's not my decision. I will embargo the story until we have your official response, but we need it quickly, 48 hours and less. I am certain the station's management will weigh your response to the story very carefully before they make a final decision."

Greg Good's quiet southern drawl blossomed.

"Lord have mercy."

12.

"So, between us, are you entertaining second thoughts?"

Ben was sitting on the couch in the living room. Emily had pulled an easy chair up to the coffee table and they were nibbling on grilled cheese sandwiches, his with tomato, hers with tomato and bacon. A bag of potato chips was open between them and the stereo was tuned to classical WFMT, the volume set as low as it could go.

"Greg scared me. He knows his boss and if he says there will be heavy criticism, I believe him. Greg's heart is in the right place, he was looking out for me as much as for his boss, but that made it even more threatening somehow. And he was certain that Jameson was in that meeting, too. If he confirms that, then we have a direct conflict—she called Humphrey about a meeting Jameson says never happened. We'd have to think long and hard about that."

"More wine?"

"No, I shouldn't. It's getting late and another glass will make me restless all night. OK, maybe just a drop or three."

He poured a dribble for her and filled his own glass.

"He could have slipped out, of course," said Ben. "A clandestine tete a tete, then back to the fraud presentation."

"I wish I could ask him that face to face. Then I'd know for sure. Without that, I have at least a little doubt."

"Enough to hold back?"

Emily set her glass on the table and stared out the windows. She was motionless, her face impassive. Ben remained quiet, gently swirling his wine and watching it cascade down the glass.

"Beni killed herself. The notion that Joseph Burton threw her to her death is just absurd. I do not believe him capable of it, period. If he didn't kill her, she killed herself. Why?"

Ben waited, well aware that the question was not for him to answer.

"Because she had no other option. She had nowhere to turn. She couldn't give Jameson what he wanted so she was going to prison and she couldn't do that. She saw only two choices, life as a turncoat liar or life as a prisoner. She killed herself because it was the most desirable choice. I believe Tommy Jameson drove her to that choice."

She looked at Ben.

"But I'd like to be positive."

The banner read Hits 980 on MONDAY! Below it, a memo from Sam Butler had been posted. Emily read it carefully before she crafted the morning news.

Butler's memo said the station was ready to launch the "new era" of radio in Chicago. It said the advertising staff had sold out the first two weeks of the new format and the Marketing department had constructed a package of promotions and advertising which would "blitz" Chicago for the entire two week launch. Butler thanked the news department for their cooperation during the transition and for their "team spirit" which he knew the entire WEL staff shared.

In the penultimate paragraph, Butler announced that Sandy Sampson had resigned to accept an offer with an FM station in Los Angeles and that Mike Mitchell was the station's "bright new" morning deejay.

The memo closed with "Good Luck."

When the pace settled down after the 6 AM newscast aired, Emily walked back to the doors and read the memo again. Rick Healey, at his desk, waited a beat before he interrupted her.

"So, honey, you hearin' a lot of cheers and rah-rahs coming out of the sales office? Sound to you like those guys are riding high on the hog? Wandered into one of those parties they hold over there lately?"

As soon as he said it, she understood. The guys on the sales side were as dedicated to celebrating their success as they were driven to achieve it. They worked hard and earned well and they never failed to have a champagne party or a catered barbecue when they met or exceeded their goals. In really good times, the parties usually included substances more potent than champagne, although never in plain sight.

"I haven't heard a peep out of them," she said. "I bet they're giving the first two weeks away because they can't sell the format. Bargain rates, bargain commissions. That what you think?"

"'Deed I do, honey," said Rick. "Haven't seen so much as a birthday cake, myself. I hear Sam's telling 'em to sit tight, sayin' once the format lands everybody will want to jump on it. What they're running into now, nobody wants to take a chance on something new. The big accounts are all sitting, waiting."

"That's not comforting," said Emily. She turned to find Dan McIntyre listening intently to the conversation.

"What do you think, Dan?"

"I don't know what to think," he said. "I'm getting some fresh coffee."

The receptionist at the main desk paged Emily shortly after 9 AM. When Emily walked up to the desk, the receptionist handed her a manila envelope.

"Courier dropped this off, I had to sign for it. Addressed to you."

The envelope bore the insignia and address of the United States Attorney's Office, Chicago. At the top of the page, it said Statement of U.S. Attorney Tommy Jameson.

"There is absolutely no evidence to support the false claim that I or anyone on my staff conducted a meeting, clandestine or otherwise, with Benita Steinart. We did not threaten her or seek false testimony from her. The allegations that I engaged in such activity are false and I categorically deny them.

I have always been dedicated to maintaining law and order as a means of protecting the values and morals which are the heart of our nation's greatness. Those who seek a society with no moral center will use any means to defeat my efforts. These allegations are clear evidence of the depths my enemies will find to defeat me.

I have made no decision as to what action I may take against those who made these scurrilous allegations or those who broadcast them. I am, however, considering all available options.

I remain resolute in my determination to do my job as my government and my Lord intended."

The statement was on official U.S. Attorney letterhead and Jameson had scrawled his signature across the bottom of the page.

Emily carried it and Tim Humphrey's pink telephone message slip into the planning meeting.

"Okay, Emily, where are we?"

"Just got Tommy Terrific's response. He categorically denies. It's not a press release, there is no contact info on the statement, no phone numbers to call. That's pretty odd."

"So? The guy wants to make a statement, he makes it.

What's the problem?"

"Style and form, for one thing. This isn't Greg Good's style at all, it doesn't have his touch. Plus, Greg would have started calling me ten minutes after the courier had the envelope. He'd make sure I got it. Based on my conversation with him, he'd be determined to get us to drop the story. If he couldn't persuade me, he'd push hard to get the entire statement on the air. Why's he suddenly out of the picture?"

"Maybe they're hoping we'll kill the story just because Jameson denies it. Maybe Jameson did this on his own, Good wasn't involved. Or, your contact Good figures none of that other stuff is needed because we'd be sure to fold when we got this."

"Maybe. But there's something else."

"What?"

"Greg Good was adamant that Jameson was in a meeting the night Beni died, he checked his own calendar while I was on the phone with him. He was positive."

"So?"

"So, why isn't that in the statement? If they can prove Jameson didn't meet with Beni, why not convince us?"

Dean paused and pondered.

"He's setting Chase up? Jameson's no dummy. I bet he's luring Chase into saying or doing something more so Tommy can really crush him. He wants Chase hanging way out on the limb before he cuts it off. Sounds like Tommy Terrific, doesn't it?"

"Maybe. Too many maybes, Dean. It feels odd to me."

"Well, we still have that PD's message, right? Whatisname, Hammerbach?"

She held up the pink slip.

"Humphrey. It clearly says Beni called him the afternoon before the alleged evening meeting with Jameson took place. She had the message marked 'URGENT'."

"Cab driver?"

"Not yet."

"What do you guys think?"

Al Coffey said he'd be real nervous airing the story based on what they had.

"I think Dean's right—they figure a denial that strong, we kill the story. If we don't, Jameson will probably own the station by the time he's done with us. Not a good idea, pulling his chain. And what I hear, he's the kinda guy would engineer a set up, too."

Don Kipper disagreed.

"Why'd she call her lawyer, urgent, there isn't something serious going on? She wanted him to come to the meeting, she called him. Plus, I had a rock solid alibi I wouldn't sit on it, I'd cram it right down our throats, shut the story down cold. I think there's something fishy here."

"Okay," said Dean Lyon.

"I trust Emily," said Dan McIntyre.

Everyone in the room stared at him.

"You didn't ask me, but if you had, I trust Emily. If she thinks the story should air, we should air it."

"I'll be damned!" said Dean Lyon, laughing. "Dan, I didn't ask because I can't remember the last time you said anything other than hello in these meetings. You guys?"

"Can't remember one time, myself," said Coffey. "Not one."

Kipper shook his head. "Heard him excuse himself to get coffee, couple weeks ago."

"Well, I have something to say now. I trust Emily."

Lyon, still shaking his head, said, "Well, Dan, I believe I do too."

Turing to Emily, he said, "I like having Humphrey's kinda sorta confirmation. That helps. I'll let you know what they have to say."

"Okay, Dean. Thanks."

"Don't thank me yet," he said. "And in the meantime, you get your guy Good on the phone and have him explain to you why they did the statement the way they did. That'll answer our questions, I bet."

"I'll get on it as soon as we're done here."

"OK. Let's move on. Y'all remember we're doing the temporary news format starting Monday, right? Emily, you want one of the guys to come in early, help out?"

Rolling her eyes to the ceiling, Emily said, "Rest assured I have not forgotten. I've been using the time between newscasts to tinker with the style and add more stories. I think I've got it handled."

"You sure? I know Kipper here would love to get up really early, lend a hand."

Kipper made an exaggerated choking sound and feigned a faint.

"Really, Dean, I think I'll be fine. If not, I'll get Healey to handle sports for me. He did it, that morning Dandy didn't show up, I think he actually liked it."

"Wait. Healey? Our Rick Healey? Did something?"

"Yes, he did. I asked, he jumped right in. If it comes to that, I'll lean on him."

"Wonders never cease. It's a miracle. I tell you, boys, the lady works miracles."

"Who knew?" said Don Kipper. "So, get my hair to grow back, wouldja, babe?"

Emily shot him a look at "babe" but said nothing.

She called Greg Good's private line as soon as the meeting ended. There was no answer.

She tried again, using the main switchboard. She was told Mr. Good was not available. She left a message and was told that it was not possible to predict when Mr. Good might find time to return calls. The woman promised Emily she would mark the message urgent but terminated the call when Emily asked if the message could be written in red.

"You're not gonna believe this," said Dean.

He was at Emily's desk, a copy of the Jameson statement and the pink phone slip in his hand.

"They killed it."

"Butler wanted to scotch it in the worst way. Basically told me to forget we'd ever even thought about the story in the first place."

"So they killed it."

"Didn't say that."

"I don't understand."

"Nip and Tuck loved it. Kept saying it's hot. They wanted to use it on Monday morning, first day of the new format."

"You're kidding."

"Absolutely not. Nip couldn't sit still, Tuck kept nodding, thought his head might fall off."

"So we go on Monday?"

"Didn't say that."

"Okay, Dean, stop this. Just tell me."

"I reminded them that we're doing staccato news on Monday, to match the format. I told them we have to give this story all the time it needs, make sure we get it right. Can't do that, two, three sentences."

He paused, smiling.

"I reminded Sam that the rapid fire news style was his idea and told him we all want to be sure we deliver what he wants. Flattery never hurts. We're airing it tomorrow. Tuck says the buzz all weekend will get everybody to tune in on Monday when we launch."

"Tomorrow."

"Tomorrow. I need you to get all the tape in shape. I want to use both Chase and Burton, okay? And there's one more thing."

"What?"

Dean Lyon turned, leaned over and rapped on Rick Healey's desk.

"Rick, sorry to interrupt, but I need you to work on this story for tomorrow's morning news cycle."

He turned back to face Emily and gave her a stop sign.

"Do not say a word, Emily. Not one word until you hear what I have to say."

Good Morning, Chicagoland! You're on the El with Morning Mike and before we bring you the morning news, weather and sports, I gotta remind you to be here on Monday when we're going to give you a whole new way to enjoy all your favorite music, big prizes every hour, too. Great music and you can win big. WEL's about to get a whole lot hotter!

I got this morning's Great Eight, eight hits in a row right after the news. Stay tuned, though, because Dan McIntyre has an important and explosive story for you. I'll catch you on the flip side. Here's the news. Dan...

Good morning, Chicago. I'm Dan McIntyre with WEL News. We have an exclusive breaking story for you this morning involving allegations of wrongdoing by United States District Attorney Tommy Jameson. Here is our WEL special report...

In an exclusive interview with WEL News, Chicago developer, entrepreneur and civic leader Cary Chase has accused U.S. Attorney Tommy Jameson of threatening Benita Steinart with a 25 year prison sentence unless she provided false testimony against Mr. Chase in a drug case. Ms. Steinart committed suicide within hours of the alleged threats.

Ms. Steinart was the executive manager of Chase Mansion, directing all social and charitable activities at Mr. Chase's expansive home on the near north side. Last summer, Ms. Steinart was a passenger in a vehicle which contained hundreds of pounds of cocaine. At the time, US Attorney Tommy Jameson held a press conference announcing an investigation of Mr. Chase's involvement in that drug deal. No charges against Mr. Chase have been brought.

The two men arrested with Ms. Steinart, Donny Marsh and Grant Wilson, pled guilty and are serving their sentences in Federal prisons. Ms. Steinart, who maintained her complete innocence, had yet to be sentenced at the time of her death.

In our interview, Cary Chase charged that the U.S. Attorney summoned Ms. Steinart to a secret meeting in which she was encouraged to perjure herself by implicating Mr. Chase in drug trafficking...

"Tommy Jameson gave her a choice between perjury and prison and she could not live with either. He is responsible for Beni Steinart's death.

"He trampled justice and fairness and the facts before him because he is convinced that I am his sworn enemy the devil. To prove it, he did everything but throw Beni Steinart out the window, plunging her to her death."

In a statement issued to WEL, U.S. Attorney Tommy Jameson has categorically denied that a meeting took place or that he threatened Ms. Steinart in any way. Mr. Jameson called the charges "scurrilous."

Cary Chase's close friend and advisor, attorney Joseph Burton was the last person to see Ms. Steinart alive. He confirmed for us that she was despondent and frightened...

"She was terrified. She said Jameson was a bully—that's the word she used—and he scared her. She was certain he'd crush her if it came to that."

WEL has confirmed that Ms. Steinart contacted her attorney, Public Defender Tim Humphrey, with an urgent message on January 6, the day Chase alleges her meeting with Tommy Jameson took place.

We are continuing our investigation into the circumstances surrounding Benita Steinart's death, so stay tuned for more news as it develops.

I'm Emily Solomon Winter, WEL News."

13.

$\mathcal{A}$s she moved to leave the broadcast booth, Dan McIntyre swiveled his chair around and whistled.

"You have a fine sound, Emily. Excellent delivery."

"Thank you, Dan. That means a lot to me."

Dean Lyon and Rick Healey were waiting at her desk when Emily came into the bullpen. So was Max. Don Kipper and Al Coffey were leaning against the studio window and both toasted her with coffee mugs. There was a bouquet of flowers on her desk.

"You were great, Emily," said Dean. "Crisp, tight, got it all in. Nice job."

Emily's smile shone bright.

"Thanks. And thanks to you too, Rick—I know you worked hard on the intro."

"Dean's idea. He didn't think you should write your own intro. I didn't really do much," said Rick. "Once I heard the story, I figured it stood on its own. I did make Mitchell use 'important and explosive.' Thought 'allegations of wrongdoing' might help, too. Didn't want the audience driftin' away."

"Wow, Rick. Thanks."

"My pleasure."

Dean Lyon said, "You understand you made history today."

"Really, Dean? The first woman on the air at WEL? Golly, it never entered my mind."

"Yeah, well it's about damn time, you ask me," said Max. "Couldn't be prouder of you, Emily." He stepped forward and handed her a doughnut.

"Max! You just called me—"

"Yeah, I did. Emily Solomon Winter. I gotta say, I liked the way that sounds. Gotta run, parked the cab on the street, flashers on. Had to be here, though. Plus, I had orders to deliver these," Max pointed to the flowers. "You sounded great. Just great."

As Max scurried out, Nip and Tuck appeared in the entry to the bullpen. They listened while the news staff chattered on, but when Dean Lyon looked over and spotted them they beckoned him away.

While the three men huddled in the hallway, Emily tugged the card from the bouquet and opened it.

"Brava! Hard work, superior reporting and an exquisite sense of justice reap the reward they merit. Were I any prouder, I should surely burst. All my love."

The card was written, with a fountain pen, in Ben's distinctive hand.

Dean Lyon returned to Emily's desk.

"Did you say you'd been doing some test copy for Monday's 'cast?"

"I did."

"Still got any of it?"

"Sure. Somewhere."

"Doesn't really matter. You got a few loose pages of something in that satchel?"

"Of course."

She found a couple of press releases.

"Hand them to me. Don't worry, I'm not going to read

180

any of this stuff."

She knit her brows in confusion. Dean very gently inclined his head toward the bullpen doors. Nip and Tuck were still standing there, watching.

"They want to be sure we've got the Monday news in perfect shape. I told them I would double check. They think I'm going over copy with you, like we'd have Monday copy ready to go on Friday morning. Too stupid. Anyhow, the easiest way to get them out of my hair is to do this."

He spent a moment looking at the first page in his hand and then rolled it to the bottom of the pile and gazed absently at the next page up. Emily glanced over at Nip and Tuck and reminded herself not to laugh.

"Got it. We're showing them how dedicated we are, how hard we're working to get it right?"

"Yup. That's not what matters."

"What does?"

"What matters is, they are not reading this copy. They are not allowed anywhere near newsroom copy, ever. I told them I'd review with you, but they'd have to shoot me to get their hands on it."

She pulled her reporters' notebook from the satchel, flipped it open and began scribbling in it. Every now and then, she'd look up at Dean and nod or tilt her head to show she was paying careful attention. Over Dean's shoulder, she could see Nip and Tuck absorbing it all.

"That should do it."

He pointed to something on a page and handed it to her. She looked at it and nodded.

Dean went to the doors and joined the two consultants, nodding vigorously and pointing at Emily. They appeared satisfied.

When she moved the flowers to a corner of her desk, she found a white envelope. Her name was typed on the envelope, but it was otherwise blank.

She held it up.

"Rick, you know anything about this?"

"What?"

"This envelope. Did it come with the flowers?"

"I dunno. Didn't notice anyone put it there."

She grabbed a letter opener and slit the envelope open. It contained six legal size pages, crisply folded.

She was holding a copy of U.S. Department of Justice Pyramid & Ponzi Prosecution Protocols (WORKING DRAFT). It was styled as a memo from D.A. Fraud Team/Chicago to All Senior Staff/Chicago. It was single-spaced and dense with long paragraphs and at least 25 footnotes and annotations.

In the middle of the last page, below the last paragraph, a rubber stamp box had been applied with blank spaces for initials and a date below capital letters which said APPROVED.

Emily left her desk and walked out to the WEL lobby and reception area.

"Hi, Kathy. Do you have a minute?"

"For you? You bet! What's on your mind?"

Emily held up the envelope and its contents.

"Who delivered this to us?"

The woman looked at the envelope then took it and turned it over twice.

"Never saw it before. Where'd you find it?"

"It was on my desk this morning. I don't know when it got there. I found it under the flowers."

"Oh, well, the flowers! That cab driver guy busts in here, has to be at your desk before you get off the air, wouldn't sign in or anything, just smiled at me and walked right on into the bullpen. Kinda cute, that guy. All he had was the flowers, though. He had his arm around them and he had a hat in his other hand. No envelope I saw. I'd know if I sent to you from here, that's for sure."

"Okay. Thanks."

"Uh, Emily?"

"Yes?"

"Way to go this morning. It's about time."

Emily blushed.

"Thank you."

"Nah. Thank *you*. Lot of us gals think it's long overdue, getting one of us on the air. Sorry I couldn't help with that envelope. Is it important? "

"Tell you the truth," said Emily, "I don't have any idea. Maybe."

Back at her desk, Emily sat and placed a call.

"Hi, pal. It's your bride."

"Hurrah, my love! Well played, indeed. You were terrific this morning. Just terrific. Great story, of course, but you sounded so professional, so polished, quite as though you've been on the air all your life. This may sound a little odd, but I think you sound even better on the air than you do in person. It is elusive on so little evidence, but there's something more compelling about you on the air. You sound so, what? So—"

"If you say 'cute,' mister, I will become most irritated."

"Heaven forefend, ma'am, certainly not that. No. More authoritative? A smidgen more energy? A sense of power? Maybe not. Ah, I ramble. The point is that it was thrilling to hear you on the air and I for one hope to have that thrill far more often."

"And I would love nothing more than to fulfill that hope, sir. In the meantime, however, I have a question."

"Yes?"

"Did you send an envelope along with the beautiful flowers I got this morning?"

"Those rapscallions! I wrote it out myself and they forgot to include it? I'll cancel payment."

"No, no, Ben. I got your card, it was lovely. There was an envelope under the flowers, though, it's a copy of some weird prosecution guidelines. I think it's the thing Greg said Jameson was in a meeting about the night he supposedly met with Beni. I thought perhaps you had something to do with this?"

"Not I, m'lady, not I."

"It had my name on the envelope, so I'm supposed to have it but I don't know why."

"What is the content of the document?"

"Pyramid schemes, I think. I haven't had time to read it. There's so much of it, the pages look solid black. I scanned it and I didn't see anything related to the Grant-Marsh prosecution. I'll read it later, but I don't know why."

"It is, as the King of Siam was wont to observe, a puzzlement. Could I persuade you to bring the document home with you that I might give it my attention?"

"I had planned to ask just that."

"I already knew that, further evidence that my exquisite extrasensory perception grows stronger every day. That ESP workout exercise tape I bought is worth every dime, I must say."

"Ben, this is serious."

"Of course it is. And of course, I'll give it my most careful scrutiny this evening. Perhaps Greg could enlighten. Is he still speaking to you?"

Emily snorted. "Who knows? I've already called him, private line and switchboard. Nothing. I don't suppose you have heard from him?"

"Nary a whisper."

"Drat!"

"Language, my dear, language! The FCC has no tolerance for inappropriate language. It harms our well being and leads innocent children astray. 'Drat' must be on the list. Now that you are an on-air personality, attention must be focused on such matters. Perhaps I could develop a list of forbidden words for you?"

"Good bye, Ben."

"Ta."

Mike Mitchell used the last hour of the Friday morning show to tease the Hits 980 format. He didn't allude to what he was doing, but the prolonged sets and the rotating top 25 format were there, just as they would be on Monday's launch and thereafter.

Emily listened as she worked on the Noon news. Mitchell went from "Best of My Love" to "Lonely People" to "Black Water" to "My Eyes Adored You." Through the morning, Emily heard all four of those multiple times, interspersed with less frequent airings each of "Some Kind of Wonderful" and "Fire." "Big Yellow Taxi," the only one she liked, sat at 24 on the playlist, so she heard it only once.

When she heard "Boogie On Reggae Woman" for the second time, followed by "Have You Never Been Mellow," she rose from her desk and turned the nearest speaker all the way down.

Between Noon news assignments, Emily received several calls from friends and colleagues congratulating her on her work. Later in the morning, Sam Butler dropped by her desk to say he was impressed with her work even if he was terrified of what it might bring down on the station. She thanked him and assured him, because he asked, that she was prepared for Monday's format-friendly changes to the news.

The odd memo nagged at her through the day. She was frustrated that she couldn't determine why she had it and the fact that she did have it began to make her increasingly nervous. Greg Good's words, "this could cost you your job," triggered a suspicion that Federal agents were poised to swoop into the bullpen and arrest her for possession of stolen documents. She pictured an agent threatening her with the evidence— "your fingerprints are all over a private internal government document"—and promising to ruin her life. While she thought the idea far-fetched, she was also keenly aware that exactly such a promise had been made to Beni Steinart.

After the Noon news, she placed another call to Greg Good, to no avail, and then to celebrate Friday she walked through the Loop to the Mallers Building and treated herself to a cheeseburger. Happily full, she rode up to the 15th floor and tried on several pair of Frye boots and fleece-warm moccasins and browsed the leather briefcases and purses. She didn't buy anything, but she was far more relaxed leaving the building than she had been entering. When she left, she varied her pace and crossed streets unnecessarily to be sure she didn't have a tail. She found her behavior as absurd as it was rational.

Emily arrived at Ricardo's a bit ahead of her usual time and was surprised to see The Rules Committee already in full session. She checked her satchel, got a drink from the bar and headed to the booth. As she made her way, she sensed that some in the room were stopping their conversations as she walked past. Before she could figure that out, she arrived to discover that every member of the Committee had a white table napkin at their neck.

As she stood before them, Kirstin Bonner raised her hand and on her downbeat the group removed their napkins to reveal large red, white and blue campaign buttons. The buttons said:

EMILY SOLOMON WINTER
WEL NEWS!

As her colleagues cheered and Emily teared, several in the room shouted in her direction and raised their glasses to her.

Mary Massey spoke first.

"It's not just that you broke through," she said. "You did it with a story so hot that everybody in this room is jealous. You pulled the tiger's tail. It's all they're talking about, you know. The whole room is buzzing. My News Director wants to know how we can piggy-back on it."

"My editor wants to know how come I didn't catch this story," said Lois Lipton.

"You cover courts," said Emily. "There wasn't a trial. It was all plea bargaining."

"You think I didn't point that out? He implied that if I was a guy, maybe we wouldn't have gotten scooped."

The table exploded.

"You told him it was a woman who broke the story, right?"

"Ignorant sexist."

"That's never-date-him stupid."

"Chauvinist pig!"

Emily laughed with them.

"I don't suppose you asked him if he actually heard the report?"

"Once my blood pressure backed down to a mere red alert, I did ask him that."

"And?"

Lois grinned. "He hadn't heard it. Some pal of his called and mentioned it."

"You're kidding."

"Oh, yeah," said Lipton. "So I told him who broke the story."

"Just that gently?" asked Bonner.

"Well, I can't say I wasn't forceful. I'm not sure I kept my voice down and I may have used a few unsuitable words. And I may have questioned his heritage. And his intelligence."

Emily frowned and Lois laughed.

"Relax, my friend. He'll never admit it, but for the first time since I started there, I think he's glad there's a woman on his staff. He said 'I won't get scooped by a broad again' and told me to go find good stories like 'that other chick.'"

"Chick," said Marcy Marcus. "That one's really annoying, isn't it? Just as bad as the Brits with their 'bird.' We're all pretty but oh so fragile, right? Men!"

"All the more reason to celebrate Emily's breakthrough," said Bonner. "We work our way up, eventually we'll be able to turn around and bring somebody up behind us. I've hired twice for Cary, women both times. Imagine what a newsroom would be like if

Mary or Emily sat in the News Director's chair."

"Not me," said Emily. "I'd be a lousy boss and I'd be even worse in the carpeted suites, executives and I don't mix well—they'd hate me and I'd return the favor. But Mary? I'd take a cut in pay and go back to the Cop Shop overnight to work for her."

"No, you wouldn't," said Massey. "I'd have you on the streets every day, where you belong. None of this occasional reporting nonsense, on radio no less. Speaking of which, Emily, what's the deal with all the hype? You guys got billboards everywhere, you're all over local TV, what's happening on Monday?"

"Oh, I heard about it," said Lois Lipton. "Word all over town is, they're going to play nothing but pop hits. Two different people told me Sandy Sampson left because the new format is so boring he couldn't stand to work with it. Nobody expects JD the DJ to last. So, what's up, Emily?"

"Sampson got a great gig in L.A., bigger market, bigger station. And a big pay bump too, I hear. Far as I know, Decker's not going anywhere."

"I miss Sandy," said Lipton. "Mitchell's nice enough, but he's not very funny."

"Air talent comes and goes," said Massey. "Nothing new there. But, what about the news side, Emily?"

"They say nothing will change. We're going to tweak morning drive during the first couple of weeks, but they aren't cutting our time. After that, we're told we go back to normal. "

"You trust them?"

"I trust Dean Lyon and he's navigated this pretty well so far. The two consultants who dreamed this thing up, I don't know what to make of them, never mind what they're doing. I'm as eager as you guys to see what happens."

Late on Saturday morning, Emily padded down the hall to the living room and found Ben in the recliner on the platform. He was sipping coffee and nibbling at a sweet roll as he focused intensely on his reading material.

"Morning, pal," said Emily, walking to the windows and taking in the view.

"Indeed it is," he said. "Sleep well?"

"Very."

"Coffee's on."

"Thanks."

She called to him from the kitchen while she organized coffee and nosh.

"Are you working? Looks like a brief to me."

"I am fulfilling a promise," he said. "I am on my third reading of Pyramid & Ponzi Prosecution Protocols. The prose sings but the narrative thread is weak. I do like that alliterative title, I must say. Do you supposed they called it 'Pequod' in the office?"

She leaned around the kitchen entry.

"What?"

"Four Ps in the title, P Quad, as in the Melville opus."

"Ah. I get it. Did you say third reading?"

"You would prefer I approach this lackadaisically? One must be thorough."

"But one need not endure cruel and unusual punishment. Isn't it dull?"

"It never rises to the level of dull, alas. It is comprehensive. It is also tedious beyond measure."

"I guess you love me, huh?"

"Such is my fortune."

"So? Any thoughts?"

"Well, first and foremost, you are correct that there is no connection to the cocaine case involving Ms. Steinart. It is not mentioned and that is no surprise—that case has no place in this document."

"Then why would someone want me to have it?"

"The obvious seems the most plausible, I think. Somebody delivered it to a reporter so that questions would be asked."

"And that took three readings?"

"Third time is the charm, it would appear."

"You know, I pretty much had the same conclusion about fifteen minutes after the thing was delivered."

"I concede that my analysis does not overflow with subtlety. But my conclusion is no less firm—you're being told to look into this."

"Whatever this is. So, any chance you'd join me in a walk in the park and brunch somewhere? I'd love to get outdoors for a bit."

"Delighted."

After brunch, they wandered down Clark Street, carrying on their conversation. They eventually found themselves within a block of Wrigley Field, a sizable detour from their path home.

"I can make it back," said Emily, grinning, "but if you want to grab a cab, I'd be okay with that."

"I've a better idea. As long as we've come this far, let's cut over to the inner Drive and drop in on Greg and Alicia. We can visit with them and we'll be right on the bus line home when we leave."

"What? You, of all people, want to 'drop in' unannounced? You're not going to call them first, beg their forgiveness for the untimely intrusion? You sound so—"

"Spontaneous?"

"Well, yeah, that. But, so informal, so casual. I'm just a bit surprised, is all."

"Those who do not welcome change cannot evolve. I like to imagine I am capable of growth."

"Wonders never cease. Let's give it a go."

They walked another several blocks north and then east toward the lake. They entered the lobby of the high rise apartment building and approached the desk where a bellman sat. He turned down his radio as they approached.

"We're here to see Mr. and Mrs. Good, please," said Ben.

"I'll ring 'em." He flipped through the pages of his directory and then picked up an intercom phone.

"No answer," he said. "They expecting you?"

Ben shot Emily a look.

"No. The visit is spontaneous."

"Too bad. Nobody home."

"Thank you, sir. Would you pass this along to them when they return, please?"

Ben extracted a business card from his wallet, wrote "Dinner?" on the card and handed it across the desk.

As they exited the bus at Wellington, Ben took her hand.

"Deviations from accepted protocol do not always work, I see."

"True," said Emily. "But evolution, as I understand it, is a slow steady process."

"Smarty pants."

"Guilty."

14.

Good Morning, Chicagoland! I'm Morning Mike at the mike and you're riding...um, you're riding high on Hits 980. We've got more of today's top music right after this morning's news with Dan McIntyre.

Hits 980, all hits all the time...here's Dan with today's news.

Thank you, Mike. For Hits 980, I'm Dan McIntyre. It's currently thirty-two degrees with snow flurries and winds kicking up. Expect the temperatures to remain in the low thirties throughout the day. Let's check traffic with Robert Roberts. Robert...

...Thank you, Rob. Hits 980 traffic is brought to you by McLaughlin Chevrolet in Skokie, who remind you to drive carefully on our slick streets this morning. Here's the Hits 980 News.

The Cook Country grand jury has indicted a local retired dentist on murder for hire charges. The dentist allegedly paid a pharmacist to kill two business partners.

Secretary of State Henry Kissinger and Russian leader Andre Gromyko will meet today. They'll talk about trade and arms.

President Ford has approved a deal which will allow Iran to invest three hundred million dollars in struggling Pan American Airways.

We'll take a break from Hits 890 News, but I'll be back with more, and sports, right after these important messages...

We have a quick update from Merrill Chevrolet traffic...Thanks, Robert.

Here's a round-up of news in the race for Mayor.

Mayor Richard Daley calls rival Bill Singer's campaign "a political machine from New York." The Mayor says his own organization is "a human machine made up of neighbors."

Candidate Ed Hanrahan invited reporters to question him without restriction on a radio program which aired this weekend.

And Alderman Bill Singer spoke to a Baptist church on the South Side.

We'll be right back after this break...

In other news, police in Rome sprayed tear gas at the audience during a Lou Reed concert.

The Post Office is expected to announce that first class stamps will soon cost thirteen cents.

Over the weekend, thirteen year old Ted Kennedy, Junior beat his dad in a ski race. The younger Kennedy recently lost a leg to cancer.

We'll be right back after this traffic update...

...Let's bring you up to date on sports now, courtesy of Ace Hardware.

Montreal beat the Blackhawks last night.

The Bulls smothered the Braves.

And on the college basketball scene, Duke beat DePaul.

I'll be back with one last story after this brief pause...

Finally, a leader of ERA Central has charged that ERA supporters in Illinois are being subjected to "one of the dirtiest campaigns imaginable." Anti-ERA advocate Phyllis Schlafly denies that her followers engage in dirty tactics.

I'm Dan McIntyre and you're up to date on Hits 980. With all hits all the time, here's Morning Mike Mitchell.

Great job, Dan. Thanks. Good morning, Chicago. I've got ten hits in a row for you right now on Hits 980. We'll kick it off with the Eagles, Best of My Love and Average White Band's Pick Up The Pieces. This is Hits 980, Chicago!

"So, how long do we have to do this?"

When Dan McIntyre came out of the broadcast booth, he centered the news copy on his desk and took his coffee mug down the hall to the break room. Rick Healey left his desk and walked over and read the copy.

"Dean says two weeks," said Emily, "the launch phase."

"And then?"

"Then we go back to writing stories instead of headlines, bring back taped interviews, beef it up again."

"Good. It's pretty thin now."

"As far as I'm concerned, the only thing thinner is Phyllis Schlafly's position on the ERA. Funny part is, it's much harder to write. Every one of those stories demands three, four more sentences minimum— leaving just about everything out is more challenging than including it. Weird, isn't it?"

"Don't know about that, but it sure is wrong. I know everybody thinks I'm just dead weight around here, but I know what news should be and this isn't it. I'm not saying you did wrong, mind you—when the suits dictate, we all gotta follow—but it sure isn't what we've always given our listeners."

"Agreed."

"There's something else."

"Yes?"

"Dan's not comfortable with it and you can hear it. He's better than this. They're wasting good talent."

"You should tell him," said Emily.

He snorted. "Right."

Healey saw McIntyre moving down the hall. He tamped the copy straight and laid it dead center on the desk and loped, with enough agility to surprise Emily, back to his own desk. By the time McIntyre sat down, Healey was buried in the Sports section.

Emily took a call from Dean Lyon. With the phone cradled on her shoulder, she made the few small changes he suggested. His notes made the copy move along even faster. He complained angrily to Emily about Butler's notion of news to match the music while he improved its delivery.

When she ended the call, Healey lowered his newspaper and rattled it at her.

"Rick? Something else?"

"Just wonderin'. You know that story you aired last week, the chick went out the window?"

"She was a woman, Rick. She didn't hatch eggs or preen her feathers, she worked hard and she had friends and family."

"Yeah. Well, I'm wonderin', you got any idea how much time you put into that thing, before it got broadcast? All of it is what I'm askin'—not just when you were on the clock, but all totaled?"

"For the last week, it's all been on assignment."

"Yeah. And the work you did the day we reported her death was our clock, too. What about in between?"

"Rick, I don't have any idea. Lots of hours, I guess."

"You didn't keep track?"

"Never occurred to me. Why?"

"You think 20 hours? More? 40?"

Emily sat back and ran through it. She'd spent at least three hours in newspaper archives digging up the background on Beni's prosecution. She'd visited the Virginia Hotel and interviewed Mavis and Bobby Banks and then the kid behind the lunch counter. She'd traveled to meet Mrs. Steinart. Her initial meeting with Tim Humphrey, her conversations with Greg Good and Kirstin Bonner—all of it had been off the clock.

"Honestly, Rick, I just don't know. I'd guess somewhere between those two, more than 20, less than 40, but I'm not even sure of that. Could be higher, I suppose."

"Huh." He snapped the paper back in place and resumed reading.

The phone on Emily's desk rang.

"WEL Newsroom."

"Emily, Mary Massey."

"Hey! What can I do for you?"

"Do you know Troy Coburn?"

"Never heard of him."

"Her."

"Never heard of her. Who is she?"

"Troy Coburn is the under-fed junk yard dog currently protecting our crusading D.A. Tommy Jameson from attack."

"What? Who's attacking Jameson?"

"By her definition, I am. Can you believe that? You didn't think the rest of us were going to let you have the Chase Jameson fight all to yourself, did you?"

"I saw the Sun Times used the gist of our story in their city news wrap yesterday," said Emily. "Barely two 'graphs. I sort of figured it would die over the weekend because there's no place to go with it. Jameson denies what Chase says, Chase doesn't have anything else to say—there's not much there to work with for now."

"Jameson won't even deny."

"What?"

"That's where this Troy Coburn person comes in. She's fielding all press calls to Jameson and she is rude and impossible. She refused to give us a copy of the statement he gave you and when I asked why she said, I'm not making this up, she said 'Because I said so.' She sounds like she's about 15 years old. She told me that if we pursued your story—she called it 'that pile of rock station crap'— she'd see to it Jameson never spoke with us again, about anything."

"Wait, Mary. I need to back up. You called Jameson's press office, right?

"Who else? Of course, that's who I called."

"And they didn't send you to Greg Good?"

"No. I asked for him. By name. Switchboard patched the call through and Troy answered."

"Did you—"

"Ask to talk to Good himself? You bet I did. We go back a ways, Greg and I. Troy—who names a girl Troy, anyhow?—Troy said 'I'm handling this now.'"

"I don't understand."

"Neither do I. I know you and Ben are close to Greg and his wife, thought you might be able to give me a heads-up about what's going on."

"Mary, on my honor, I don't have the faintest idea. We haven't heard from Greg in days and, for Ben at least, that's very unusual. And now you tell me he's either not on the job or he's been taken off his press work, I'm concerned."

"I'm sorry, Emily. I didn't mean to spring this on you. I figured you'd already know something. Pretty clumsy."

"No, no, I'm glad you called. At least now I can start asking around, see what I can dig up. I'm grateful. Really."

"OK, but I'm still sort of embarrassed."

"Let it go, please."

"OK, I guess. One more thing, just between us, okay?"

"My lips are sealed."

"I listened to y'all this morning, driving in."

"And?"

"It's really awful. Noisy and boring. Sorry again."

"Yeah. They didn't give me a vote. Some of us are hoping, once it's up and running smoothly, they'll make some adjustments, get a little more flexible."

"That was judiciously stated, my friend. You think it's awful, too."

"No comment. But thanks again for the heads-up about Greg Good. If I hear anything, I'll let you know."

"See you Friday. Bye."

Emily sat for just a moment, trying to imagine what had happened to Greg. None of the options she could conjure up were pleasant—he'd been demoted, he'd been suspended, he'd been fired, something had happened which put him entirely out of reach—and she cut herself off.

"Hello."

"Hi, it's me."

"Good morning."

"Ben, I'm really worried about Greg. I just got a call, Greg isn't handling press for Jameson, there's somebody new doing it. They weren't home on Saturday, we haven't heard from them. Has he called you, has he been in touch?"

"He has not."

"I'm worried."

"Let's not be hasty. I know many of his regular haunts. We use the same gym, I know his favorite spots for lunch, several of his colleagues at work, I even know his favorite gas station. I'll make some calls right now and try to determine his whereabouts. I'm sure there's a reasonable explanation."

"Thanks. I have some work to do right now, but when I get a break I thought I'd call a few women I know, Alicia's friends. Maybe they'll know something."

"Well, then, let us proceed. I'll call as soon as I know something."

"Me, too. Bye."

During the morning planning meeting, Dean Lyon had asked Emily to pare the report on foster care down from five segments to three.

"It's running too long, even for the Noon 'cast. See if you can't tighten it down."

Emily was sorely tempted to ask if her job description had been altered from News Writer to News Reducer, but the editing challenge intrigued her so she nodded. Dean looked less than pleased and she wondered if the decision to cut the series had been his.

It was hard work. The copy cuts she made helped, but Emily was forced to find ways to cut interview segments entirely to meet the time constraints. She did her best to maintain the flow of the story. Even with the station's skillful engineer at her side, the project took a long time to complete.

It was well past the lunch hour when Emily was able to sit at her desk and rifle her rolodex to find Alicia Good's friends. She came up with three contacts; two were on lunch break and the third, who lived in the suburbs, didn't pick up the phone at all.

She called Ben. He was awaiting at least three return calls and had yet to contact another few but had no more to report.

She plucked Greg Good's card from the rolodex and dialed the private line he had provided on the back of the card. It rang 15 times before she disconnected.

Ben rode past his usual stop, riding further down Sheridan Road to the Goods' apartment building. He spoke with the bellman at the desk, who had not seen the Goods in a few days, and then took the elevator down to the garage and checked the parking space with the number which corresponded to Greg's home. The space was empty.

He left the building and walked several blocks to the gas station nearest Greg's building and spent some time chatting with the guys who ran the place.

"I think they're on a road trip, a vacation," he told Emily when he came in the door. "I don't think there's anything about which to be alarmed."

"Tell me."

"Well, their car isn't in its space and you know they only use it on weekends."

"That's it? That's not enough—"

"I've more. I ventured to the station Greg uses, which I know to be the only station he'll use unless he's out of town. They service the car for him, too. So, last Friday, Greg drove into the station and filled the tank. He did so in the middle of the afternoon."

Ben appeared to be done.

"That's it? I mean, that's all?"

He nodded. "As far as I'm concerned, that's all we

need."

"Are you being deliberately obscure? I don't get it."

"Greg never fills the tank, Emily. It's a quirk. He's convinced that it is more economical to buy a specific amount of gas. He believes that he saves money by putting only five, six, seven dollars into the tank rather than filling it up. I have suggested to him on several occasions that his theory is pure folly. Eventually, he will spend the amount it takes to fill the tank. That is as inevitable as wind off the lake. And, of course, there's the matter of having to visit the station more often and the additional use of gas each visit entails. Still, he insists that he is—"

"Ben, please. Stop. What does this have to do with anything?"

"I'm sorry, perhaps it is murkier than I imagined. If Greg filled the tank, it can only be because he knew he'd be out of town the next time he needed gas. He wanted to get as far as possible before he had to use a strange gas station. He filled the tank because they're going on a trip."

"'They'. Who, they?"

"Did I neglect to mention that Alicia was in the car as well? Confusing testimony, that. My apology. They were both in the car with a full tank. Alicia was with him, the car was fueled to go a great distance and it was the middle of the day."

Emily nodded. "To beat the Friday night exodus, ahead of rush hour."

"You've got it."

"Road trip," said Emily.

"Road trip. A perfectly plausible conclusion, I believe."

"Did Greg mention this to you?"

"He did not and I admit that troubles me just a little. Yet, I remain confident that nothing is amiss here. I think they took off, just the two of them, for the fun of it."

"I hope so," said Emily.

15.

"*H*its 980 News."

"Is this Emily Winter?"

"Yes."

"Hello. My name's Wes Clark. Joseph Burton said I hadda give you a jingle."

"I see. Why?"

"I drive a cab. Mr. Burton, he said you'd wanna talk t'me."

Emily drew a deep breath.

"Did you take a fare to the Federal Building early in January? Her name was Steinart, Beni Steinart."

"January 6. Miserable weather, nobody was out, I was lucky to catch any fares that night. I was sittin,' nothin' goin' on, she comes outta the hotel and hails me. Luck, right? Drove her from the Virginia to the Fed Building, dropped her off maybe 6:20, 6:25. Didn't catch a name."

"You're sure of the time?"

"Lady, we keep logs. This one was easy to find, too, 'cause I had maybe three fares that night, not like when a convention hits town, drivin' 'em all over the place until

203

they sorta all moosh together, barely got time to write 'em down. Not like that at all. Plus, once she got in and got her hat and scarf off, she was a babe and a half. Really fine, I'm sayin'. Keepin' an eye on that one in the mirror, not exactly tough duty. Great to look at, even if she was kinda off."

"Off?"

"Well, yeah. She was real jumpy, for one thing, didn't sit still much. And how many people get outta my cab, go right past the front doors and down the garage ramp instead?"

"Mr. Clark, I would like to arrange to interview you, on tape, so we have your story on the record. If that's okay, when would be convenient for you?"

"You mean, like for radio? Talkin' to a recorder, you play what I say? On the air? For real?"

"Absolutely for real, sir. Absolutely."

Max pulled his cab to the curb in front of the WEL studios and Emily climbed in.

"This is kind of upside down, isn't it? Me picking you up after work, 'stead of dropping you off before."

"My lucky day, Max. I get to see you twice and it's just not Holy Cow o'clock."

"So where we going?"

"Mr. Clark's favorite bar," said Emily. "Near Addison & Clark."

"Wrigley? We're goin' to a Wrigley Field bar? It's February. This guy knows the Cubs aren't playing, right?"

Emily laughed.

"He lives in the neighborhood, Max. The place is his regular spot, he said he'd be comfortable talking to me there and I agreed."

"In a bar? Middle of the afternoon? Need to keep a sharp eye on this guy."

"That's why you're here, Max. That's exactly why."

"I been sniffin' around, like you asked. Nobody seems to know much about him, but a couple guys, Acme Cab the outfit he drives for, say they don't hear nothing bad about him. He's been drivin' a while, they say. I did that, you asked, and I got my instructions for this meet, too. Don't worry about me."

"Max, I only worry about you when I can't keep an eye on you."

"That's most of the day, Emily Solomon Winter."

"Exactly. Handsome guy like you, out on the loose chauffeuring lovely ladies around in a nice clean new cab, you might find yourself in compromised circumstances. Max. What would I tell the family?"

Max grinned.

"Tell 'em they should be so lucky."

The bar was almost empty. There were two business men in suits, ties loosened, sitting at the bar finishing sandwiches and beers. There were tables of varying sizes in rows down the center of the room, but only one under the television set was in use by three men in maintenance overalls gathered around a couple of empty pitchers. Three booths lined the wall closest to the door and a lone man was seated in the center one.

"Mr. Clark?"

"You Winter?"

"Yes," she said, extending her hand. "Nice to meet you."

"Take a seat. Who's he?"

"Max, my driver. It's pretty cold and damp out there, I couldn't leave him on the street. He's not going to be in the way, I promise. Max, why don't you find a seat, I'll holler when we're done here."

"Yes, ma'am," said Max. While Emily settled into Clark's booth and organized her recorder, Max strolled until he found the table he needed. He positioned himself so he could hear everything they said. If the bartender stayed out of his line of sight, he could also see Clark's face and upper torso in the big clear mirror behind the bar.

She had anticipated a fuss about Max's presence. It

must have seemed a little odd and she had worried that it might make Wes Clark suspicious, but he seemed to take it in stride.

The interview went quickly and smoothly. As soon as the recorder had been checked, Emily asked the cab driver to describe his encounter with Beni Steinart. He confirmed that she had hailed him near the Virginia Hotel and directed him to the Federal Building Plaza. He described Beni in rich detail and while Emily flinched at a few salacious remarks, she was convinced that it was indeed Beni who had ridden in his cab.

He said he thought it weird that somebody wanted to go to the Federal Building after it was closed. It worried him enough, he sat in the cab while she walked across the plaza—"makin' sure a lady that fine didn't get into no difficulties might need some help."

And Wes Clark watched as she walked past the entrance to the building to the garage ramp.

"Babe walked right down that ramp, I'm tellin' ya. Like she knew what she was doin', you know? I figured, her car musta been down there, she was comin' back from some meeting or something, she was gonna drive home. She walked down that ramp, I watched until I couldn't see her no more."

"And what time was that?"

He pulled a small notebook from his shirt pocket and flipped through the pages.

"Picked 'er up 5:55. Dropped 'er, 6:23."

"Can I see that log?"

"Sure. Won't make no sense to you."

He passed it over. Emily took several minutes to figure out how he charted his activities and several more to decipher his handwriting and what appeared to be a whimsical approach to spelling.

"I see now," she said. "1Femail, 555P, 623DO—that's pickup and drop off, right?"

"You got it, hon."

"And this other number, that's the fare?"

"Yup. Pretty short run and the clock didn't add much 'cause there was so little traffic we never sat nowhere except for red lights. You can see for yourself it ain't like I could retire for the night after she climbed out."

Emily shut her recorder off and double checked to make sure she had what she needed.

As she did so, Max got out of his seat and approached their booth. He put his hands on the table and leaned across until he was ominously close to Wes Clark, staring at him.

"Two things pal," said Max. "First, I'm the driver but that ain't all I do for the lady. I find out you been slingin' some stuff at her, I hear this story's bogus, you got a serious problem on your hands. You get my drift?"

Emily was stunned. She hadn't expected this but she was even more shocked by Max's demeanor. To even think of Max as threatening was nearly impossible and yet here he was, displaying enough menace to make the bartender set a glass aside and look over at him.

"I gotcha, pal. Really. I'm givin' the lady the straight dope, honest. You wanna see my log, too?"

"Nah," said Max. "I said two things, remember?"

Clark seemed to shrink a little.

"Yeah. What else?"

"She tip you?"

"Huh?"

"The fare, this young lady you been talkin' about here. She tip you?"

Clark's face relaxed.

"Tip shoulda been a buck, maybe a buck and a half. She didn't have small bills, left me all her change, tip was 4 bills plus."

Max studied Clark for another few seconds and then pushed himself away from the table.

"Ready when you are, ma'am."

Emily gathered her satchel and slid out of the booth,

Max leading the way. As they walked past the end of the bar, Max paused and leaned toward the bartender.

"Sorry, sir, didn't mean to alarm you. Just making sure we weren't getting hustled."

"No problem, buddy," said the bartender. "Wes, he's a regular, tips okay, but third, fourth drink, he gets hostile, nobody 'round here much likes him. I was sorta hopin' you'd pop him one."

"Nah," said Max, laying some cash on the bar, "but I'll pop for his next round."

"So," said Emily. "You're the expert. What do you think?"

Max was sitting in the driver's seat but they hadn't pulled away from the curb.

"He sounded legit to me and he wasn't all squirmy or nothin', sittin' there. Story seems okay, the pickup and drop and all. Not hard to figure this guy watching her all the way across the plaza, probably thinkin' stuff I can't talk with you about. Guy's kinda a letch, huh? "

"Kinda. So, this isn't a set up? I didn't think he was rehearsed. He didn't sound like he'd been coached, did he?"

"Nah. I'm not sure the guy's got the smarts to keep a lie that big straight. Just wasn't that slick. And his log'd be hard to doctor, so much later. He's on the up and up, you ask me."

"I am asking you, Max. Why did you ask about the tip?"
Max smiled.

"Double check. Most tips, you're glad to get them but they don't stand out. If he'd said he didn't remember, it wouldn't have surprised me, but he was real clear because she tipped him so big. It were me, I'da remembered that, too."

"Pretty sharp, Max."

"Yeah, well, I don't want to mess this up. It sealed the deal for me, the tip. He drove your pal that night, just like you reported."

"And I have to tell you, Max, that's a big relief. There's no more doubt now. She went there the way Chase described it and that puts us on solid ground. Of course, I had one very clever source working deep background for me. Thanks, Max."

"Deep background, eh? That sounds important, Emmy. We headed home now?"

"Yes, thanks."

"Off we go, then."

The drive took about ten minutes. For the entire ride, Max whistled softly to himself, a happy, meandering tune of his own making.

"So, you have solid confirmation," said Ben. "She went to the Federal Building on the day and at the time Chase alleges. She used the entrance protocol they claim Jameson specified and you have a witness. That second point, the garage entry, is critical. It's so unexpected, so unique that it adds significant credibility to their story."

"It does. I'm not sure where it leads, though. I think Dean will want us to air it, but I don't think Jameson will give us anything when we ask him. Massey says they aren't talking to anybody about this."

"He's stonewalling? Are all in government by their very nature incapable of learning from others' mistakes? The lessons of Watergate are fresh yet they remain stunningly obscure to those most in need of education."

"A cover-up created to hide a significant abuse of power. It does have a familiar ring, doesn't it?"

Ben smiled and gestured toward the platform in the corner.

"I have a complete library devoted to the subject," he said.

"But, here's the thing," she said, "Greg would never handle a problem this way. He's too savvy about managing press. He's careful and strategic. This is clumsy. I can't figure out why he's out of the picture. Do you suppose he's been fired?"

"That strikes me as nearly inconceivable. Jameson is bound for electoral glory but everyone knows that Greg is the wizard behind the curtain. Plus, had he been fired, I am all but certain that he would have contacted me.

"No. Were one to surmise, the stonewall strategy would be Jameson's, probably over Greg's strenuous objections. Greg is principled, as we know, so if Jameson rejected his best counsel, I can imagine Greg asking to be relieved of executing a strategy he knows to be flawed. Rather than lose him over the dispute, Jameson sends Greg on a vacation of indeterminate duration, maybe gives him some extended out of town assignment, dependant on how long the Chase story remains alive."

"That sort of makes sense. And if you're right, it explains Troy Coburn. She's is waging the campaign Jameson wants. I'd still like to hear from Greg, though."

"You're in radio, my dear," said Ben, "a realm in which nothing exists unless one hears it. But I cannot disagree— I'll be comforted to hear from him as well."

Emily crafted Tuesday morning's newscast with a bit more facility than her inaugural effort on Monday and she managed to add two more stories to the package. The copy mirrored precisely the pace Sam Butler and Dean Lyon wanted, but Dan McIntyre's style and delivery just didn't mesh with the staccato format. McIntyre delivered Emily's fast-paced, energetic news briefs slowly, with authority. He sounded uncomfortable and he ran nearly two minutes long in the 6 o'clock broadcast.

Nip and Tuck were in the bullpen, monitoring everything. McIntyre shaved some time off his delivery for the 7 o'clock newscast, but still ran more than a minute over. When McIntyre came out of the broadcast booth and set the copy on his desk, Nip scurried over to Tuck, a stopwatch in his hand, and whispered, his arms flailing. Tuck nodded and rose from his seat, moving toward Dan's desk.

"Whoa, pal! Hold it right there. Where do you think you're goin'?"

Tuck paused and gaped at Rick Healey, a mixture of surprise and disapproval in his eyes.

"I beg your pardon?"

"You're not planning to interfere with our news operation, are you?"

"I intend to keep the new format on track and on time," said Tuck.

"Not by messing with the news. No sirree."

Healey moved around his desk. Emily saw his fists were clenched and rose, moving to his side.

"Take it easy, Rick."

"Listen to her," said Tuck. "You have no business with me."

"You take one more step toward our news anchor, it's going to be my business in a big hurry."

"Rick!"

"Sorry, Emily, but I've had enough." He turned to face Tuck. "You and that pipsqueak can screw up the station's sound all you want, I guess, 'cause some fool gave you the power to do that. We built a powerhouse rock and roll station here, you know. I think you're probably going to ruin it, but there's nothin' I can do about that.

"But nobody, not even the New York nitwits hired you two, gave you the power to mess with our news and I'm not about to let it happen. Bad enough it sounds like tabloid headlines."

"If the news runs long—"

"Yeah, yeah. News runs over, you won't be able to play *Lonely People* or some other *Billboard* junk what, four times this hour?"

"Correct. If the news runs long, the format is disrupted."

"So, you talk to the News Director about that. He's not around, you talk to the Assistant News Director—that

211

would be me, Bucko—but you don't come near the rest of the news staff. You hear me?"

Dan McIntyre had been listening, transfixed. As Tuck gathered himself to respond to Healey, McIntyre stood and assumed a ramrod military stance.

"Rick, I believe I can deliver this copy in the specified time frame. I'm not accustomed to this pace and I haven't adapted well. I assure you I will bring the 8 and 9 in on time."

"I appreciate that, Dan," said Healey, turning his attention to Tuck. "Case I didn't make it clear, buddy, it would give me a great deal of pleasure to put you back in that chair. Any chance, any chance at all you're going to make me do that?"

Tuck glowered but didn't speak. Instead, he turned and walked straight to the bullpen door, snapping his finger at Nip who followed him out.

"Thanks, Rick," said Dan.

"Any time," said Rick. "Thanks for backing me up."

"Hey," said Emily. "You guys keep chattering away like this, how's a girl supposed to get any work done?"

At 8, Dan McIntyre ran exactly 4 seconds long. At 9, he ran 10 seconds under. He came out of the broadcast booth looking utterly exhausted, but he smiled at Rick Healey and winked at Emily.

In the morning staff meeting, Emily gave Dean Lyon a synopsis of her interview with Wes Clark.

"Well, that should keep Butler off our backs for a few days," said Dean. "He's been pounding down the Maalox, terrified that Jameson is going to pull our license or something 'cause we lied about him. You got good tape from this Clark guy?"

"Yes. All the details Chase gave us, the guy says it happened exactly that way."

"Let's air it. You want to give Jameson's people 48 hours again?"

"I don't think we need to be that generous, Dean. They've completely shut down on this. I will certainly give them a call, but I'll give them just a couple of hours, more if they want to give us something. "

"OK. I'd like it to lead tomorrow morning, but there's no room for a story like this in morning drive right now. Tell them we air tomorrow, up top in the Noon 'cast.

"I thought you had a good relationship with Jameson's guy, Good. He won't give you something we can use?"

"He's not handling this anymore. I don't know why and it looks like he's on vacation so I can't find out what's going on. My pal over at 'BBM-TV tried to get them on the record about Beni. They refused. I gather they were not gracious about it, either—they wouldn't even provide a copy of that statement from Tommy Terrific we got before we aired the story."

"They're still hoping it'll just blow over, I bet. Maybe a second solid story will get 'em to pay attention."

"Maybe," said Emily.

"Got another thought for you, just in case. When you call, see what they say about Good. He's Jameson's alter ego, right, the genius behind the man? If something's wrong there, it might be a story in its own right."

"Of course, I'll ask," said Emily.

"This is Troy."

"Hello, Ms. Coburn, I'm Emily Winter, WEL News. I'd like—"

"Stop!"

"Excuse me?"

"You heard me. Stop. Shut up. This office has nothing to say to you, now or ever."

"I am working on a story—"

"Don't care. You are a liar, your work is pure fabrication. As far as Mr. Jameson and I are concerned, you don't exist."

"That may be, but I have a witness who confirms that

213

Beni Steinart visited the Federal Building early in the evening of the night she died. Our information clearly supports the charges Cary Chase leveled against the United States District Attorney. We're airing the story on our Noon News tomorrow."

The line went dead.

Emily called Cary Chase. Joseph Burton happened to be in Chase's office, so she reported the details to both of them. She told them what she had gotten from the cab driver.

"That's encouraging," said Chase. "Very encouraging."

"I'm still hunting down her ride back to the hotel," said Burton. "I've checked all the major cab operations, a couple of the smaller ones. I wonder, did she take a bus back to the Virginia?"

"Maybe," said Emily. "The ride back to the hotel isn't nearly as important as what Clark gives us. All the unusual circumstances Beni described to Mr. Chase are there."

"Please. Cary."

"Cary, then. That second cab ride would be nice to confirm, if it exists. But the arrival time and that strange entry provide strong corroboration."

"Excellent," said Chase. "I know he denied it all earlier, but what does Jameson say about this now?"

"Absolutely nothing. They aren't talking to me or anybody else in the press. They're in a black out."

"That's ridiculous," said Chase. "He can't just walk away from this. That's not right."

"My boss thinks they're trying to ride it out, let it die."

"Nonsense. He has to answer for this. He must."

"Easy, Cary," said Burton. "Ms. Winter is an ally, remember? She's on our side."

"Sorry, I didn't mean to shout at you," said Chase. "Is there more you need?"

"Yes, but first, I'm not on anybody's 'side' in this. I know it seems that way, but I've given the D.A.'s office everything I've given you and I'll report both sides."

"Quite right," said Burton. "My mistake."

"I just need to be clear. For the story, I'd like to have Mr. Chase's response to this news."

"Cary. Can we do that on the phone?"

"We can," she said. "Give me a minute to patch my mic into the phone and we'll be all set."

I'm Dean Lyon, Hits 980 News Director and this is the Hits 980 Noon News. Our first story today reveals new information about the death of Beni Steinart. WEL has secured confirmation of several of the charges made by Cary Chase against U.S. Attorney Tommy Jameson. Here's Emily Solomon Winter with the latest...

WEL News has confirmed that on January 6 this year, Chase Mansion executive Beni Steinart went to the Federal Building after the building was officially closed. We have also confirmed that Ms. Steinart entered the building using the garage exit ramp. The afterhours meeting and the unusual entry are important elements in charges made by Chicago developer Cary Chase, Ms. Steinart's employer, against U.S. Attorney Tommy Jameson.

Mr. Chase alleges that in a private meeting that evening, without Ms. Steinart's attorney present, the U.S. Attorney threatened to imprison Beni Steinart if she refused to implicate Chase in a drug dealing scheme. Jameson has previously denied to WEL that such a meeting took place. His office refused to comment on this latest development in the story.

Cab driver Wes Clark of Huntington Fleet Cab Company told WEL News that he drove Ms. Steinart to the Federal Building that night.

"When she got out of my cab, she didn't go to the front doors, the main entrance, like everybody does. It was probably locked anyhow, since it was after the building is closed. But she went all the way across the plaza and down the exit ramp into the garage. I thought that was kinda odd, but I figured her car was parked down there."

Mr. Clark's taxi log for that evening confirms that Ms. Steinart hailed his cab near the Virginia Hotel, where she had rented a room for the night. They arrived at the Federal Building at 6:23 PM. Mr. Chase has charged that the secret meeting between Ms. Steinart and D.A. Jameson took place at 6:30 that evening.

Ms. Steinart, who Mr. Chase says was confronted with a choice between perjury and prison, took her own life in a leap from her room at the hotel in the early morning hours after the alleged meeting with District Attorney Jameson.

In an exclusive interview with Hits 980, Cary Chase again criticized the District Attorney.

Tommy Jameson is sworn to protect our rights, not violate them. Honesty and integrity demand a full accounting of his role in Beni's untimely and unnecessary death. His silence is a violation of the trust placed in him."

WEL will continue to investigate the circumstances surrounding Cary Chase's allegations and Beni Steinart's death. For Hits 980 News, I'm Emily Solomon Winter.

16.

Ben's family staged a birthday celebration, so Emily couldn't attend The Rules Committee meeting.

The family, especially cousin Ronny, Jr., were impressed that Emily was a "real" reporter now and it gave Emily great pleasure to stand aside and let Max tell the story of the cab driver interview he had vetted for her. It was nice to be with them all and Emily was delighted that Max was so happy, but it was all muted.

The first week of Hits 980 had been taxing. The change in the rhythm and content of the playlist and the temporary news format left the entire WEL staff feeling unsettled and out of place. Her concerns about Greg Good weighed heavily, as did the seemingly endless struggle to put an end to the Beni Steinart story.

Mike Mitchell had learned to live with the odd hours, although not without persistent complaining. His replacement in the mid-day slot, Bret Garner, was a transplant from Milwaukee recruited by Nip and Tuck. Since his previous station had already converted to the Nip and Tuck system, Garner was comfortable with the format, but so far there had been little spark or verve in his work.

Jon Decker, more dour and downhearted by the day, followed the format precisely as it had been designed, holding firmly to the Red-Blue-Red-Blue-Red-Green-Red pattern and playing long blocks of music. Now and then, Decker would comment on a song or an artist, but his notes were brief and listless and something in his tone left an emptiness hanging in the air. In the long music blocks and the extended commercial breaks which they generated, Decker often left the studio and wandered the halls of the station. He never spoke with anyone and his demeanor suggested it would be unwise to approach him.

While she was fretful about JD the DJ, Emily was even more perplexed by Greg Good's absence. She and Ben had contacted everyone they could think of. Ben had even communicated with their law school alumni office to see if they had heard from his classmate. Nothing resulted. She checked the mail eagerly every afternoon when she got home, hoping to find a post card signed by Alicia and Greg and sent from some wonderful locale.

And she had no idea how to draw Tommy Jameson out.

At about 9:30, Emily set her birthday cake on the arm of the couch where she sat and leaned back into the cushions. In a few minutes, she was asleep. Ben gently stirred her awake and, as she leaned on him every step of the way, they got in Max's cab and he drove them home. She slept all the way.

It was nearly Noon on Saturday when she shuffled down the hall to the living room. It was a sunny day and the room was warm and bright. Ben was in the recliner reading his Breslin book and she stepped up on the platform to give him a kiss.

"Sleep well, did we?" Ben reached out and took her hand.

"I'd say so," she said.

She got a cup of coffee and shifted two dining table chairs so she could face the windows and prop her feet up. The newspapers were stacked on the table but she didn't bother with them.

Instead, she watched a small boy in the park making repeated efforts to pedal his bicycle upright and in a straight line while the boy's dad stood by, a set of training wheels and a pair of pliers on the sidewalk beside him. The youngster couldn't quite manage it until his dad ran alongside the bike, steadying it with a hand on the seat. She couldn't hear the child's shout of joy when he finally flew off on his own, but she did supplement the father's dance of celebration, his arms high above his head, with her own quiet round of applause.

While Ben continued reading, Emily took her coffee cup and the papers to the couch. She dozed for most of the day and then set about preparing for a dinner date. They had a nice meal and arrived back in the apartment early. Emily was in bed and sound asleep by 9:45.

After brunch and a walk on Sunday, they spent the afternoon watching a *Thin Man* movie. When it ended, Emily went into the kitchen to throw together a pot luck supper. While she organized the food, Ben resumed reading.

She had laid out a sort of antipasto plate—cold cuts, bread and condiments for sandwiches, some fruit, a bowl of corn chips, a beer for Ben and a root beer for Emily—when Ben shouted.

"Genius! Absolute genius!"

Emily moved to the kitchen doorway.

"You called, my love?"

Ben grinned.

"You are indeed the resident genius in this household, pal, but I reference another in this instance."

"Someone has taken my place?"

"Impossible. No, I was merely admiring a marvelously subtle, simple device."

"I see. I gather you wish to share?"

"With pleasure. Breslin writes that John Doar, the counsel to the House Judiciary Committee investigating the President and his minions, used a system of filing cards to keep the whole thing straight. He and his staff had a card for everybody involved in the break-in and the shenanigans that followed. Sometimes an individual might have several cards, loaded with information, but there was a card for everybody, thousands of them."

"Three by five?"

"What?"

"The cards. Were they three by five cards?"

"It is immaterial."

"Not to me."

"Very well, then, three by five."

"Good. You keep talking, dear, I'm just going to bring the food to the coffee table. I can still hear you."

"So, Doar and his team were trying to trace the origins of the cover-up, the steps the administration took once the scandal began to close in on them. This is when the Washington Post was breaking new Watergate stories every day, the New York Times had its own investigations afoot and the networks had reporters working on it full time, too. And, ominously from the White House perspective, Congress was taking it all very seriously. So the White House was in a full state of siege.

"Well, Doar used the cards and White House logs and meeting minutes to track everybody. He finds that they all went to a meeting one afternoon in the President's office. There's no question about what they discussed. They assessed the damage and went over the evidence, to be sure, but most of all they wanted to find a way to protect Nixon and save the administration. As we know now, the ways and means they eventually adopted were far more sinister than the original break-in."

"What does this have to do with cards, Ben?"

"There was a second meeting in the White House, later

that same night. Everybody who was in the first meeting, the one in Nixon's office, was in the second meeting. Haldeman, Mitchell, Erlichman, Dean, the whole cover-up crew, all the key players are in the second meeting."

"Ben, this is really fascinating, really. But I'm getting hungry and it's getting late. The food's all here. I have to work tomorrow, you know."

"But this is so magnificent. Doar laid all the cards from the first meeting, the one in the afternoon, on a table in front of him. But when he compared the first meeting with the second one, he saw something different and he took one card off the table."

"Ben, please."

"The President wasn't in the second meeting, Emily. Everybody else was, but Nixon was all by himself in the Oval Office that night. He wasn't in the room."

Emily stared at him.

"That's it?"

"Oh, it's so clever. They have to do anything they can to contain the scandal and for these guys, that means violating bribery laws, concealing or destroying evidence, coercing witnesses. The second meeting was to create and execute a criminal conspiracy."

"Yes, dear. I knew that."

"But, don't you see? They created a criminal enterprise designed to protect the President, so the one person who could never be associated with it in any way is the President himself.

"He sat alone in his office so he could honestly claim that he didn't participate in planning the cover-up. He knew exactly what they were doing, of course, which is exactly why he couldn't be there— they're planning crimes and he can't be one of the criminals. Doar used index cards to bring down the President of the United States. Imagine that! It is so simple, so perfect—a work of genius."

"Are there more books about Watergate coming out?"

"I have no idea, m'love. 'Tis a strange question, though. Why do you ask?"

"I love you more than anything on this earth, Benjamin Winter. You know that, right?

"I do."

"Then don't be offended when I gently suggest that your obsession with the intricacies of Mr. Nixon's impeachment has grown, how shall I say this, just a little tedious."

Ben set his book aside, considered what she had said, smiled and walked over to sit beside his wife on the couch.

"I accept and agree. My fascination with everyone from Sam Ervin to John Sirica to Rose Mary Woods has run its course. I may have gone somewhat beyond the pale, truth be told. But my affair with one of the most thrilling adventures in law and democracy shall henceforth come to an end."

He gave her a kiss.

"I am nearly done with the Breslin book, m'love, and then I'm all yours."

"I could wish for no more," said Emily.

The news staff all gathered in Dean Lyon's office for the Monday morning planning meeting. They sat in their usual seats for nearly fifteen minutes before Lyon came through the doors and wheeled his chair around his desk. Before he sat, he returned to the door, closed it firmly and then pulled on the chains to snap the blinds on the windows facing the hallway shut.

He sat, his face grim and his shoulders slumped, and paused for a moment or two before he spoke.

"Sam Butler has been fired," he said.

Everyone reacted instantly and the noise level in the room rose rapidly as each tried to be heard above the others. It got so loud that Dean Lyon stood up and clapped his hands to quell them.

"Be quiet, please," he said. "One at a time, I'll answer

your questions if I can. Kipper?"

"What the hell happened, Dean? Butler been skimming profits or something? He finally bag that secretary, the one in advertising? She file a complaint or something?"

"No, Don. It's nothing like that."

"What then?"

Lyon leaned in and spoke very softly.

"Even before we launched Hits 980, the network had a research firm in place to do polling, audience tracking. They tracked all last week. The report came in on Friday afternoon."

"Uh-oh," said Emily.

"Yeah, uh-oh is right. The surveys showed a steady drop, day by day, every single day. These audience research guys project that, in the next formal book when the Neilsen people do it for real, we'll be number four or five in the market. Maybe lower than that."

Gasps greeted the news.

"There's more." said Lyon. "Our morning drive numbers are the worst of all. I think Sandy's departure has a lot to do with that, but the new format didn't help either. Too much all at once. Mitchell is drawing about half of what Sampson did. We aren't number one in morning drive anymore. WEL is in deep trouble."

Lyon sat stock still, his hands splayed on his thighs, his head down. The group was silent for a moment and then Emily had a dreadful thought.

"Dean," she said, "who's replacing Sam?"

Lyon looked up, his eyes cold, his chin set.

"No shouting, okay?"

They nodded.

"Nip and Tuck."

Dan McIntyre choked on his coffee, coughing violently until Al Coffey reached over and sharply slapped him on the back three times in rapid succession.

"They can't do this," said McIntyre, his voice gurgling. "It's not right."

"Right has nothing to do with it," said Kipper. "They got all the power, those two bozos. I knew they'd kill us. I just knew it."

"Their assignment is temporary," said Lyon. "They'll finish the transition, cement the new format and then they'll stay until the network picks a new GM."

"You," said Emily.

"What?"

"You, Dean. They should make you GM. You know the business side well, you've got a lot of seniority around here, everyone respects you. They should give you the job."

Lyon laughed, but his eyes showed no mirth.

"Not a chance. Thanks for the vote of confidence, but even if they're fool enough to offer it, I'm not foolish enough to say yes. Next six months, maybe a year or more, this place is going to be in chaos. They've invested so much in this Hits stuff that they'll probably have to stick with it, but if it doesn't take hold and the numbers keep falling, they'll have to dump it and find something else."

Coffey snorted. "I nominate the format put us number one until last week."

"Ain't that the truth. The point is, the station's in for a rocky ride. I think they're going to have to search some, find somebody who wants to take over this mess. It won't be me."

"Tuck scares me," said McIntyre. "And that little guy, I think he's on hippie drugs or something, running around like a hamster all over the place. I don't like them."

"I know, Dan. It's not going to be easy but we all know how to pull together, stick together. I think the best we can do is do our best, give the audience professional newscasts every time. Change is part of this business, guys, no way around it and not much we can do about it. Other questions? Okay then, let's put the Noon news together."

When they came out of the meeting, Rick Healey was at his desk scribbling notes. He watched as McIntyre settled in at his desk and Kipper and Coffey got their coats and headed out to cover stories. When Emily got to her desk, he stood and moved closer.

"Dean told you all, right?"

"Yeah," she said. "Too bad. Sam wasn't the most loveable guy around, but he did a good job until this Hits thing and that's hardly his fault. Neither is losing Sandy."

"He would have stayed if they hadn't changed the playlist? I think that's right. But it's the nature of this mean cold business. So, for the Noon 'cast, are you in the field or stayin' here?"

"Here. Doing some phoners and setting up the stock interview. Probably writing intros for Coffey's City Hall story. Kipper's covering a Cubs news conference."

"Good. I was hopin' you'd be around. Here's the deal. This place is going to be in turmoil from now until who knows when. Before it gets totally out of control, it's time to make our move."

"What are you talking about, Rick?"

Instead of answering, he turned and picked up the pad he'd been working and headed for the doors.

"I need to spend a few minutes with HR and accounting," he said. "Don't go anywhere."

Thoroughly perplexed, Emily watched him walk down the hall. Then she reached back and turned the speaker behind her desk all the way off and patched her recorder into the phone. She chased down two interviews, one of which involved several transfers and at least as many "please hold" delays, and took a feed from Al Coffey.

Most of an hour had elapsed when Rick Healey came down the hall. He paused by Dean Lyon's office to glance in and then moved quickly to the bullpen.

"Come on," he said, crooking a finger repeatedly. "He's in there and he's alone."

"Rick, what on earth are you talking about? What is this?"

"This is good news, Emily. Move it along, we need to

talk to Dean."

She rose and followed him, uncertain that she should do so and far too curious not to.

When they reached the door to Dean's office, Rick turned and looked straight at her.

"Follow my lead. Don't say anything unless I ask you to. Got it?"

She nodded, now even more uneasy.

"Good. Let's go."

Dean Lyon was at his desk working through a large stack of papers. He looked up when they entered and a querulous scowl crossed his face.

"Rick, Emily. Something I can do for you?"

"Dean, we need to talk," said Healey.

"Something wrong?"

"Not as far as Emily is concerned, but the suits may not be thrilled."

Dean looked genuinely puzzled and Emily was so nervous she stepped forward, prepared to tell her boss she had no idea what was going on. Healey turned to face her and his flashing eyes persuaded her to be quiet. She wasn't happy to do so.

"Rick, what is this all about?"

"Overtime, Dean. A whole lot of overtime plus a whole lot of golden overtime on top of it."

"Whose?"

"Emily's, of course."

"You're kidding."

Healey feigned a look of hurt.

"Dean, please. When was the last time this shop steward talked about overtime with you, I was kidding? Never is when. You know when we're talking union I'm all business."

Lyon met Healey's eyes and held them. Emily watched them both, evaluating their resolve. As she concluded that Rick Healey had the more determined stare, Dean spoke.

"Why don't you guys take a seat, we'll talk this over."

Rick Healey sat on the edge of the couch and laid his notepad on his lap. Emily sat in the club chair so she could see both faces.

"I wasn't paying a whole lot of attention when this Steinart thing first came up, didn't much care one way or the other. But then it got hot and then we put Emily on the air, not once but twice now, and I got to thinking.

"Here's what we agree on, Dean. She's part-time. She's union 'cause she sailed through the probation period, but she's still part time."

"We do agree on that," said Dean.

"Good. I haven't talked with Emily about this in detail, so I don't have exact figures, but I have a general picture. I figure that at least 60 percent of the work she's done on Steinart was after hours, Dean. Overtime."

"Really?" Dean looked at Emily and found her staring at Healey with a look of astonishment so genuine that Dean actually chuckled aloud.

"Really." Healey flipped a couple of pages of notes and began reading.

"Starts with a visit to the Virginia Hotel, same day we aired the story 'bout the babe whacked herself. Travel time and field work—check out the room the babe stayed in, gather information from the desk staff and the resident on the same floor as the babe's hotel room. Probably over 4 hours, we'll call it 3 point 5.

"Research, the narcotics bust the Steinart chick was nailed for, at least 5 hours, that's archives, interviews with reporters, background info, CPD sources."

"Travel and professional time, gathering information from the babe's mom, 4 more hours."

Dean held up a hand.

"Okay, Rick, I got the picture. What's the bottom line?"

"That's only part of the picture, Dean. This list is just what I gathered on my own, without Emily helping. I haven't read it all to you, got a couple more items on it, but it's only what I know sort of hearsay. This list is incomplete because we don't have Emily's input. Yet.

"But even on this incomplete list, there's a lot of *golden* overtime. Weekends, hours beyond the daily overtime cap, that's all golden, Dean.

"And I know you've already figured this out, but just to get it on the table and then out of the way, there's no question that Emily was authorized to do the work. Even if she was freelancing in the beginning, everything she did led to the stories management aired—you put her on the air, Dean, so you clearly authorized the work that led to broadcast material."

Dean shifted in his chair, leaning forward.

"Rick, you and I have been through this before, so let's not waste a lot of time, okay? Of course, Emily's work was authorized. I personally directed her to make follow up calls after we reported the suicide.

"I won't quarrel with a reasonable number once you two figure it out. But I insist that since she landed the interview with Joe Burton, she's been on the clock on this story. You're not going to stick me for those hours, too, Rick."

Rick smiled.

"Of course not, Dean. We want to be fair."

Both men sat back in their seats.

"So to save you some time," said Healey, "I just now sat down with HR and Accounting."

He pulled a sheet of paper from under his pad, glanced at it and handed it to Lyon.

"This is based only on my estimate. HR flagged the hours they think are golden and I'm good with their evaluation. Emily and I will sit down and we'll get you a solid final count, but based on my guesses, this is the number HR estimates."

Dean took the page and tilted it so he could read it under his desk lamp. He scanned it and then looked like he was going to whistle. Instead, he looked over to Emily.

"Have you seen this?"

Emily hesitated, still in shock, her mouth open.

"Go ahead, answer that," said Rick.

"Dean, I had no idea what this meeting was about until three minutes ago. I haven't seen this, this paper. I didn't know Rick was doing this. I'm so sorry, Dean. If I'd known—"

"Hush, Emily," said Dean. "Before you say anything more, you should take a look."

He handed the HR document to her.

Emily scanned the document and then stared first at Rick Healey and then at Dean Lyon. "You guys aren't kidding me, are you? Is this some sort of joke?"

They both smiled and shook their heads.

She looked at the document again, focusing on the number at the bottom of the page. Then she broke into a gale of giggles which lasted long enough to take her breath away.

17.

"That's it, kiddo. Congrats. We can go now."

"Actually, Rick, I need to do some planning with Emily, now's as good a time as any. Can you stay a couple minutes longer?"

"Sure, Dean."

"Good. Rick, you take good care of your people. If I weren't management, I'd be damn glad to have you on my side."

"Thanks, Dean. Sorry to bring this up in the middle of all this turmoil, but frankly—"

"You think the place may be producing more lay-offs than hires pretty soon, you wanted to move ahead of a revenue drop. I'd do the same in your shoes. It's a smart move."

"Yeah. I don't like what I seeing and hearing, but I'm not about to let those two jokers get away with anything, I can tell you that."

"Maybe you should tell them," said Dean, chuckling. "It might scare them all the way back to Manhattan."

"We can only hope," said Healey as he left the room.

When the door closed, Dean swiveled his chair around to face Emily.

"Dean, I'm so sorry. I really had—"

"No need, Emily. First, Rick did what he's supposed to do and I wasn't kidding, he's good at it. Second, he's right. You have worked this story without compensation and we owe you. Thing makes me laugh, I told them, when your hire first came up, they should make it full time. Make it a real job with a real salary, but no, they wanted to save money. Now it looks like they didn't save a dime and it may cost even more. Life's a hoot, isn't it?"

"But, Dean, it's a lot of money. I mean, it's a *lot* of money."

"All of it well earned. And the way you earned it is what we need to talk about. I want to know where you are with Chase and Jameson."

"We're still trying to find out how she got from the Fed building back to the Virginia, although even if we find it I'm not sure it's air worthy. We need Tommy Jameson. Until he stops hiding and slamming doors on us, we're stuck where we are."

"Not what I wanted to hear," said Dean. He shifted in his seat and held her gaze. "I had a good relationship with Sam Butler. We clashed and fought, but I trusted him and he trusted me. We could work together, work stuff out, the way I did with Rick just now. Sam knew I was going to give him a first class news operation and I knew he'd leave me mostly alone to do just that."

"And now?"

"Now, I just don't know. I don't trust Armento and Carroll—"

"Who?"

"Sorry. Gus Armento, Aaron Carroll—Nip and Tuck's real names."

"No kidding! I'd completely forgotten."

"We may all pray to forget them both soon enough. Anyhow, my point is, I don't have a relationship with them like with Sam. I don't trust them. They really like the format we're using for AM drive news and even though Sam promised it would be short term, I don't know if they'll honor that. And they've been unhappy about our half hour at Noon since before they got here. I'm going to try to manage them, but I just don't know."

"I'm sorry, Dean. You've built a great news operation here, it would be a shame to take it apart."

"I don't know that they'll do that, but I don't know that they won't, either. That's my point about the Jameson story. If we've got anything, if you've got leads, let's get it all in shape so we can air it as soon as possible. Honestly, I don't know how much time we've got."

"I get it, but I'm not sure what I can do. Chase called him out again last week and it didn't generate a peep. We've aired two stories which line up with Chase's charges but Jameson just says 'Nope, didn't happen' and keeps his mouth shut. I really thought the second story, we put Beni in the building and confirmed she used the specified entrance, I really thought that would force them."

"And instead they went to their bunker and slammed the door shut."

"It's so frustrating I want to scream," said Emily. "We've got a great story here and we can't air the ending because we don't know what it is and the only person who can tell us how it ends won't talk to me or anybody else, period. Did I tell you this new press person, Coburn, actually told me to shut up when I called her last week?"

"How polite, never mind politic," said Lyon. "It isn't worth much, I know, but in my experience, somebody proclaiming innocence who won't step up to prove it probably isn't innocent."

"I think the 5th Amendment has something to say about that, boss."

"That's not what I mean, smarty. If he's got proof he didn't drag that girl into a meeting and down to her death, where the hell is it?"

"Nobody wants to see it more than I," said Emily.

"Well, I hope you find it soonest. Use all you can to move it along, Emily. Sooner is better because later may not exist at all."

"I understand," she said. "Not sure what to do, but I understand."

"Okay," said Dean. "Back to it, then."

She saluted. "Right, boss."

Dean called to her just as she was pulling his office door closed.

"No day dreaming about what you're going to do with all that money, rich girl. Work, work, work!"

"Troy Coburn? She's working for Tommy Jameson? I don't believe it!"

Emily and Kirstin Bonner were enjoying lunch at a bistro in the lobby of one of Cary Chase's downtown office buildings.

While they waited to be served, Kirstin had recounted the dramatic change Emily's interview had wrought in her boss.

"He didn't think it would ever get on the air, you know. He told me that no matter how much he believed Beni, he could see how shaky the story appeared. I think the interview by itself went a long way toward bringing him back—he was shifting his focus before you left the room, right? But he really came back when you got it on the air. He made everyone in the office come into the conference room and listen to it."

She trusted her new friend so Emily didn't particularly care that she blushed. Their salads arrived and they chatted about this and that between bites until Emily brought the conversation back to Beni and Jameson. She was relating her conversation with Greg Good's replacement when Kirstin broke in.

"Troy is hell on wheels. She's bright and very skillful, but she can't resist being an aggressive thug. I think she decided that the only way she was going to make it in a predominately man's world was to out macho everybody. She's as gentle as barbed wire."

"How do you know her?"

"After the Art Institute, but before Cary, I spent a couple of years in Donna Penny's PR shop. You know they handle some work for Cary, right? That's how I got the offer from him. Anyhow, Troy came in about three months after I did. She had great instincts, every bit as good on strategy as Penny herself is, and nobody's better, so Donna put up with her.

"But, boy, was Troy brutal. She muscled in on accounts she wasn't assigned because they had higher profiles. She elbowed everybody more than once and she went out of her way to undermine other women in particular. She never stopped manipulating. She has a nasty mouth on her, too. If Jameson wants to treat the press like scum, she's the perfect candidate."

Emily's fork was suspended mid-way to her mouth. Her gaze drifted into space and she sat motionless for so long that Kirstin grew concerned.

"Emily? Emily? Are you feeling all right? Do you need some water or something?"

It took several moments until Emily blinked and focused on her companion again.

"Sorry. I'm fine," said Emily. "I just had a funny idea. Maybe not so funny, actually. Do you have a relationship with Coburn now?"

"We're both on the Marketing Committee at the Chamber, we're in a couple of professional associations together. I guess we see each other once a month or so."

"Do you speak, interact?"

"Oh, sure. She's only cold to me now, not mean, because I'm not a rival any more. She's riding roughshod over the Chamber committee, but she has good ideas so I'm just going along."

"And her strategic instincts are strong?"

"Press strategy and tactics, she's among the best. What are you—"

"I'm going to ask you something, I want you to feel absolutely free to say you don't want any part of it. You say no, no it is. Okay?"

"You look a whole lot like you have some serious mischief in mind. Are you scheming?"

"Maneuvering would be more like it. Or maybe stabbing in the dark. It's nothing illegal or anything. Maybe you'll tell me it's too absurd and that'll be that. But I do have a scheme."

"Well, you brought my boss back from the dismal depths, so I owe it to you to at least listen."

"This isn't for me," said Emily, "It's for Beni. Here's what I have in mind."

At about ten o'clock on Wednesday, the next day, Kirstin called to say that the call had been made and it had gone well.

"She didn't slam the door on me," said Kirstin. "She didn't kill it outright."

"All we can do now is wait," said Emily. "At least I've got lots of practice at that."

On Wednesday morning, Nip and Tuck walked into the morning news staff meeting unannounced, interrupting Dean Lyon.

Before Dean could say anything, the door swung open again and Rick Healey barged in, glowering at the two as he did. He forced his way between the new station managers and took a position against a wall near Dean's desk.

"You got something to say to the news staff, you want all senior staff in here, right? All of us?"

Tuck nodded.

"Damn straight."

"We have some matters to discuss with you," said Nip. "We have invested a lot of time going over the survey numbers our research firm has generated. We've analyzed our age demographics to see who really likes what we're doing, we've examined audience geography to find out where they live. We also paid a lot of attention to the competition, the stations trying to win our audience."

Under his breath, Don Kipper said "No need to try. Just walk up and take 'em, we're giving the ranch away" and Al Coffey gave him a sharp nudge.

"We are going to make some subtle shifts in our programming, but those changes will be gradual. In the meantime, however, we are convinced that young suburban listeners compose our strongest potential audience. We think they want something different on the AM dial and we want Hits 980 to give it to them."

Nip stepped back and Tuck moved forward.

"We believe the news concept we have used for morning drive since the launch of our great new playlist is exactly what our audience wants. Rapid fire news so the kids don't switch us off, lots of traffic reports so Mom and Dad won't leave the station the kids like, that's what we're after.

"So we're extending the launch phase news programming into the indefinite future."

"Damnit," said Dean. "You haven't discussed this with me. I'm the News Director here. How dare you do this without consulting me? How dare you?"

"We're doing what is best for the station," said Tuck. "I'm sure that's what you wish as well, isn't it, Mr. Lyon?"

"What about what's best for the public? We have an obligation to serve the community, it comes with the damn FCC license. We don't serve them well with skimpy headlines and a couple of traffic reports in a five, six minute newscast."

"Three," said Tuck. "Starting tomorrow morning, we'll air three traffic segments in each minute morning drive newscast."

Lyon rolled back in his chair, his arms to the ceiling.

"In our time slot? 3 traffic breaks? That's not news, it's a joke."

"Two of the stations we're competing with have no news at all, just traffic," said Tuck. "We're hoping to get younger adults to tune in because they like our music but still want to be informed."

"Well, we sure as hell won't be the ones informing them," said Rick Healey. "We'll be feeding them news candy."

"Are you two quite done?" Dean rose, gesturing toward the door. "Given what you've told us, we have a lot of work to do here."

"We are not done yet," said Nip.

The room fell eerily quiet. Dan McIntyre had buried his face in his hands and now and then he gently rocked back and forth a little.

"The Noon news," said Dean. "Of course. Why keep airing the best mid-day news block in the city, radio or television? Who needs that?"

"Well, you're right about one thing. We believe that an important mid-day segment of our audience does need it," said Nip. "Stay at home moms. We give them traffic updates in the morning and their kids really like our playlist, but the moms want something to entertain them around lunch time."

"*Entertain* them?"

"We're keeping the half-hour news block, Mr. Lyon," said Tuck. "The network executives disagreed, but when they heard about the changes we have in mind, we won them over."

A series of groans, curses and angry shouts greeted "changes we have in mind."

"Go ahead," said Dean when the room quieted enough so he could be heard, "tell us what else you have for us."

"We'd like a few minutes of news right at the top of the program, just like morning drive."

"At the top? News is all we do at Noon." Lyon's

contempt was rich and thick.

"And then we're going to provide a wide variety of entertainment updates. Interviews, movies openings, special events around town, celebrities dropping in, that sort of thing. It will be a sort of gossip column on the air, full of fun news, news about fun stuff. We'll probably want to throw in a hit now and then, just to remind them who we are—perhaps we'll just use the top five, the best of the best."

"When do you propose to do this?" Healey's fists were clenched again.

"It's a significant change, but we think a few days will give you plenty of time to get it ready."

Dean leaned forward. "We have stories working, right now stories. We've got a series on the County's foster care system which is ready to go. Emily's work on the Steinart suicide isn't done. If you give us a pittance in the morning and next to nothing at Noon, what are we supposed to do with stories like that?"

Nip and Tuck exchanged a look and Nip spoke.

"Well, as you know, we think the Cary Chase story is hot—sensational and exciting, two of the city's biggest names involved, pretty young victim, all that's great. If something else comes up on that one, you let us know and we'll see what we can do."

"And foster care?"

"We still have the FCC requirement for community programming, as you say. So we're keeping the Sunday night community affairs show. You can air the foster care series there."

Dean Lyon started to speak but Rick Healey jumped in ahead of him.

"Nobody listens to that show, you fools. Tom Adams, the guy who hosts it, tapes it in advance? *He* doesn't listen to it. You're throwing high quality work into a swamp. 'Community programming?' The words don't belong in your mouth."

Healey was advancing as he spoke, his voice rising. As he moved forward, Dan McIntyre looked up, stood up and moved to the center of the room, directly in Healey's path.

"Don't do anything foolish, Rick. You've worked too hard earning all you have, good job, good money, your union work matters to everyone. Don't waste it on these two. I don't want that for you."

Healey relaxed a bit.

"Sorry, Dan. I didn't mean to upset you."

"No problem, Rick. Let's just not make this worse than it is."

"Good thinking."

As Healey moved back and McIntyre resumed his seat, Dean Lyon stood.

"Do you gentlemen have more to share with us at this time?"

Again the two checked with one another; this time, Tuck spoke.

"We are done for now," he said. "Thank you for—"

"Then kindly get out of my office," said Dean. When the door closed behind them, he added "And don't ever return."

When the Noon news wrapped, Dean Lyon came out of the news studio with Dan McIntyre trailing close behind. They came to the space which separated Rick Healey's desk from Emily's.

"We're going to ride the elevator down to the first floor, walk out the door, turn left and walk straight into Bernie's Bar," said Lyon. "I don't know about you guys, but I need to tie one on. Dan's in. I told Kipper and Coffey, they're headed to Bernie's now. So, you two?"

Healey was headed for the coat rack before Lyon finished.

Emily hesitated and then said, "Well, I've never felt more like one of the guys, but I'm going to head home. I don't think it would be a good idea for me to drink right now, it'd just make me feel even lousier. I could go along and order Shirley Temples, but you all would never let me hear the end of that. I think I'm better off going home."

Lyon said, "You change your mind, we'll be easy to find."

"Yeah," said Healey. "Bernie's, look for the table, four guys crying in their beer."

"Single malt," said McIntyre. "I won't drink beer."

"Figures," said Healey. "You're still welcome, Dan."

"Thanks, Rick. So, what are we waiting for?"

Emily shed her satchel and changed into fleece pants, a big floppy sweater and oversized wool socks. She brewed a cup of tea and carried it into the living room where she tuned in WFMT and then settled into the Danish lounge chair on the reading platform.

Cozy and comfortable, she watched the park and the lake, playing over in her mind the wretched meeting with Nip and Tuck and the consequences of it. Writing headlines and traffic intro's had become her primary assignment. No phone interviews to flesh out a story, no deadline driven tape editing, no sports beyond scores. Even her occasional stories tweaking the boys in the newsroom were gone.

And while she enjoyed the occasional celebrity story, she couldn't imagine a half hour of news filled with them and the thought of spending her time interviewing the latest fad made her feel even more dismal.

She made a conscious effort to set her frustration and anger over her job aside but then quickly drifted to the Beni Steinart story. She hoped that her ploy with Kirstin Bonner to lure Jameson into an interview would work, but she knew it was a long shot. And even if he took the bait, Emily harbored doubts that she had enough to expose him. Joseph Burton's account of Beni's last hours, Tim Humphrey's phone record and Wes Clark's cab log were all solid evidence of a secret meeting in Jameson's office. Still,

Emily wasn't sure those pieces of the puzzle were sufficient to solve it, especially if Jameson continued to deny it all. Being so near but still out of reach agitated her at least as much as the damage Nip and Tuck had done, so she concentrated on pushing both of them aside.

She gazed at the lake for a bit and then found herself staring at Ben's Watergate library and, to distract herself, she took the Breslin book form the top of the pile and began leafing through it. A slip of paper slid out; Ben had used it to mark the section about John Doar and the index cards. Smiling, Emily started to read.

Two pages later, she jumped out of her chair, flew off the platform and raced to her satchel. She dug among the papers until she found the D.A. office memo about pyramid prosecutions. She walked back to the windows and tilted the pages to catch maximum natural light so she was certain of what she saw.

When Ben came through the door that evening, she was waiting for him. She gave him a hug and a long warm kiss.

"You, sir, are the absolute best," she said, grinning at him.

"I am assuredly not complaining, no fool I, but have I done something special to merit such a lavish welcome?"

"You sure have, Benjamin Winter, you sure have."

"May I know what that something might be?"

"Of course," she said, bouncing on her toes. "President Nixon wasn't in the room!"

18.

As soon as she had made the last of the changes for the truncated morning news copy, while Dan McIntyre was on air racing through the 9 AM news slot, Emily got on the phone.

She called the U.S. Attorney office's main number and explained what she sought. She went through several transfers, carefully telling each new phone contact that she was a WEL reporter.

Eventually, she talked with the secretary whose boss had drafted the pyramid prosecution document. Emily told the secretary she had only one or two questions to ask of the author, questions related to a story the station was pursuing. She promised the interview would be as brief as possible and, after a short hold, Eric Buss came on the line.

Emily asked three questions. Buss answered all of them.

"I promised to be brief and I'm good to my word, sir. Thank you and good-bye."

She spent the balance of the morning contacting

publicists representing arts and entertainment clients, seeking stories to suit the changes in the Noon news. She told those she spoke with that the new Hits 980 News & Entertainment at Noon show, "launching soon," was eager to hear pitches—"entertainment stories, interviews, previews, let us know." After each call, she pictured her phone messages rising ever higher, lamenting that this particular reporters' dream—stories pouring in—was going to generate an avalanche of amusing information but hardly any news.

Dean Lyon had sworn to remain in his job until Nip and Tuck's temporary reign ended so he could "teach the next GM what news is all about." Emily shared with everyone except Rick Healey a sense of conflict. She hadn't yet taken steps, but she was certainly thinking about other options and opportunities. She knew the two field reporters were in the same position, trying to protect their future but unwilling to abandon their boss. Dan McIntyre, whom everyone was certain would be the first to go, had not shared his plans or thoughts with anyone.

Like Dean, Rick Healey wasn't going anywhere just yet. He had only a year left to earn his fully vested handsome pension and he pronounced himself determined to "stay right here and drive those two idiots crazy until I can tell 'em both to shove it."

She was consolidating her notes from the entertainment calls she'd made when the switchboard buzzed her line.

"Emily, somebody named Troy on line two for you. Sounds like she's pretty angry, you want to duck, I'll take a message."

Emily grabbed a notepad and cradled the phone on her shoulder so she could take notes.

"No, no. I've been hoping for the call. Please put her through.

"This is Emily."

"Tomorrow at 11 AM, the United States District

Attorney will issue a statement regarding the Beni Steinart matter to you and then he will take your questions about his statement. We will distribute the same statement to all other press the following morning—it will be exclusive to you until then.

"You are to arrive at this office promptly at 10:45, when I will instruct you on additional ground rules and restrictions, all of which will be non-negotiable. You either accept my terms or there is no interview, no advance on the statement. Do I make myself clear?"

"Abundantly," said Emily, hoping her voice didn't betray her enormous smile. "10:45 tomorrow, the U.S. Attorney's office, Federal Building. I will be there."

Emily rose from her desk and literally ran across the bullpen and out to the door, racing down the hall and slamming open Dean Lyon's office door.

"I got him," she shouted. "Jameson is going on the record, tomorrow, Noon. It's exclusive, Dean, we got it!"

When she paused for a response, she realized Dean was looking to her left.

Dan McIntyre was sitting on the very edge of the couch, his face pale.

"I'm so sorry, Dean. I should have knocked. I'll just go now, I can come back when it's more convenient."

"Stay Emily, please. Dan and I were just finishing up."

He rose and walked over to McIntyre, extending his hand. McIntyre gave Lyon a grateful smile and a hearty handshake and walked to the door. As he passed her, he paused at her side.

"You're one of the really good ones, Emily. You have a genuine feel for radio news. Congratulations on the interview. I know you'll do it justice. Good luck."

She turned to face Dean, her smile again bright. She found him gazing at the closed door, his eyes deep with regret, and realized what she had interrupted.

"Oh, dear," she said. "He's leaving us, isn't he?"

"Yes," said Dean. "Two week's notice. He's going

freelance. He'll get lots of voice work, probably more than he can handle. He'd be a great TV announcer, of course. I said I'd give him all my TV contacts but he doesn't want to work in news anymore. He said 'it doesn't taste good.' Funny expression, isn't it? Doesn't taste good."

"How long has he been here with you? Years, right?"

"Lots of them. I stole him from WIND about twenty minutes after they made me News Director, nine years ago plus. We were interns at WGN, two summers in a row, long before that. We talked about that just now, how a run like ours isn't very likely these days. It's all job hopping and format shifting and whatever the trend is until it isn't a trend any more. It does leave a sour taste, doesn't it?"

"I'll miss him. My copy always sounded great when he read it."

"Yes it did. Of course, the phone book sounds great when he reads it. No offense."

"None taken, I know what you mean. You know what's the real shame? He and Rick just realized they have too much in common to be at war. They were getting along, just lately, you saw how Dan protected Rick in that meeting, we all did. Now Nip and Tuck have spoiled that, too."

"Yeah, but we keep fighting back, right? When you're ready, we'll figure out what to do. I'll handle Nip and Tuck when the time comes."

She told him about the call from Troy Coburn.

"What's this about restrictions?"

"They won't matter. His statement will open all the doors I need opened."

"What, you're going to tell me you know what his statement is going to be?

You can't possibly know that."

Emily grinned. "As a matter of fact, I know exactly what he's going to say."

"How? How do you already know?"

"It was my idea."

"Really? This should be good. I need coffee. You? OK, let's walk and talk, head to the break room."

"You and Troy Coburn have something in common," Emily had told Kirstin Bonner at their lunch.

"Which is?"

"You both want to put an end to the dispute surrounding Beni's death. You want your boss to be able to do what he does best and he can't do that with Beni's death and his pain and anger getting in the way. She and her boss want the dark cloud in his otherwise bright future to blow away."

"True," said Kirstin "even if we each want entirely different conclusions. Where does that lead?"

"Well, if your mutual best interests point to putting the Beni Steinart matter to rest, why not suggest that if Jameson drops the charges against Beni, you'll convince your boss it's time to move on. Her name will be cleared, she can rest in peace, the feud will end and both bosses get what they want."

"Cary will never accept that."

"Of course not," said Emily with a twinkle. "You aren't promising Cary Chase will let it go, you're promising to try to persuade him to let it go."

"You're a little scary, you know that? This is diabolical."

"Thanks," said Emily. "I like it too."

"I'm still not entirely clear. Why would Jameson even consider this?"

"Two good reasons," said Emily. "First, he really does want this to go away. If the deal is as good as it appears, he can put it behind him and go become Governor."

Kirstin held up one finger. "Two?"

"Two, what's he got to lose? The changes against Beni are useless to him, he has no leverage over her anymore. There's no point in holding those charges open. Dropping the charges won't matter to him, so it's an empty gesture that makes him look good."

"And what about Troy? She'll shoot this down on the spot."

"Not if she thinks it was her idea," said Emily.

Kirstin thought about it for a moment and then started laughing.

"So, I call Troy and say, what? 'Hi how you doing, let's make a deal'?"

"Would you be comfortable calling her because you really need her help to get Cary off this crusade he's on, does she have any ideas?"

"Play to her oceanic ego. Of course. This is starting to get delicious."

"I'm just working with what you told me. And if she doesn't come up with dropping the charges on her own—"

"I think she will," said Kirstin, "she does have the touch, remember."

"If she's that good, we're all set. But if you need to, hint at it without saying it. Either way, once she sees it, I think she'll want it."

"There's something else I can use, she'll like it. Even if Cary refuses to back down, dropping the changes against Beni turns the tide in Jameson's favor. If he releases her and Cary keeps up the attack, Jameson will be the decent guy who did the right thing and Chase is the crazy zealot. I can tell her that's one of the arguments I'll use with Cary.

Emily nodded. "That's good."

"It just might work," said Kirstin.

"And when it does," said Emily, "I am going to interview Tommy Jameson."

"Of course you are," Kirstin said, laughing, "who else would they call?"

"You're kidding, right?" Dean Lyon's eyebrows could not rise any higher. "You have this pal of yours, works for Cary, call Jameson's gunslinger and Jameson ends up doing exactly what you want him to do?"

"Not just Jameson. We had to get Coburn to sell it to

him. When Bonner told me how savvy Troy is, how big her ego is, I saw the opening. She could carry a good idea to her boss, solve a problem and show him how smart she is. It worked and if I read it right, she's convinced she's in control. She thinks they can handle me."

Lyon lifted his coffee cup high.

"Here's to those who underestimate you, Winter. May they live and learn."

Ben's pot roast was excellent and they had a lively conversation over dinner, but Emily cut it short to clear the dining room table so she had enough room to spread out all the tools necessary to give herself a manicure before she went to bed.

She was about half done with her left hand when Ben finished cleaning in the kitchen and sat across from her with what remained in his wine glass.

"You are confident? You are prepared? I know a bit about preparing clients for testimony, if I can be of service..."

Emily looked up, a brush poised over her ring finger.

"You can select something amusing to watch," she said. "I'm as ready as I'll ever be, but I'm nervous, too. A background distraction would be welcome."

"Something silly should not be terribly difficult to locate among the evening's network offerings. It is, after all, what they do best."

"Cynical, sir. Cynical."

"When it comes to television these days, what else can one be? Before we become part of the evening's vast audience, may I ask a question?"

"Shoot."

"Why do you do that?"

"What?"

"Your nails. I noticed your hands—they're grand, by the by, simply exquisite—when you were setting the table earlier and your nails looked just fine."

Emily looked closely at the brush in her hand and plopped it back in its bottle.

"Can't let it get dry, the brush gets all sticky" she said. "I know my nails were okay earlier, I just did them last weekend."

"Hence my question."

"I'm not sure I can explain this," she said. "Tomorrow is critical, Ben, it's probably the one and only chance I'll have to find out what really happened to Beni. I have to focus on that, nothing but that. I'm doing my nails so I don't have to worry about them."

"But, as I observed and you confirmed, they were already fine. Why would you worry about them when you already know there's nothing about which to worry?"

"Because." She took the brush from its bottle and began applying polish where she had left off. "Just because."

"You cannot believe I will be satisfied with that."

She looked up and smiled.

"Of course not. I am doing my nails before an important meeting, whether they need to be done or not, because it is what girls do."

"Ah," said Ben. "I see. 'Tis an explanation which by definition evades the masculine mind."

"Now and forever, my fine fellow. Now and forever."

19.

Troy Coburn was extremely thin. She wore a pale yellow pantsuit with snug, straight lines which made her appear even thinner. Her hair was a muted red with faint orange highlights and her face was pale but for a splatter of freckles on her sharp nose.

Despite her nervous tension, Emily had to stifle a grin when Coburn met her in Tommy Jameson's outer offices. Her very first thought was that Troy Coburn looked like nothing so much as a pencil.

Coburn did not extend her hand or a greeting of any sort.

"The United States Attorney will read a statement to you. You may use it on the air. We will give you a copy of it when you leave.

"You will confine your questions exclusively to the content of the District Attorney's statement. Any issue which is not mentioned in the statement is entirely off limits.

"We have allotted twenty minutes for the interview. You will cease recording when that time has lapsed.

"If I decide you have violated or are preparing to violate any of these restrictions, I will terminate the interview immediately and Mr. Jameson will leave the room.

"Any questions?"

"You will be joining us for the interview?"

"Of course I will. Do you have any questions which aren't as stupid as that one?"

"No, thank you. I'm ready when you are."

Emily had been over the interview dozens of times, shaping her questions, anticipating Jameson's answers, speculating about the specific content of the statement. She walked into the U.S. Attorney's office confident but wary. She had forgotten what an imposing figure Jameson cut and when he rose to welcome her she felt very small indeed.

Jameson was tall and solid, hefty without being heavy. He stood with his shoulders back, his suit cut well to accentuate a fit figure and an impressively broad chest. He had the slightest hint of a tan, the look of a man who had recently spent a weekend golfing in a climate far sunnier than Chicago's. He looked confident.

He didn't smile when she entered the large room, but he did extend his hand as she neared his desk. The desk was broad and ornate with papers neatly organized; a space had been cleared in front of the chair they had set up for Emily. She located the nearest outlet and ran an extension cord to her tape recorder; she dared not risk losing a moment of the encounter to a battery failure.

He made pleasant chat while she organized her equipment, asking about the weather, making sure she had enough room for everything. There was a single sheet of official stationery in front of him on the desk and when Emily had checked her sound levels, he picked it up. Coburn sat on a couch against the wall where she could keep both Jameson and Emily in full view. She had a copy of the statement on her lap. When Jameson looked at her, she gave him an encouraging smile.

"I have directed my staff to petition the Federal District court to dismiss all charges against Benita Ann Steinart.

"In the wake of her untimely and unfortunate death, I do not believe that any further purpose can be served by pursuing Ms. Steinart's involvement in the trafficking of illegal narcotics.

"I extend to her family and friends my sincere sorrow for their recent loss, but I wish to assert once more that I had no direct involvement in her suicide. I share with those close to Miss Steinart the hope that, with my action today, she can at last make her peace with our Lord."

He put the page down and looked directly at Emily, full of confidence. He glanced over at Coburn and she nodded firmly.

"I'll take your questions now," he said.

"Do you expect the court to honor your request?"

"Of course I do."

"When will the charges against Ms. Steinart be officially dismissed?"

"I hope by the end of next week. We are dependent on the court's calendar, of course, but we will seek an expedited hearing."

"Have you informed Ms. Steinart's attorney of your decision?"

A flash of surprise crossed his face and he again looked over to Coburn. She shook her head once.

"I do not believe he has learned of our decision yet," said Jameson. "As soon as we are done here, I'll make sure he is notified. By day's end at the very latest."

"May I take a moment to read the statement?"

Before he could answer, Coburn rose and strode across the room to hand Emily a copy. Emily read it quickly while Jameson waited and Coburn went back to the couch.

"Can you explain what you mean by 'no direct involvement'?"

He didn't hesitate.

"Ms. Steinart made the decision to take her own life. It is most regrettable that she made that choice and I sincerely wish she had not made it, but it was hers and hers alone."

"Why do you believe she made that choice?"

He hesitated for a moment, his eyes drifting as he searched for the right reply.

"As I say, the choice was hers. I am a skillful attorney, but I do not have the training or expertise to explain an act that rash."

Emily thought the response had been rehearsed.

"Do you believe that the pressure of the charges against her contributed to her decision?"

"I do not have the training or expertise—"

"Did the threat of a long prison sentence cause her to consider taking her own life?"

"Stop!" Troy Coburn was on her feet instantly. "There is absolutely nothing in the statement which justifies that question. You are to confine your questions to the statement."

"Ms. Coburn, the statement clearly implies that Mr. Jameson may have had an indirect role in her death," said Emily. "Would you like me to read that portion to you again?"

"It doesn't say that," said Troy.

"'...no direct involvement...' I'm quoting, Ms. Coburn. No direct involvement suggests that *in*direct involvement might exist. I'm trying to find out precisely what the statement, your statement, means. You want the public to understand your position, don't you?"

"There is no way I'm going to permit you to go over all that crap you've broadcast. Cary Chase is a liar. We have denied his lies and no further comment is necessary. You will ask only about the statement or I will terminate the interview."

Emily turned to face Jameson.

"We do have your earlier denial of Cary Chase's charges, sir. Would you prefer that we use that statement when we air our story?"

Jameson looked at Coburn. She folded her arms across her chest and shook her head vigorously.

"No. We want you to report on my announcement. That's why you are here."

"Since you issued that first statement, we have verified that Ms. Steinart came to the Federal Building on the evening January 6, after the building was closed for the day, just as she has said she was instructed to do. She used the parking garage to enter the building exactly as she told Mr. Chase she had been instructed to do. We have also confirmed that she tried to contact her attorney to seek his counsel about a meeting with your office.

"Your previous statement does not address these new developments. Surely you and Ms. Coburn want the public to know how you view those facts."

"Stop. I mean it, Winter. Shut up right now."

"Troy," said Jameson, holding up his hand.

"No, sir! I will not permit this. The interview is over."

"Mr. Jameson? Are we done here? Do you wish to leave all the circumstances surrounding Beni Steinart's death unaddressed? Are you content to remain silent?"

Ignoring Coburn, Emily watched as Jameson weighed his decision. He didn't rush and both women held their breath.

"Troy, I want to put this matter to rest once and for all. We have done nothing wrong, I have done nothing wrong. Ms. Winter is correct, the public has to know that I had no role in this woman's unfortunate death."

"Sir, I must insist. We had an agreement, the statement and the statement only. This woman represents the interests of those who oppose your mission, your crusade to make Chicago clean and righteous again. She and Chase are the enemy, sir. You don't want to help them."

Emily thought the appeal to Jameson's mission had

persuaded him. She was considering how to goad him further, to push harder before Coburn called somebody to escort her out of the building.

Before she could decide what to say, she saw a look of calm resolve settle onto Jameson's face.

"No, Troy. You were right that we should do this, dropping the charges is the right thing to do. So is telling the truth."

"Sir—"

"Trust me, Troy. I can put this matter to rest right here and now."

"Don't give her anything, sir. This is not what we planned."

He waved her off and turned to Emily. He leaned into the microphone just a little.

"Here is the truth. Mr. Chase's allegation of a surreptitious meeting is entirely false. I cannot explain her cab ride or her fanciful account of entering our building through the garage and I have no idea why she called her attorney before she killed herself. None of that makes any sense because the meeting did not take place."

He looked confident again, relaxed and in control.

"Cary Chase accuses me of abusing Benita Steinart in a secret meeting. He claims that I drove her to her death. It is blasphemy.

"The meeting did not take place. I can prove it."

Emily's heart leapt to her throat. She was certain she knew what was coming but she was terrified that she might be wrong. She briefly closed her eyes to gather her wits while Jameson reached across his desk and picked up a large leather bound calendar.

He flipped through a handful of pages until he found what he sought. He smiled and nodded and then spun the book around so it faced Emily, pointing to the bottom of the page.

"There!" he said. "The evening of January 6, correct? That's when this supposed meeting took place? 6:30, right?"

"Yes," said Emily.

"See for yourself, then. The senior staff in this office participated in a meeting to finalize a document we had been asked to prepare for the Justice Department, a new set of pyramid prosecution protocols. The meeting started at 6:00, it ended about 7:15."

"Yes, I see that," said Emily.

"It was an important initiative and leading it was an honor for my office, a vote of confidence from D.C. I wanted to be certain it was the best we could deliver. I was in this meeting"—his finger stabbed the calendar page—"with my senior staff during the time Cary Chase claims I was threatening Ms. Steinart."

"No, sir," said Emily. "You were not."

Jameson gasped and some of the color drained from his face.

Coburn leapt to her feet.

"How dare you? Who do you think—never mind. Sir, I am going to call building security. This cannot continue."

Jameson held up his hand and fixed his gaze on Emily.

"Are you calling me a liar?"

"No, sir. Not precisely. It's true you were in that meeting when it started. You weren't there when it ended."

Emily leaned over and removed two items from her satchel, her copy of the pyramid protocols and a small battery-powered tape player.

"I believe this is the document which was the subject of the meeting?"

Jameson took it from her.

"How did you get this? Who gave this to you? You are not authorized to have this."

"I don't' have any idea," she said. "I have a guess, but it it's only a guess. It was delivered to my desk anonymously and it tells an important story."

She punched a button on the portable player and sat back as they all listened.

"Mr. Eric Buss, are you the attorney in the U.S.D.A.'s office who conducted a briefing session on draft prosecution guidelines for pyramid schemes?"

"Yes, that was my project. Pyramid & Ponzi Prosecution Protocols. We called it P-Quad. It had been through several iterations and I thought it was ready to submit. Tommy Jameson wanted to have one more staff review, so we scheduled that meeting."

"Were the protocols submitted to Washington?"

"No. P-Quad is still pending final approval from D.A. Jameson."

"It wasn't approved in the meeting on January 6th?"

"No, it wasn't. Mr. Jameson left the meeting about twenty minutes after it started. He said he'd be back, but he never made it. I don't know where he went, but he never signed off on the final version. I'm still waiting."

Emily shut down the portable recorder and pointed to the protocol document on Jameson's desk.

"You can see for yourself, sir, on the last page. The approval box is empty. You didn't approve the protocols because you weren't in the meeting when it ended. You left the meeting just before Beni Steinart arrived at your office and you didn't come back.

"You weren't in the room, sir. You were in a meeting with Benita Steinart."

Coburn sprang, moving toward Emily, but she froze mid-way when Jameson exploded to his feet with such force that his chair spilled over and careened across the floor behind him.

Jameson raised his arms above his shoulders, his outstretched hands pointing upward. He rolled his head back and stared at the ceiling. And then he bellowed.

"I am innocent. I have done nothing but serve my Lord."

Emily remained perfectly still. Troy inched her way closer to the desk.

Jameson lowered one arm and leveled it, pointing at

Emily's forehead.

"You are an instrument of this evil cabal. Your station plays godless anthems to drug abuse and promiscuous sex. You spew lies for Satan's agents."

Jameson's voice boomed, his words flowing in a rhythmic cadence.

"Cary Chase is sin incarnate. He plies his charms and his guile to seduce innocents into a godless life. He welcomed the drug dealer Wilson into his home, the man was a permanent guest. He used Benita Steinart to manage unbridled debauchery in that wretched mansion, adultery and sodomy and heaven only knows what else.

"Drugs are instruments in his hands. Drugs keep Cary Chase's victims compliant and eager to follow his vile orthodoxy. When Chase's guest Wilson went to buy drugs, Chase's trusted employee was there every step of the way. She knew what was happening, how could she not know?

"They were all determined to destroy our way of life until I stopped them. But, oh Lord, I could have done much more. So much more.

"I gave her every chance. I told her she had an opportunity to save thousands from a life of sin and an afterlife of damnation. I told her I needed her help, but she wouldn't help me."

"And so you scared her to death," said Emily.

"She had to understand, she had to see that her failure to serve our great cause would cause great harm. I showed her harm, I showed her the wages of sin. All she had to do was join the crusade. If she had done so, if she had seen the light, she would still be among us today, poor girl."

Jameson turned and righted his chair. Wheeling it back to the desk, he collapsed into it. When he spoke again, there was genuine sorrow in his eyes.

"The devil's grip on her was stronger than my own and I failed. I was called to drive evil away and I did not meet the call. I regret only that."

He folded his hands and lowered his head as if in

prayer.

Coburn spoke very quietly.

"This is over, you are done. You can see the District Attorney is not himself. You must consider leaving that tape here. I'll arrange for a fresh interview—you pick the time and place—under more suitable circumstances."

Emily smiled.

"You know better. You granted the interview, I agreed to all your conditions. You authorized me to use what I gathered here on the air. We were on the record and as far as I'm concerned, we still are."

Coburn's eyes registered shock and she glanced at the large tape recorder on Jameson's desk. It was still recording and Emily could all but hear her mind racing.

"You did not have permission to record me," she said. "And I do not grant it. You cannot broadcast what I just said. You must not."

"You're right, you were not the interview subject," said Emily. "I won't use what you said. I'll also leave the protocol document with you. Mr. Jameson suggested that I am not authorized to have it and I accept that. But everything else is on the record."

"You're going to destroy the career of a great man, you know," said Coburn. Her tone was resigned.

"No, I am not. I am going to report the facts as they have been revealed. Mr. Jameson will have to decide what to do. So will the public and appropriate officials." Emily caught and held Troy's gaze. "I am just the reporter."

She shut down the large recorder and moved it and the miniature one into her satchel.

With a dejected look which made Emily feel a little sorry for her, Coburn walked with her to the door. Jameson remained his chair, still in his prayerful pose. Emily thought she heard him muttering, but it was too faint to understand.

Emily pushed the elevator button and turned to Troy.

"I'm sure you believed him. I'm sorry he didn't level

with you, but it's obvious that he didn't. You trusted him and there's no harm in that."

Coburn didn't respond.

"I think Greg Good figured out that Jameson was lying. I think you're here now because Greg got fired or quit, I don't know which. What can you tell me about that, off the record? I ask because he's a friend, a close friend, and my husband and I are worried about him."

Coburn held Emily's eyes for a moment, calculating.

"I'm sorry," she said, "It is our policy never to comment on internal personnel matters."

And then, without saying it aloud, she formed the words "on leave."

The elevator doors slid open and Emily stepped into the car. She held her hand against the door to keep it open.

"Ms. Coburn, if you really intend to deny a reporter access to your office, you should remember to let the switchboard know. Between that and the empty approval box, it's pretty clear that the devil really is in the details."

20.

Dean Lyon was on his way into the Noon newscast when Emily got back and gave him a quick summary of the interview. He told her to do whatever it took to get a response from Cary Chase immediately and to ask the news staff to assemble in his office as soon as the Noon 'cast wrapped.

She played the tape for everyone so they knew what they had and then Dean disbursed them to various assignments. Don Kipper was sent to try to secure reactions from the Attorney General or a Justice Department media relations officer. With a sly grin to Emily, Lyon asked Rick Healey and Dan McIntyre to work up intro copy. He sent Emily to the editing bay to create tape for broadcast and he told Al Coffey to back up anyone who needed it until 3:30, when he was to begin calling city desks, assignment editors and segment producers and wire services to offer a heads-up to a WEL special newscast at 4:20.

He asked them all to take special care to avoid alerting Nip and Tuck to their plan.

"I'll take care of that," he said, "but with all that's going on, I just don't see how I'll have time to tell them until about 4:15."

Friends, I know how you love your Hits 980, but we have an important breaking news story to share with you. I'm going to take a short break so we can deliver a WEL special report. Here is WEL's Dan McIntyre in our newsroom...

Thank you, JD. In an extraordinary development, United States Attorney Tommy Jameson has acknowledged that he had a clandestine meeting with Benita Ann Steinart just hours before she took her own life. D.A. Jameson also acknowledged that he threatened to send Ms. Steinart to prison for 25 years if she failed to implicate her employer, businessman Cary Chase, in a drug transport and trafficking case involving millions of dollars worth of cocaine.

Two of those arrested by the FBI in Chicago last year are now serving sentences, but U.S. Attorney Jameson never closed the case against Ms. Steinart, who was a passenger in the car with the two convicted men. Cary Chase charged that Jameson had threatened Beni Steinart with 25 years if she didn't implicate Chase himself in the drug deal. Chase learned of the threat in a phone conversation with Ms. Steinart shortly before her death. When first confronted with the charges, the U.S. Attorney firmly denied them.

Today's reversal came in a one-on-one interview conducted earlier today by WEL's Emily Solomon Winter, who has previously reported facts which appeared to confirm Cary Chase's allegations about the secret meeting. Emily...

Thank you, Dan. In our interview with District Attorney Jameson in his office this morning, Mr. Jameson offered proof that he had not conducted a meeting with Beni Steinart. He claimed that he was in a staff meeting at the time Cary Chase charged he was meeting with Ms. Steinart. When WEL presented evidence which clearly contradicted the District Attorney's statement, Mr. Jameson told WEL:

"I am innocent. I have done nothing but serve my Lord... I gave her every chance. I told her she had an opportunity to save thousands from a life of sin and an afterlife of damnation. I told her I needed

her help, but she wouldn't help me...She had to understand, she had to see that her failure to serve our great cause would cause great harm. I showed her the harm, I showed her the wages of sin. All she had to do was join the crusade. If she had done so, if she had seen the light, she would still be among us today, poor girl."

WEL contacted Attorney General Edward Levi's office for a response. Here is WEL reporter Don Kipper with that story.

The U.S. Department of Justice and the Attorney General are withholding comment about Tommy Jameson's revealing interview today while expressing their sympathy to the Steinart family. Shortly after our request for their comment, U.S. Justice Department officials visited WEL and asked for a complete transcript of WEL's interview. WEL General Managers provided the Justice Department with a taped copy of the complete interview. A statement from the Department is expected following their review of the WEL interview. Now, here's Dan McIntyre with more.

That's WEL News's Don Kipper with reaction to Tommy Jameson's now-confirmed attempt to generate perjured testimony against Cary Chase. Thanks Don.

Cary Chase also spoke with WEL this afternoon. For that, we go back to Emily Solomon Winter.

Dan, Cary Chase told WEL that he is satisfied with the outcome. Here's what he said:

"Beni Steinart could not give Tommy Jameson evidence that I am a drug dealer because it does not exist and it never did. She would not lie to Jameson and so he threatened her with prison. She decided to end her life rather than make an impossible choice. I was determined to see the U.S. Attorney held to account for his behavior and now that he has given us the truth, I am confident that his superiors will take appropriate action rapidly."

Chase also said:

"I suppose it is a measure of justice that Mr. Jameson's world has been shattered, just as he shattered Beni's life and the lives of so many of us who loved her so dearly. I cannot forgive him his actions, but I believe his precipitous fall from grace will exact dramatic and painful professional and personal penalties. Perhaps there is some justice in that."

There is one more aspect of this story to report. To wrap it up, here's Dan.

Thank you, Emily. The original purpose of the WEL interview this morning was to announce that the U.S. Attorney's Office plans to drop all outstanding charges against Beni Steinart. A representative of the D.A.'s office, Troy Coburn, told WEL News late today that the office will submit that request to the courts tomorrow. WEL will keep you informed as that process unfolds.

For the entire Hits 980 news team, I'm Dan McIntyre. Now, let's get back to all hits all the time with JD the DJ. JD, it's all yours...

"Dean, you're a genius," said Emily.

They were all on the carpet in the General Manager's office, where a television set sat atop a credenza.

Lyon was standing to one side of the set, dialing from one local newscast to another.

Wherever he landed, the story was about what the U.S. Attorney and presumptive next Governor of Illinois had said and done. Whatever they said, all the channels showed the same footage. Reporters, camera crews and photographers from every newsroom in town, all denied access to Jameson's office, had set up shop at the top of the exit ramp from the Federal Building garage. When Jameson's car motored up the ramp, they closed in and began screaming questions at the closed window.

Inside, Tommy Jameson stared straight ahead. There were a lot of news people surrounding his car so the drive up the ramp was slow. Depending on which station they watched and how far up the exit ramp he had moved, viewers could see the cost the short drive extracted. By the time he reached the street and pulled away, his face was contorted with anguish.

"He might as well be in hand cuffs," said Coffey.

Dean Lyon turned to Nip and Tuck, each seated on a corner of Sam Butler's desk.

"There," he said. "That's why we broke your precious

format. Anybody in town tunes in TV news, they're going to be talking about us, this station, all evening and later ahead of the late night shows, gentlemen. Not to mention the newspapers. It'll rule morning drive tomorrow, too. WEL is front page news."

Both listened, Tuck still and silent while Nip fidgeted. Neither spoke.

"Because we know exactly what we're doing," said Rick Healey. "You think the timing, giving them all enough time to catch up with the story for the early evening newscasts, you think that was an accident? Your news crew just did more to lift WEL up in a little under ten minutes than you bozos have done since you got here. Whaddya say we go back to a real morning newscast tomorrow? Most of Chicago will be tuning in, listen to what we're doing—let's give 'em the real deal."

The two exchanged glances.

"We'll consider it," said Tuck.

"But we'll need a little time," said Nip.

"So we need our office back," Tuck said, sliding off the desk. "If you all would be so kind..."

The next day on the ride in, Emily scanned the morning papers to confirm that the Jameson story was front page news while she listened to Max brag and crow. When they reached the station, Max leaned over and back to pop open the door for her.

"So, you got more on this Jameson creep for today?"

"I don't know, Max," she said. "None of the papers have anything we don't already have and we poured it all into the broadcast yesterday. I'll work on it if we see something worth chasing."

"You oughta use that interview again, use it all morning."

"Maybe, Max, maybe. It's still fresh. But the thing is, I don't know what our news will be this morning."

"Gotta be Jameson, right? There is no other story today, you ask me."

"No, that's not what I meant. I mean, I don't know what kind of news we're doing today, headlines and traffic or the old news format—it's not clear."

"Oy," said Max. "Well, good luck."

"Thanks, I'll probably need it."

"Headlines and traffic at 6, 7 and 8," said Rick when she walked into the bullpen. "Not my choice, but I'm under strict orders."

He nodded to a corner of the room where Nip and Tuck were huddled.

"They did me the courtesy of informing me, letting me tell you. I got 'em trained that much," he said. "They'd already called Dean last night to tell him. He fought again and lost again."

Nip and Tuck walked over to join them. Tuck spoke.

"We thought it over. We know we'll have a bigger audience this morning than we've had in a while, so we're going to give them the Hits format, no changes. We want them to hear it and love it."

"You're kidding," said Emily. "That great big audience will be tuning in to hear the news, you know. So we're going to give them headlines and traffic? That doesn't make any sense."

"That's because these two are stupid beyond science's capacity to measure stupid," said Rick. When Nip bristled, he added, "but they run the show, so let's get going."

"Wait," said Emily, "what happens at 9?"

"We'd like you to do a recap of the Jameson story. Take the whole news slot, wrap the story around traffic," said Tuck.

"In headlines? You want me to give Jameson and Beni's death a sentence each? Are you kidding?"

"We are not."

She weighed fighting back but Healey caught her eye and gave her a look and a shrug which said "Lost Cause."

"Okay," she said. "I'll get the tape edited and draft copy for Dan right after I put the 6 to bed. It won't be very informative, but maybe Dan can sell it."

"No," said Nip.

"No, what?"

"We want you to do the nine o'clock newscast."

"By yourself," said Tuck.

Emily walked to McIntyre's desk and stood beside him.

"We have a news anchor," she said. "It's his job to bring our audience the news. I'll do an intro and outs and I'll report if you want me to, but Dan's the anchor. He's the best there is, far better than I. He's the voice of WEL news."

"Not for long," said Nip.

"I don't care. As long as he's here, he does the news."

"You don't understand," said Tuck. "We all know Dan is leaving. We need a morning news anchor. We think you're perfect for the job."

Dan McIntyre stood up.

"It's okay," he said, "take the 9, Emily. They're smart to find a spot for you and you'll be good at it right off the bat, I bet."

"I won't do it, Dan."

"I appreciate that, Emily, but this is a chance for you to—"

"No. I won't do it. Not while you're still here."

He looked at her and smiled, shaking his head gently.

"Rick?"

"Yeah, Dan?"

"Dean coming in before 9?"

"Nope. He's got a breakfast meeting, be here closer to 10."

"That makes you acting News Director, right?"

"Right as rain."

"Well, boss, here's the thing. I got a tiny little something in the back of my throat, not too serious yet but I don't want to take any chances. I'm pretty sure I can get through the early hours, but if I could rest the pipes at 9, I'd appreciate it."

"You're right, Dan, we can't take any chances. Emily, I need you to take Dan's slot on the 9."

"Rick—"

"You really want to take on the boss, girl? You want to get yourself in a lot of hot water, have management bring you up, insubordination charges? I were you, I don't think I'd mess with me on this one, honey."

"He's right," said Dan. "This isn't a good fight to pick."

She shifted her focus between them and found both smiling slyly.

"Ok," she said, "on the boss's orders. Thanks, guys."

She turned to Nip and Tuck.

"But hear me loud and clear, you two. This is not an audition."

They returned her gaze but did not speak.

"Rick, there's one more thing."

"What's that?"

"Quit calling me honey."

"Right. Sorry, sweetheart."

The Rules Committee secured several bags of confetti and when Emily arrived at the table Mary Massey barked "Cover your drinks, ladies" and they showered her.

Ben was late arriving, but Emily and the Committee rolled through the evening with such zest that Emily barely noticed. When he did arrive, he didn't check his coat or head for the bar. Instead, he waved and blew a kiss, miming that he'd be right there and stood, waiting.

When he made his way to her ten minutes later, Ben had Greg Good on one arm and Alicia Good on the other.

"I apologize for removing the lady from your midst," said Ben, greeting the table. "But she and I have unexpected, albeit most welcome, guests for dinner and a pressing reservation at Twin Anchors. Ms. Winter, would you join us please?"

Emily wasn't angry, but she was thoroughly mystified.

"Why didn't you call me? You knew I was working on the story, Greg. Why didn't you call?"

"Well, at first there wasn't a reason to call. All you had was Chase's story and even you will admit it was pretty far-fetched. All I had was Tommy's denial—he told me he'd been in the P-quad meeting and I had no reason to doubt him. Plus, when you asked me about it, I checked the calendar and it said Tommy didn't meet with her."

"I remember. You were wrong."

"I was, but I didn't know that then."

"When did you know?" asked Ben, a dripping rib suspended over his dinner plate.

"When Humphrey, the P.D., confirmed that Beni had called him the same day the meeting supposedly took place, the coincidence made me nervous. So I did what Emily eventually did, I checked with Eric Buss and I found what Emily found."

"But you still didn't call me," said Emily.

"I couldn't," said Greg.

"Why not?"

"Ten bucks," said Alicia with a sneer.

"What?"

"Ten bucks. Tommy Terrific, that good guy, bought Greg for ten bucks."

Greg blushed.

"She's more or less right," he said. "When Tommy moved me from being a grunt in the AG's office in Springfield and made me his communications and strategy guy, the first thing he did was hand me ten dollars."

Ben snickered.

"That's one sly politician," he said. "He put you on retainer."

Greg nodded.

"Exactly. Every year, he acknowledged the anniversary with another ten dollars."

"I don't get it," said Emily.

"Privilege," said Ben. "Jameson retained Greg as his

lawyer so he could invoke attorney client privilege any time anything dicey came up. Greg was trapped—he knew what Jameson had done but he couldn't talk about it because Jameson was technically his client."

"But it still got ugly fast. Greg and Tommy fought about it." said Alicia.

Greg nodded. "We had the fight of our lives. I told him there was only one way to handle this, come clean, apologize and swear never to abuse power again. He was certain he could handle it with a flat out denial, he was convinced that Chase would give up sooner or later."

Emily's mouth was full so she stopped Greg with her hand while she chewed and swallowed.

"Such good food," she said. "So, he fired you?"

"No," said Greg. "He figured if he let me go, people would start asking why and that would put more focus on the very thing he was trying to hide. So, I quit."

"But Tommy wouldn't let him," said Alicia. "When Greg refused to help Tommy cover it up, Tommy ordered him to take a long vacation instead."

"He said 'Until I fix this,'" Greg said. "He was sure that he could get through it and I would come back to work with him. He was sure it would all be fine again."

Alicia said, "You gave that man all you could, you put him in a position to be Governor, maybe even President, and he rewarded you by badgering that poor girl to death and lying about it. Tommy ruined everything Greg had accomplished."

She threw her arm around Greg and pulled him close.

"My man has more integrity in his little finger than Tommy Terrific has in that huge body of his."

Emily took a bite of salad and gazed off in the distance for a moment.

"Okay, I get all that," she said, looking directly at Greg, "but didn't giving me that P-quad document violate privilege? Isn't that the same as testifying against your client?"

"It might have been an issue," said Alicia, "if Greg had given you that document."

Greg smiled.

"You didn't give it to me?"

Greg shook his head.

"I did," said Alicia.

"You?"

"Me. Greg was in agony over what Jameson had done, heartbroken that all their work was jeopardized. Their fight went on and on, in the office and then on the phone for hours, that night. It was horrible. I got up before Greg did and found the copy of that P-quad thing on our dining table. I'd heard Greg arguing with Tommy about it the night before, so I knew it had something to do with their fight but I didn't know what it was or how it fit.

"Then Tommy made Greg to go on vacation. I couldn't stand the thought that Tommy might actually get away with it. I didn't know what that pyramid paper was all about, but I knew it was important so I made a copy and sent it to you."

"Tell her how," said Greg with a smile.

"Oh, that. Our doorman, Howard, his son's in high school and a couple of times a week he comes to our building so he and his dad can ride the bus home together. Nice kid, seems smart and capable, so I put the paper in a blank envelope and paid Howard's kid to make sure it got to your desk."

"That's not the best part," said Greg. "Tell them what you paid him."

"Jameson's retainer for this year," said Alicia. "I paid the kid ten bucks."

21.

On Monday morning, Max pulled into the driveway, the cab wet and the wipers brushing against a cold mist which fell just short of rain. As Emily left the lobby, a gust of wind caught the door and drove her forward and she struggled to gain her balance, nearly dragged down when the wind caught her satchel flush on and spun her around.

Max jumped out of the cab and caught her, taking the satchel and tossing it in the back seat before he got her seated.

"You okay, Emmy? You got walloped, huh?"

"It was a little scary for a moment there, Max. Thanks for grabbing me. I didn't want to drop the satchel, get the equipment wet or dirty. Nice way to start the day, right?"

Max settled into the cab and turned so he could face her fully.

"It's not going to get any better, Emmy."

"Why? What's going on?"

He grimaced and nodded to the newspapers under the satchel. Emily shifted so she could see.

The *Tribune* was on top, sporting a banner headline

which read JAMESON RESIGNS.

The by-line on the story read Lois Lipton, Tribune court reporter.

Emily gasped when she saw the headline but smiled in admiration when she began reading. She read all the copy on the first page and then checked the other two front pages. Both had sent reporters out to background the story. WEL's report and Cary Chase were quoted in all three papers, but Lois and the Trib had the resignation scoop.

Max pulled the cab out of the driveway and Emily opened the paper to finish reading Lipton's story. In a telephone conversation initiated by Tommy Jameson, the U.S. Attorney told Lipton that he was leaving his position effective immediately to "maintain the integrity of the office and address some deeply troubling personal matters with my family and my church."

As the cab pulled on to the outer Drive, Max checked his passenger in the mirror.

"You okay, Emily?"

She looked at him through the mirror and began chuckling.

"Troy Coburn."

"What? Who's that?"

"I didn't mean to, but I made her look bad and now she's paid me back. Fair is fair."

"You shoulda had that story, Emmy. You did all the hard work."

"That's the point, Max. She gave it to Lois just so I would not get it. She made me pay for my sins."

"Just not right," said Max.

"Max, it's okay. Really. Jameson did the honorable thing by stepping aside and my work, no, you helped, so it was *our* work, had everything to do with that. Beni's story has been told and nobody can disparage her anymore. So, the way I see it, Max, we got the job done and that headline proves it."

"You look at it that way," said Max, beaming, "I gotta say, Yeah, we done good."

As soon as the nine o'clock broadcast aired, a secretary walked up to Emily's desk.

"They want you in the office," she said.

"They, who? What office."

"I'm sorry. Mr. Armento and Mr. Carroll in the General Manager's office."

"Ah," said Emily. "Let's go, then."

The two were perched on the corners of the desk again and Emily wondered if either of them ever actually sat behind it.

"We're officially making the changes in news permanent," said Nip. "We're keeping the morning drive format and we're launching Hits 980 News & Entertainment at Noon later this week.

"So?"

"We want you to replace Dan McIntyre. Full time, a substantial boost in pay, you'll handle morning drive and co-host at noon—"

"No."

Her response was quick and sharp.

"This is a great opportunity, Emily," said Tuck. "Great for your career. Plus, with our network connections, we can talk about getting you some national air time, too."

Emily chuckled.

"The network ran our story on Jameson coast to coast, fellas," she said, "I've already cracked that ceiling."

"Yes, you're the first ever woman to cover hard news for the network" said Nip. "That's just an example of how far we think you can go."

"Not with you."

"You should consider this more carefully," said Tuck. "Perhaps you'd like to talk it over with your husband—"

"Don't say it," said Emily. "You're going to say the man in my life is going to talk some sense into my addled little head. Don't. The answer is no."

"We'll leave it open," said Tuck.

"Leave it open as long as you wish," she said. "Is that all?"

"Yes."

"Then I'm going back to work. Bye."

"You turned them down, right?" Dean Lyon had his feet on his desk, his chair swiveled so he could look out the window.

"Of course I did."

"Good. I told them you would, glad I read it right."

"I can't replace Dan."

"Of course you can," he said, "but you shouldn't. You belong on the street."

"Thanks."

"Don't thank me yet," he said. "The boys over there in the carpeted suite didn't tell you the whole story."

"No, but I can guess."

"Go ahead," he said, smiling. "You're usually two steps ahead of most of us anyhow."

"Not you," she said. "It'll be years before I'm that sharp. But this one is pretty obvious—if all they're doing from 5 to 9 is headlines, they don't need a writer. They can rip headlines from the wires and read them. My job is obsolete."

"Almost," said Dean. "Rick's going to keep his shift and write headers. He wants somebody in the shop every day to keep an eye on them."

"So, where do I fit, then?"

"I still need somebody to write and produce for Noon," he said.

"Really? Dean—"

"Let me finish. I need somebody to do that, I don't want it to be you."

Standing by the couch, Emily put a hand back to steady herself as she collapsed into it.

"You're letting me go?"

"I like to think I'm sending you off to be the great reporter I know you to be," he said. "Giving you one fluff assignment after another isn't exactly driving an innocent woman to her death, but it would be a crime. You're too good for what we're doing, Emily. You need to go where you can shine.

"I told those two idiots you'd turn them down and I told them when you did I'd cut your hours, give you a shift doesn't make the bags under your eyes permanent. So from now on, you'll come in for the morning planning meeting, stay through Noon, that's it. Job's yours as long as you need it. But as soon as you can, Emily, you have to go."

"You've given me everything. Beni's story, air time, network exposure, it all comes down to you, Dean. I can't just walk away."

"You can and you will, Emily. I'm the boss and I'm giving you a direct order."

"But—"

"Nope, no buts. I've put together a list of stations I think might be interested in you, places I know somebody, I can put in a good word. I'm not shoving you out the door yet, Emily, but if you don't find something sooner rather than later, I will."

When she got back to her desk, she found a sheet of WEL letterhead on her desk. It was a typed letter of recommendation signed by Rick Healey, Assistant News Director & Shop Steward.

"Use it anywhere in town, doll," Rick said. "Go get 'em and when you do, knock 'em dead."

On Thursday afternoon at 4:45, as the sky was darkening and the rush hour was at the starting line, JD the DJ cued a block of ten songs in a row and walked out of WEL's main broadcast studio. Decker and his engineer moved quickly to the elevator, a canvas duffel bag slung over Decker's shoulder. They rode the elevator to the parking area in the basement and tossed the bag onto the passenger seat of the station's mobile broadcast van and drove it out of the garage and onto the bridge which crossed the Chicago River at Michigan Avenue and Wacker Drive.

Decker pulled the van into the center lane of the bridge, grabbed the duffel bag and climbed out of the van, locking it behind him. His engineer threaded a long microphone cord through a slit at the top of the passenger window and then locked himself in.

On his engineer's cue, John Decker began broadcasting live from the bridge, inviting any so inclined to join him. Cars and trucks tried to dodge around the parked van, but it didn't take long for traffic to back up in both directions. Soon enough, both Michigan and Wacker were in gridlock, blaring horns and angry shouts echoed off the walls of the surrounding buildings as a crowd grew steadily.

In the cacophony, Jon Decker solemnly declared the death of "Hits 980." For the next several minutes, with the crowd cheering him on, Jon Decker took one tape cassette after another out of the duffel and heaved them over the railing into the icy water below.

The cassettes flew off the bridge in order, red, blue, red, blue, red, green until there were ten cassettes remaining of the original 25.

As each of the last ten sailed out the damp evening air, the crowd and JD the DJ counted down.

"Ten...nine...eight...two...ONE!"

When the last cassette lofted out over the water, the crowd exploded in a rousing cheer. As two uniformed officers came up the sidewalk toward him, Decker's engineer climbed out of the van's back door and set the lock before he closed it.

Friends, I'm sorry to say I have to leave you now. It has been my honor and joy to share good music with you here on the El, but the time has come for us to go our separate ways. I hope to talk with you soon, but until then, I promise you that rock and roll—good rock and roll on good radio stations—will never die.

The two officers drew near and Jon Decker stood tall, one arm raised above his head.

JD the DJ signing off, friends. Shine On, Chicago! Shine on and on...

Then he rifled the keys to the van over the railing and into the river, waved good bye to the crowd and walked down the Avenue, his long coat flapping and his head bent low against the wind.

Emily and Ben were the last to arrive at the Friday night dinner party. Ben had run late at the office and the cab driver who picked them up at Ricardo's was so timid that the drive took ten or twelve minutes longer than it should have. They were at least fifteen minutes late when they rang the ornate doorbell at Chase Mansion.

"My regret, sir, for our tardiness," said Ben when the elevator opened to the fourth floor. "It is entirely my fault. I'm Benjamin Winter, Mr. Chase, Emily's husband."

"It's a pleasure to meet you, Benjamin. Do you prefer that to Ben?"

"I'm Ben to most, but I am content with either depending on your preference."

"Well, in either event, I am Cary. Hello, Emily. I'm delighted that you could join us. The others are in the living room but they've got drinks and one another, so they're good for the moment. Let's steal away and I'll give you a quick tour. Lay your coats on that table, they'll be ready when you leave. Please, follow me."

The residence was elegant. Its colors and tones were subdued, the art work carefully arranged. Ben gasped when they rounded a corner and came upon an Andrew Wyeth. A few minutes later, Emily thought she might have to restrain her husband when he saw the library.

"You do understand that my husband would live in the

281

room for the rest of his life. I'd advise you to keep an eye on him all night long, Cary."

"I would not consider moving into this magnificent room without you, m'lady. But if you'd care to join me—?"

"Allow me to intercede," said Cary, laughing. "The room is not for rent. You're welcome to browse when you have time, I'll lend anything in here."

"On that you can rely," said Ben.

Chase swept them along, delighted to share his home with them and clearly pleased that they appreciated its warmth and charm as much as did he.

They arrived in the living room, a very large room with several small seating arrangements and an expansive area in front of the fire place which featured several couches and comfortable chairs.

The fireplace sparked and popped as the large logs burned slowly down and Chase had the group circle around it. He stood by the marble mantle and raised his glass to the only thing on that mantle, a black and white photograph of Beni Steinart in a subtle frame. She wore a lovely cocktail dress and she was cheerily welcoming guests in the entry hall at Chase Mansion. She was beautiful and happy.

"She will always be here," said Cary Chase. "She will always be missed, she will always be loved and as long as we remember her glorious smile—that smile right there, the one which lights up this room just as it lit up this house—she will live in our hearts and our souls."

They stood in silence for a long time.

"I know she will always be here," said Chase with a grin, "because right now she is reminding me that if I cause us to linger here any longer, I will ruin the chef's timing. He can get cranky, so let's eat."

Cary Chase sat at one end of the table, Emily at the other. Barbara Burton, Joseph's wife, and Joseph sat on one side of the table, Kirstin Bonner next to Ben on the other.

Chase had only recently returned to his home, but during his absence from it, under Kirstin's direction, the staff had kept it at the ready. During their tour, he said the staff had made it feel as if he'd never left.

In the very first lull in the conversation, Kirstin Bonner leaned forward and caught Emily's eye at the end of the table.

"So, what's the story, Emily? Is Kup right? Have you been fired? Are you really off the air at the station?"

Ben tensed, but Emily laid a hand on his knee.

"I'm afraid that Kup got it wrong this time," she said. "It's true that I'm leaving, but it's hardly under a cloud and they've given me time to find a new job. I'll be fine.

"I was shocked at first, but now I'm eager to move on. The neat thing is, Dean Lyon says the only candidates they've talked with so far are women."

"Amen to that," said Barbara Burton.

"Anybody in town'd be lucky to get you," said Joseph. "You did magnificent work on this story. Just magnificent."

"I'll say," said Barbara. "What we liked most of all was the shot they all got of Jameson's car driving up the exit ramp, every reporter in town screaming at him to say something."

"It seemed kind of just," said Joseph. "They all caught him on the same ramp he used to sneak her into the building. I liked that."

"I relished that irony as well," said Ben. "But his letter of resignation provided far greater satisfaction. It lifts one's spirits to see a free press doing precisely what the founders intended, holding miscreants to account, righting wrongs."

Kirsten asked, "Where will you go? Print? Television? All news radio?"

Emily shrugged and turned both palms up.

"I don' have any idea. My plan was to take a few weeks and think about it, spend some time learning to stay up late and sleep in. I got a nice sort of bonus check for overtime.

I figured that and the reduced hours they're giving me would give me the room to take my time."

"But fate intervened," said Ben. "Our financial status took a dramatic turn."

"They're converting our building to condos and we love our place too much to let it go," said Emily. "So that check isn't a cushion anymore, it became most of the down payment. It's gone and I have to find some work pretty quickly."

"We'll hire you here and now," said Kirstin. Cary Chase nodded enthusiastically.

"You want to handle press for the cab association?" said Joseph Burton. "If you do, you're hired."

Emily laughed.

"Well, that's grand, I must say, but I think I belong on the other side of the microphone from you newsmakers."

"Our loss," said Cary Chase, "but at least you're not leaving Chicago."

"Never!"

"Good," he said, "Chicago needs you. You belong here."

"Well, she's not allowed to leave in any event," said Ben. "It would break the rule."

"What rule?" said Chase.

Ben put his arm around Emily and grinned.

"The rule that says we have to have winter in Chicago, or course."